THE USBORNE
INTERNET-LINKED
CHILDREN'S
WORLD
ATLAS

Stephanie Turnbull and Emma Helbrough
Designers: Stephen Moncrieff and Andrea Slane
Consultant cartographic editor: Craig Asquith

Cartography by European Map Graphics Ltd
Map design by Laura Fearn and Keith Newell
Consultant: Dr. Roger Trend, Senior Lecturer in Earth Science
and Geography Education, University of Exeter

CONTENTS

Here you can see dramatic cloud formations at sunset over a desert in California, U.S.A. Below is a large sandstone arch, shaped by the weather over many years.

INTERNET LINKS

Throughout this book we have recommended websites where you can find out more about maps and places around the world.

To visit the sites, follow these simple steps to go to the **Usborne Quicklinks Website** where you will find links to take you to the websites:

1. Go to **www.usborne-quicklinks.com**
2. Type the keyword for this book: **atlas**
3. Type the page number of the link you want to visit.
4. Click on the links to go to the recommended sites.

When using the internet, make sure you follow the internet safety guidelines shown on the opposite page, and displayed on the Usborne Quicklinks Website.

Internet links
For links to all the websites described in this book, go to **www.usborne-quicklinks.com** and enter the keyword "atlas".

Help

For general help and advice on using the internet, go to the Usborne Quicklinks Website and click on "Net Help".

To find out more about using your web browser, click on your browser's Help menu and choose "Contents and Index". You'll find a searchable dictionary containing tips on how to find your way around the internet easily.

Here are some of the things you can do on the websites recommended in this book:

- Explore online maps of all the countries in the world.
- Take virtual tours of different countries, and listen to their languages.
- See satellite images of Earth's landforms, from the River Ganges to the Swiss Alps.
- Explore an Egyptian pyramid and go on a photo safari in Africa.
- Browse encyclopedia guides to the countries of the world.

Site availability

The links in Usborne Quicklinks are regularly reviewed and updated, but occasionally you may find a site is unavailable. This might be temporary, so try again later, or even the next day.

Websites do occasionally close down and when this happens, we will replace them with new links in Usborne Quicklinks. Sometimes we add extra links too, if we think they are useful, so when you visit Usborne Quicklinks, the links may be slightly different from those described in your book.

Computer not essential
If you don't have use of the internet, don't worry. This atlas is a complete, self-contained reference book on its own.

Extras

Some websites need additional programs, called plug-ins, to play sounds, or to show videos, animations or 3-D images. If you go to a site and you do not have the necessary plug-in, a message should come up on the screen.

There is usually a button on the site that you can click on to download the plug-in. Alternatively, go to Usborne Quicklinks and click on "Net Help". There you can find links to download plug-ins. Here is a list of plug-ins that you might need:

• **QuickTime** – lets you play video clips.

• **RealPlayer**® – lets you play video clips and sound files.

• **Flash**™ – lets you play animations.

• **Shockwave**® – lets you play animations and enjoy interactive sites.

Computer viruses

A computer virus is a program that can damage your computer. A virus can get into your computer when you download programs from the internet, or in an attachment (an extra file) that arrives with an email. We strongly recommend that you buy anti-virus software to protect your computer and that you update the software regularly. You can buy anti-virus software at computer stores or download it from the internet. To find out more about viruses, go to Usborne Quicklinks and click on "Net Help".

Macintosh and QuickTime are trademarks of Apple computer, Inc., registered in the U.S.A. and other countries.

RealPlayer is a trademark of RealNetworks, Inc., registered in the U.S.A. and other countries.

Flash and Shockwave are trademarks of Macromedia, Inc., registered in the U.S.A. and other countries.

Internet safety

When using the internet, make sure you follow these simple safety rules.

• Ask your parent's or guardian's permission before you connect to the internet. They can then stay nearby if they think they should do so.

• If you write a message in a website guest book, or on a website message board, do not include your email address, real name, address, phone number or the name of your school.

• If a website asks you to log in or register by typing your name or email address, ask the permission of an adult first.

• If you receive email from someone you don't know, tell an adult and do not reply to the email.

• Never arrange to meet anyone you have talked to on the internet.

Note for parents

The websites described in this book are regularly checked and reviewed by Usborne editors and the links in Usborne Quicklinks are updated. However, the content of a website may change at any time and Usborne Publishing is not responsible for the content of any website other than its own.

We recommend that children are supervised while on the internet, that they do not use internet chat rooms, and that you use internet filtering software to block unsuitable material. Please ensure that your children read and follow the safety guidelines above. For more information, go to the Net Help area on the Usborne Quicklinks Website at **www.usborne-quicklinks.com**

WHAT IS AN ATLAS?

An atlas is a collection of maps. This atlas helps you explore our world and find out more about its varied landscapes, famous cities and amazing sights.

What maps show

A map is an image that represents an area of the Earth's surface, usually from above. Unlike a photograph, which shows exactly what an area looks like, a map can show features of the area in a clear, simplified way. It can also give different information, such as place names. Symbols are often used to mark features such as volcanoes and waterfalls.

Which way is up?

Although the Earth doesn't have a top and a bottom, north is usually at the top of maps. But it is sometimes more convenient to reposition a map, so north might not necessarily be at the top. Some maps have a compass symbol that indicates where north lies.

Wolf volcano

Darwin volcano

San Salvador

Fernandina

Alcedo volcano

La Cumbre volcano

Isabela

Santa Cruz

Sierra Negra volcano

Cerro Azul volcano

This simple map of the central Galapagos Islands names the main islands and their volcanoes.

Floreana

This is a satellite image of part of the Galapagos Islands. Using the map on this page, can you identify the islands shown in the photograph?

Physical and political

Physical maps indicate natural features such as mountains, deserts, rivers and lakes. Political maps focus on the division of the Earth's surface into different countries. Look on pages 18–19 for a political map of the world, and on pages 20–21 for a physical map. Most of the maps in this atlas show physical features as well as country borders, cities and towns.

Map scales

The size of a map in relation to the area it shows is called its scale. Some maps have a scale bar, which is a rule with measurements. It tells you how many miles or km are represented by a certain distance on the map. Other maps show these relative distances just as numbers. For example, the figure 1:100 means that 1cm on the map represents 100cm on the Earth's surface.

The scale of a map depends on its purpose. A map showing the whole world is on a very small scale, but a town plan is on a much larger scale so that features such as roads can be shown clearly.

1:97,600,000

| 0 | 1,000 | 2,000 | 3,000km |
| 0 | 1,000 | | 2,000 miles |

This map of Europe is on a small scale so that it all fits onto one small map.

1:8,500,000

| 0 | 100 | 200 | 300km |
| 0 | | 100 | 200 miles |

This map of Denmark is on a larger scale to show more detail.

Internet links

For links to the following websites, go to **www.usborne-quicklinks.com**

Website 1 Political maps of every country in the world, with helpful facts.

Website 2 An online guide to scale, with a test-yourself quiz.

This is Mount Rushmore, a huge sculpture of four U.S. presidents, which is one of the most famous sights in the U.S.A. Throughout this atlas you will see pictures of many more well known landmarks from around the world.

Using this atlas

The maps in this atlas are grouped by continent. There are seven continents, which are (from largest to smallest): Asia, Africa, North America, South America, Antarctica, Europe and Australasia and Oceania. Each map section is accompanied by photographs and satellite images showing some of the continent's most impressive sights. You can look up many of these places on the maps.

THE EARTH FROM SPACE

Modern technology has enabled scientists to make more accurate maps of the world than ever before. Even remote places, such as deserts, ocean floors and mountain ranges, have been mapped in detail, using information from satellites that observe the Earth from space.

What is a satellite?

Artificial satellites are machines that orbit, or travel around, the Earth. They observe the Earth using a technique called remote sensing. Instruments on the satellite monitor the Earth from a distance, and send back pictures of its surface. Satellites also monitor moons and other planets.

This satellite monitors the Earth 24 hours a day. It uses powerful radar that pierces through clouds. This means that the satellite can provide images of the Earth in all weather conditions.

Satellite movement

Some satellites orbit the Earth at a height of between 5km (3 miles) and 1,500km (930 miles), providing views of different parts of the planet. Others stay above the same place all the time, moving at the same speed as the Earth rotates to give a constant view of a particular area. These are called geostationary satellites. They travel at a height of around 36,000km (22,370 miles).

Internet links

For links to the following websites, go to **www.usborne-quicklinks.com**

Website 1 Look at detailed satellite pictures of any part of the world.
Website 2 Find out more about remote sensing and how satellites are used.
Website 3 How satellites monitor natural disasters, with a satellite jigsaw.

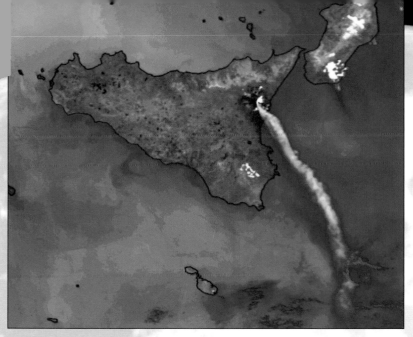

This satellite image of Sicily was taken in July 2001. It shows the volcano Mount Etna erupting. You can see smoke from the volcano on the right of the picture.

Satellite uses

Satellite pictures can be used to help predict and monitor natural hazards such as volcanic eruptions. They can also help scientists to observe the effects people have on the environment, for example the destruction of rainforests in South America. Satellite images are often artificially shaded to highlight relevant features, for example forests, so that they are easier to see.

Remote sensing

Satellites use a range of remote sensing techniques. One type is radar, which can provide images of the Earth even when it is dark or cloudy. Radar works by reflecting radio waves off a target object. The time it takes for a wave to bounce back indicates how far away the object is.

Powerful cameras provide pictures of the Earth's surface. Often, infrared cameras are used. Different surfaces reflect infrared rays differently, so infrared images of the Earth are able to show its various types of land surfaces, such as deserts, grasslands and forests.

This satellite image of the Earth is shaded to show different types of land. Deserts and other dry regions are red, and areas with lots of vegetation are orange.

DIVIDING LINES

The Earth is divided up with imaginary lines that help us measure distances and find where places are. There are two sets of lines, called latitude and longitude.

This arctic fox lives in northern Canada, very near the Arctic Circle line of latitude.

Latitude lines

Lines of latitude run around the globe. They are parallel to each other and get shorter the closer they are to the two poles. The latitude line that runs around the middle of the Earth is called the Equator. It is the most important line of latitude as all other lines are measured north or south of it.

Longitude lines

Lines of longitude run from the North Pole to the South Pole. All the lines are the same length, and they all meet at the North and South Poles.

The most important line of longitude is the Prime Meridian Line, which runs through Greenwich, in England. All other lines of longitude are measured east or west of this line.

Other lines

The Equator is not the only named line of latitude. The Tropic of Cancer is a line north of the Equator. The Tropic of Capricorn is at the same distance south of the Equator. Between these lines are the hottest, wettest parts of the world. This region is called the tropics.

The Arctic Circle is a latitude line far north of the Equator. The area north of this includes the North Pole and is called the Arctic. On the other side of the globe is the Antarctic Circle. The area south of this includes the South Pole and is known as the Antarctic.

Latitude lines

Longitude lines

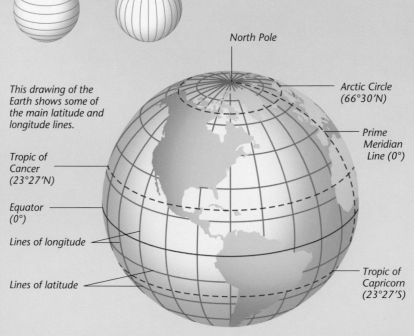

This drawing of the Earth shows some of the main latitude and longitude lines.

North Pole

Arctic Circle (66°30'N)

Prime Meridian Line (0°)

Tropic of Cancer (23°27'N)

Equator (0°)

Lines of longitude

Lines of latitude

Tropic of Capricorn (23°27'S)

Internet links

For links to websites where you can find out more about latitude and longitude and explore the world in an online game, go to **www.usborne-quicklinks.com**

Using the lines

Lines of latitude and longitude are measured in degrees (°). The positions of places are described according to which lines of latitude and longitude are nearest to them. For example, a place with a location of 50°S and 100°E has a latitude 50 degrees south of the Equator, and a longitude 100 degrees east of the Prime Meridian Line.

Exact locations

The distance between degrees is divided up to give even more precise measurements. Each degree is divided into 60 minutes ('), and each minute is divided into 60 seconds ("). The subdivisions allow us to locate any place on Earth. For example, the city of New York, U.S.A., is at 40°42'51"N and 74°00'23"W.

The steamy rainforests of Malaysia lie near the Equator. Many apes, like the one shown here, live in these rainforests.

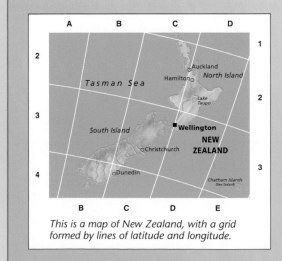

This is a map of New Zealand, with a grid formed by lines of latitude and longitude.

Using a grid

Lines of latitude and longitude form grids on maps. The maps in this book look similar to the one on the left. The columns that run from top to bottom are formed by lines of longitude and marked with letters. The rows running across the page are formed by lines of latitude and are numbered.

All the places listed in the map index on page 130 have a letter and a number reference that tell you where to find them on a particular page. For example, on the map on the left, the city of Christchurch would have a grid reference of C3.

HOW MAPS ARE MADE

The process of making maps is called cartography. Map-makers, or cartographers, compile each map by gathering information about the area and representing it as an image as accurately as possible.

Internet links

For links to websites where you can watch movies of maps made from satellite images and find out how to make a globe from a flat piece of paper, go to
www.usborne-quicklinks.com

Creating maps

Many sources are used to create maps. These include satellite images and aerial photographs. Cartographers often visit the area to be mapped, where they take many extra measurements.

In addition, cartographers use statistics, such as population figures, from censuses and other documents. As the maps are being made, many people check them to make sure they are accurate and up-to-date.

Map projections

Cartographers can't draw maps that show the world exactly as it is, because it is impossible to show a curved surface on a flat map without distorting (stretching or squashing) some areas. A representation of the Earth on a map is called a projection. Projections are worked out using complex mathematics.

There are three basic types of projections – cylindrical, conical and azimuthal, but there are also variations on these. They all distort the Earth's surface in some way, either by altering the shapes or sizes of areas of land or the distance between places.

A cartographer uses an electronic distance measurer to check the measurements of an area of land.

Cylindrical projections

A cylindrical projection is similar to the image created by wrapping a piece of paper around a globe to form a cylinder and then shining a light inside the globe. The shapes of countries would be projected onto the paper. Near the middle they would be accurate, but farther away they would be distorted.

Cartographers often alter the basic cylindrical projection to make the distortion less obvious in certain areas, but they can never make a map that is completely accurate.

This picture of a piece of paper wrapped around a globe illustrates how a cylindrical projection is made.

Below is a type of cylindrical projection called the Mercator projection, which was invented in 1596 by a cartographer named Gerardus Mercator. It makes countries the right shape, but makes those near the poles too big.

This cylindrical projection makes countries the right size in relation to each other, but some parts are too long. The projection was created in 1973 by Arno Peters. It is called the Peters Projection.

Conical projections

A conical projection is similar to the image you would get if you wrapped a cone of paper around part of a globe, then shone a light inside the globe. Where the cone touches the globe, the projection will be most accurate.

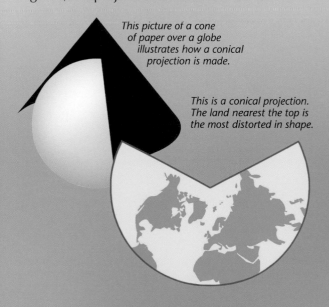

This picture of a cone of paper over a globe illustrates how a conical projection is made.

This is a conical projection. The land nearest the top is the most distorted in shape.

Azimuthal projections

An azimuthal projection is like an image made by holding paper in front of a globe, and shining a light through it. Land projected onto the middle of the paper would be accurate, but areas farther away would be distorted.

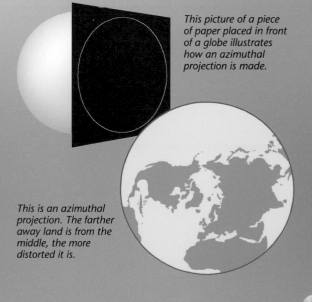

This picture of a piece of paper placed in front of a globe illustrates how an azimuthal projection is made.

This is an azimuthal projection. The farther away land is from the middle, the more distorted it is.

THEMATIC MAPS

Maps that represent information on particular themes, like the ones on these pages, are known as thematic maps. They help you to identify patterns and make comparisons between the features of different areas.

Earth's resources

The Earth contains all kinds of useful resources. Rocks and minerals can be used as building materials, and fuels such as coal, oil and gas contain energy that can be turned into heat and electricity.

Countries with large amounts of natural resources can become very rich. For example, Saudi Arabia, in western Asia, has large oil and gas reserves, which it exports all over the world.

This is an oil field, where oil is extracted from the ground using pumps. It is then piped to refineries and turned into products such as motor fuel.

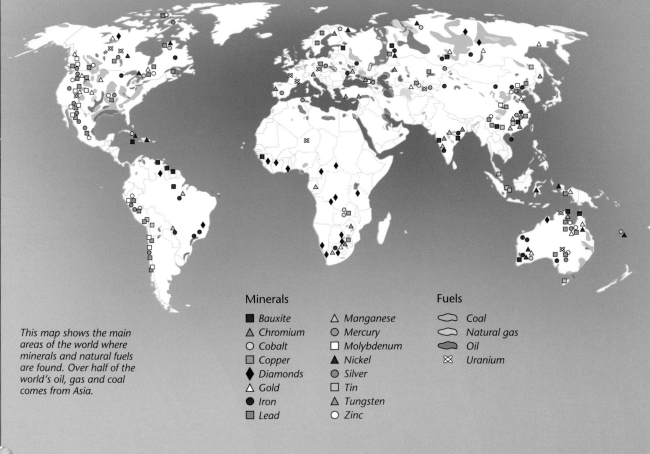

This map shows the main areas of the world where minerals and natural fuels are found. Over half of the world's oil, gas and coal comes from Asia.

Minerals

■ Bauxite
△ Chromium
○ Cobalt
□ Copper
◆ Diamonds
△ Gold
● Iron
▨ Lead

△ Manganese
○ Mercury
□ Molybdenum
▲ Nickel
◓ Silver
□ Tin
△ Tungsten
○ Zinc

Fuels

⬭ Coal
⬭ Natural gas
⬬ Oil
⊠ Uranium

Different climates

The long-term or typical pattern of weather in a particular area is known as its climate. Climates vary across the world and depend largely on each area's latitude. The hottest parts of the world are those closest to the Equator.

Climate is also affected by other factors, such as wind and the height of the land. Oceans influence climate too – places near the sea normally have a milder, wetter climate than areas farther inland.

On this map, land is divided into five climate types. Dry areas are generally hot, but temperatures there can fall very low too. Some dry places, such as the Gobi Desert in eastern Asia, are extremely cold in winter.

- ☐ *Polar*
- ☐ *Cold*
- ☐ *Temperate*
- ☐ *Dry*
- ■ *Tropical*

World population

There are more than six billion people in the world, and the population is still growing. Experts think it may reach more than nine billion by 2050. The number of people living in a given area is known as its population density. Europe and Asia are the most densely populated continents in the world. About a third of the world's population lives in China and India alone.

Internet links

For a link to a website where you can see the population of the Earth when you were born, and find lots of other population facts, graphs and animations, go to **www.usborne quicklinks.com**

This map shows the average population density by country. The shading indicates the number of people per sq km (0.386 sq miles).

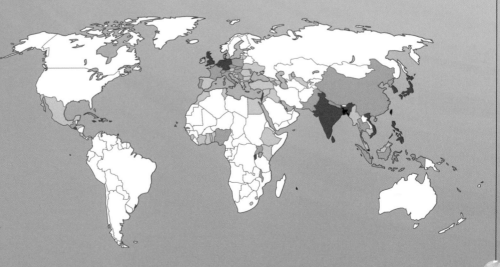

- ■ *Over 500 people*
- ■ *200–500 people*
- ☐ *100–200 people*
- ☐ *50–100 people*
- ☐ *10–50 people*
- ☐ *Fewer than 10 people*

HOW TO USE THE MAPS

Each continent section in this atlas begins with a political map showing the whole continent. The rest of the maps are larger scale maps showing the various parts of the continent in more detail.

Political maps

The shading on the political maps in this atlas is there to help you see clearly the different countries that make up each continent. The main purpose of these maps is to show country borders and capital cities. Alongside them there are facts and figures about the continents and their features.

This is a section of the political map of South America. You can see the whole map on pages 36–37.

Environmental maps

The majority of the maps in this atlas are environmental maps, like the one on the right. The shading on these maps shows different types of land, or environments, such as desert, mountain or wetland.

The main key on the opposite page shows what the different shading means. It also shows the symbols used to represent towns, cities and other features. There is a smaller key on each environmental map repeating the most important information from this key.

Finding places

To find a particular place or feature on the environmental maps, look up its name in the index on pages 130–143. Its page number and grid reference is given next to the name. You can find out how to use the grid on page 9.

The map on the right is part of the environmental map of the U.S.A. The numbered labels at the top explain some important features of these maps.

❶ The letters and numbers in the border help you to find a place you have looked up in the index.

❷ Lines of latitude and longitude are shown as thin blue lines.

❸ The names of countries are shown in large, bold type with capital letters.

❹ The thick purple lines are country boundaries.

❺ The thinner purple lines are boundaries of internal regions within a country.

Main key

Land cover:

Boreal forest
Temperate forest
Tropical forest
Temperate grassland
Savanna
Semi-desert and scrub
Hot desert
Wetland
Mountain (Only high mountains are marked.)
Tundra
Ice
Cultivation
Urban

Cities and towns:

■ National capital
● Internal capital
⊙ Major city or town
○ Other town

Boundaries:

━━━ International boundary
- - - International boundary through water
─── Internal boundary
- - - Internal boundary through water

Water features:

Sea
Lake or reservoir
Seasonal lake
Dry lake/salt pan
River
Seasonal river
Waterfall/dam

Other features:

▲ 2,490m (7,988ft) Height above or below sea level (Only a selection of elevation points are given. Places below sea level have a minus sign in front of the height.)

⁘ Ruin or other place of interest

ⅢⅢ Ancient wall

Scale:

This tells you the size of the map in relation to the area it represents. For example:

1:14,600,000

0	200	400km

0	100	200	300 miles

C   115°   D   110°   E   105°   F   100°   G   85°

COLUMBIA
ALBERTA
Lethbridge
Swift Current
Moose Jaw   ❷   Regina
Lake Manitoba
MANITOBA
SASKATCHEWAN
ROCKY
Coeur d'Alene
Great Falls
Fort Peck Lake
Estevan
❹
CAN
Brandon
ONTAR
Marath
Missoula
Lewiston
Missouri
Helena
MONTANA
Minot
NORTH DAKOTA
Yellowstone
Billings
Bismarck
rior
IDAHO
Boise
Idaho Falls
Yellowstone Lake
Grand Teton 4,197m (13,770ft)
❺
Rapid City
Pierre
SOUTH DAKOTA
Missouri
Twin Falls
WYOMING
Lake Michigan
M
Gra
Ra
Great Salt Lake Desert
Great Salt Lake
Ogden
Kings Peak 4,123m (13,527ft)
Casper
Cheyenne
NEBRASKA
Grand Island
aukee
South Bend
Salt Lake City
Provo
MOUNTAINS
Platte
INDIA
at
St. George
Grand Junction
Colorado
UTAH
Denver
COLORADO
Colorado Springs
KANSAS
India
in
Lake Mead
Grand Canyon
Colorado Plateau
❸ U N I T E D   S T A T E S
Pueblo
Wichita
Evansv
deau
Kentucky Lake
as egas
Flagstaff
Farmington
Rio Grande
Santa Fe
Albuquerque
Canadian
Oklahoma City
A
TENN
Jackson   Cha
ado
ARIZONA
Baldy Peak 3,476m (11,404ft)
Phoenix
NEW MEXICO
Amarillo
Red
his
Huntsv
o
B
Tucson
Lubbock
PI
an
AL
Me
Nogales
Agua Prieta
Ciudad Juarez
El Paso
Pecos
Fort Worth
Abilene
TEXAS
on
Mobile
Hermosillo
Ojinaga
Edwards Plateau
Austin
Gulf of California
Ciudad Obregon
Chihuahua
Del Rio
San Antonio
Rio Grande
Eastern Sierra Madre
Corpus Christi
Orleans
Mississip Delta
Los Mochis
MEXICO
Monclova
Laredo
Western Ma
f Me

Abbreviations used on map:

ARM.	ARMENIA
AUST.	AUSTRIA
AZER.	AZERBAIJAN
BELG.	BELGIUM
B.H.	BOSNIA AND HERZEGOVINA
CRO.	CROATIA
CZECH REP.	CZECH REPUBLIC
LEB.	LEBANON
LUX.	LUXEMBOURG
MAC.	MACEDONIA
NETH.	NETHERLANDS
SLOV.	SLOVENIA
S.M.	SERBIA AND MONTENEGRO
SWITZ.	SWITZERLAND
U.A.E.	UNITED ARAB EMIRATES

20° E 40° 60° 80° 100° 120° 140° 160° 180°

Svalbard
(Norway)

Arctic Circle

RUSSIA

60°

DEN FINLAND

ESTONIA

LATVIA

RUSSIA LITHUANIA

ERMANY BELARUS

POLAND

CZECH REP.

SLOVAKIA UKRAINE

HUNGARY MOLDOVA

O. KAZAKHSTAN MONGOLIA

B.H. S.M. BULGARIA

ALY ALBANIA MAC.

ALBANIA Black Sea Caspian GEORGIA UZBEKISTAN KYRGYZSTAN

GREECE TURKEY Sea ARM. AZER. TURKMENISTAN TAJIKISTAN

40°

CYPRUS SYRIA AFGHANISTAN CHINA

Mediterranean Sea LEB. ISRAEL JORDAN IRAQ IRAN

NORTH
KOREA

SOUTH
KOREA

JAPAN

PACIFIC

EGYPT KUWAIT PAKISTAN NEPAL BHUTAN

SAUDI BAHRAIN OCEAN

ARABIA QATAR BANGLA-
DESH BURMA
(MYANMAR)

U.A.E. OMAN INDIA TAIWAN

Tropic of Cancer

20°
N

CHAD LAOS

SUDAN ERITREA YEMEN THAILAND Northern
Mariana
Islands
(U.S.A.)

DJIBOUTI VIETNAM

CENTRAL ETHIOPIA CAMBODIA PHILIPPINES MARSHALL
ISLANDS

AFRICAN
REPUBLIC SRI LANKA

AMEROON SOMALIA

FEDERATED STATES
OF MICRONESIA

CONGO UGANDA MALDIVES BRUNEI

(DEMOCRATIC KENYA PALAU

ongo REPUBLIC) RWANDA MALAYSIA

TANZANIA SINGAPORE Equator 0°

SEYCHELLES NAURU KIRIBATI

ANGOLA COMOROS INDIAN INDONESIA PAPUA
NEW GUINEA SOLOMON
ISLANDS TUVALU

ZAMBIA MALAWI OCEAN

MBABWE Coral Sea SAMOA

AMIBIA MADAGASCAR MAURITIUS Islands
Territory
(Australia) VANUATU

BOTSWANA MOZAMBIQUE Reunion
(France) New
Caledonia
(France) FIJI TONGA

AUSTRALIA Tropic of Capricorn 20°
S

SWAZILAND

LESOTHO

SOUTH AFRICA

40°

Kerguelen Islands
(France)

NEW
ZEALAND

60°

Antarctic Circle

The shading on this map is there to help
you see the different countries clearly.

ANTARCTICA

20° E 40° 60° 80° 100° 120° 140° 160° 180°

80°

19

80°

160°   140°   120°   100°   80°   60°   40°   20° W   0°

Beaufort Sea

Ellesmere Island

Victoria Island

Queen Elizabeth Islands

Baffin Bay

Baffin Island

Greenland

Greenland Sea

Iceland

Arctic Circle

Alaska

Mount McKinley
▲
6,194m
(20,321ft)

60°

Yukon

Gulf of Alaska

Hudson Bay

Labrador Sea

British Isles

Nort

Aleutian Islands

NORTH AMERICA

Rocky Mountains

Great Plains

Great Lakes

Newfoundland

North Sea

40°

Appalachian Mountains

Azores

Mississippi

Canary Islands

Atlas Mountain

Tropic of Cancer

Gulf of Mexico

S

20° N

Cuba

West Indies

Greater Antilles

Cape Verde Islands

S

Hawaiian Islands

Caribbean Sea

Lesser Antilles

Guiana Highlands

Equator   0°

P o l y n e s i a

PACIFIC

Galapagos Islands

Amazon Basin

Amazon

ATLANTIC

Selvas

OCEAN

Andes

SOUTH AMERICA

OCEAN

Tahiti

20° S

Tropic of Capricorn

Easter Island

Atacama Desert

Aconcagua
▲
6,959m
(22,831ft)

Pampas

40°

Patagonia

1:88,700,000

0   1,000   2,000   3,000   4,000   5,000km

0   1,000   2,000   3,000 miles

Falkland Islands

South Georgia

Cape Horn

60°

Antarctic Circle

Antarctic Peninsula

W e d d e l l Sea

80°

160°   140°   120°   100°   80°   60°   40°   20° W   0°

ARCTIC OCEAN

20° E 40° 60° 80° 100° 120° 140° 160° 180°

Svalbard   Novaya   Severnaya   Laptev Sea   New Siberia   East Siberian Sea
            Zemlya   Zemlya   Islands

North Cape   Kara Sea   80°

Barents Sea   Arctic Circle

Scandinavia   Ural Mountains   Verkhoyansk Range

North European Plain   Ob   Yenisey   Siberia   60°

EUROPE   Volga   ASIA   Lake   Sea   Kamchatka
                                               Baikal   of   Peninsula
        Mount   Aral   Okhotsk
        Elbrus   Sea   Altai Mountains Gobi
        5,642m   Caspian   Desert Huang He (Yellow)   Hokkaido
        (18,510ft) Sea   Sea   40°
Danube   Yellow   of
Black Sea   Himalayas   Sea   Japan   Honshu

Mediterranean Sea   Zagros Mountains   Chang Jiang (Yangtze)   East
                                                              China
        Tigris   Mount Everest   Sea   Taiwan   Tropic of Cancer
Sahara   Ganges   8,850m   20°
        Arabian   (29,035ft)   N
        Peninsula   Red Sea

Sahel   Deccan   Bay   South   Philippine   Micronesia   PACIFIC
                              Plateau   of   China   Islands
AFRICA   Ethiopian   Arabian   Bengal   Sea   OCEAN
            Highlands   Sea
        Lake   Sri Lanka   Celebes
        Victoria   Sea
Congo   Kilimanjaro   Seychelles   Mekong   Sumatra   Borneo   Equator
Basin   5,895m   Melanesia
Congo   (19,340ft)   INDIAN   Greater Sunda Islands   New Guinea
        Rift Valley   Mount Wilhelm   Solomon
                             OCEAN   Java   4,509m   Islands
        Comoro   (14,793ft)
        Islands   Lesser Sunda Islands   Arafura
                                                              Sea
Namib Desert   Madagascar   Coral   New   Fiji
        Mauritius   Sea   Caledonia Islands   20°
Kalahari Reunion   Great Sandy   Tropic of Capricorn   S
Desert   Desert   Great Barrier Reef

        Drakensberg   AUSTRALASIA   AND   OCEANIA
Cape of Good Hope   Great Victoria   Great Dividing Range
                                           Desert   North
                                                          Tasman   Island
                                                          Sea   South
                                                                  Island   40°

                        Kerguelen   Tasmania
                        Islands

SOUTHERN OCEAN

                                                          60°

                                  See page 17 for key.   Antarctic Circle

ANTARCTICA

20° E   40°   60°   80°   100°   120°   140°   160°   180°   80°

NORTH AMERICA

The name "North America" can be used to mean several different things. In this atlas, North America includes Greenland, Canada, the U.S.A., the Caribbean, and the countries of Central America, which run along the narrow strip of land between the U.S.A. and South America. The continent has over 20 countries, including Canada, the second-largest country in the world.

These are columns of rock called hoodoos in Bryce Canyon National Park, U.S.A.

Arctic Circle

ARCTIC OCEAN

Beaufort Sea

Bering Sea

Yukon

ALASKA
(U.S.A.)

Anchorage

Victoria Island

CANADA

Vancouver

Columbia

Missouri

PACIFIC

OCEAN

Hawaiian Islands
(U.S.A.)

UNITED STATES

Colorado

Los Angeles

Rio Grande

Tropic of Cancer

MEXICO

Mexico City

*Ellesmere
Island*

GREENLAND
(Denmark)

*Queen
Elizabeth
Islands*

*Baffin
Island*

Arctic Circle

Godthab■

*Hudson
Bay*

Newfoundland

St. Lawrence

Montreal
Ottawa■

*Great
Lakes*

Chicago⊙

New York

■**Washington D.C.**

ATLANTIC

OCEAN

OF AMERICA

Mississippi

Houston⊙

Tropic of Cancer

**THE
BAHAMAS**

*Gulf of
Mexico*

Havana■
CUBA

Puerto Rico
(U.S.A.)

Guadeloupe
(France)

DOMINICA
Martinique (France)

HAITI

**DOMINICAN
REPUBLIC**

BARBADOS

JAMAICA

**TRINIDAD
AND TOBAGO**

BELIZE

Caribbean Sea

HONDURAS

GUATEMALA

EL SALVADOR

NICARAGUA

COSTA RICA

PANAMA

The shading on this map is
there to help you see clearly
the different countries that
make up the continent.

Facts

Total land area 22,656,190 sq km
(8,745,289 sq miles)
Total population 487 million
Biggest city Mexico City, Mexico
Biggest country Canada 9,970,610
sq km (3,849,653 sq miles)
Smallest country Saint Kitts and
Nevis 269 sq km (104 sq miles)

Highest mountain Mount
McKinley, Alaska, U.S.A. 6,194m
(20,321ft)
Longest river Mississippi/Missouri,
U.S.A. 6,019km (3,741 miles)
Biggest lake Lake Superior,
between the U.S.A. and
Canada 82,414 sq km (31,820
sq miles)
Highest waterfall Yosemite Falls,
on the Yosemite Creek, California,
U.S.A. 739m (2,425ft)
Biggest desert Great Basin Desert,
U.S.A. 492,000 sq km (190,000
sq miles)
Biggest island Greenland
2,175,600 sq km (840,000 sq miles)

Main mineral deposits Silver, gold,
copper, lead, zinc, graphite,
molybdenum, nickel
Main fuel deposits Oil, coal,
natural gas, uranium

The bald eagle is the national bird
of the U.S.A. It is not really bald,
but has white feathers
on its head.

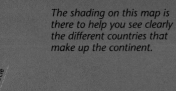

23

North America covers a huge area, from just south of the North Pole to just north of the Equator. The land in the far north is icy and barren, while southern areas are lush and tropical. The west is dominated by the snow-capped Rocky Mountains.

This satellite image of North America shows dry areas in brown, vegetation in green and icy regions in white.

Enormous parks

North America has many vast national parks. These are specially-protected natural areas where all kinds of animals live. One of the most famous parks is Yellowstone Park in Wyoming, U.S.A., which is home to wolves, black bears and many other animals. The park also has natural hot springs and geysers.

Erupting island

Half of the island of Hawaii is covered by Mauna Loa, the biggest volcano on Earth, and one of the most active. The volcano is monitored constantly to check for impending eruptions. Its biggest eruption was in 1950, when a wide river of red-hot lava flowed 24km (15 miles) to the sea, destroying roads and houses in its path.

This satellite image shows part of Mauna Loa volcano. The dark, round hole at the top is one of the volcano's craters, out of which lava and gases regularly explode.

This huge pool is a natural hot spring in Yellowstone Park, Wyoming, U.S.A. The water heats up under the ground.

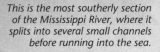

Internet links

For links to websites where you can find online tours and maps of the Grand Canyon and Yellowstone Park's hot springs, geysers and wildlife, go to **www.usborne-quicklinks.com**

This is the most southerly section of the Mississippi River, where it splits into several small channels before running into the sea.

Mighty Mississippi

The Mississippi/Missouri River is the longest river system in North America and the fourth-longest in the world. The Mississippi flows from Minnesota in northern U.S.A. to the Gulf of Mexico in the south. The Missouri begins in Montana, in the west, and joins the Mississippi in the state of Missouri. The river system is a busy shipping route, and is also vital for wildlife – migratory birds follow it as they fly south in the winter.

The deepest valley

The Grand Canyon, in Arizona, U.S.A., is the world's largest gorge, a deep valley that stretches over 400km (250 miles). In some parts it is 1.6km (1 mile) deep, and up to 29km (18 miles) wide.

The Grand Canyon was carved out by the Colorado River, which eroded the rocky land over many thousands of years. It is possible to hike down the sides of the Canyon, but they are so steep that it takes a whole day to get to the bottom.

Running from top left to bottom right of this satellite image is the jagged Grand Canyon, in the flat, dry state of Arizona, U.S.A. Smaller valleys join the main canyon.

The northern part of North America consists mainly of Canada and the U.S.A. and has many large, dynamic cities as well as forests, deserts and other vast natural spaces.

Huge clouds of spray and mist rise from Horseshoe Falls, one of the two spectacular waterfalls that form Niagara Falls. The falls divide the U.S.A. (left) and Canada (right).

Cold country

Canada has extremely cold, snowy winters, especially in northern and eastern areas. In the city of Montreal, an amazing 1m (40in) of snow once fell in a single day. Not surprisingly, Canada is famous for its many winter sports, such as skiing, ice-skating and ice hockey.

On the border

The border between Canada and the U.S.A. is the longest in the world, covering 6,416km (3,987 miles). In the east, the border runs through several huge lakes, known as the Great Lakes. This section of the border includes Niagara Falls, where water from Lake Erie crashes over two enormous waterfalls.

Big cities

The largest city in the U.S.A. is New York, which is also the country's financial capital. Other big cities include Los Angeles, home of the movie-making area Hollywood, and Las Vegas, which boasts the largest number of hotel rooms of any U.S. city.

At night, the casinos and hotels of Las Vegas are lit up in a blaze of neon lights.

Desert heat

Death Valley in California is the driest place in the U.S.A., and one of the hottest places in the world. The temperature in this vast wilderness has been known to reach a sweltering 57°C (134°F). The desert is generally barren, though when rain does occasionally fall, beautiful wild flowers spring up between the rocks.

An American alligator lazes in one of Florida's coastal swamps. Alligators eat birds, frogs and other animals – sometimes even small alligators.

In the foreground of this Las Vegas skyline is a replica of the Chrysler Building, a New York skyscraper. It is part of an extravagant hotel that has 12 towers, each in the shape of a famous New York building.

The sunshine state

Florida, in southeastern U.S.A., has a hot, tropical climate and is nicknamed "the sunshine state". Southern Florida is covered in swampy wetlands called the Everglades. All kinds of wildlife live there, including Florida panthers and American alligators.

Internet links

For links to websites where you can watch slide shows of U.S. cities, discover more about Canada with a map game and try a test-yourself quiz on Everglades animals, go to **www.usborne-quicklinks.com**

Central America is dominated by the country of Mexico, with its ancient ruins and crowded cities. Farther south, the countries near the border with South America have beautiful beaches, tropical rainforests and fiery volcanoes.

Here a bright wall mural is being painted in the coastal town of Cancun, one of Mexico's lively tourist spots.

City living

Mexico has a huge population, and also has millions of visitors every year. Its biggest city is the capital, Mexico City, where almost a quarter of Mexico's total population lives. The city is so overcrowded that the air is heavily polluted, and many people have poor living conditions and inadequate water supplies.

Ancient remains

These statues are in Tula, Mexico. They were built by the ancient Toltec people, and were probably columns that held up a roof.

In Mexico and nearby areas there are many remains of ancient cities. These were built by people from ancient civilizations, such as the Maya and the Toltec. The Maya had a powerful empire around AD200–900, while the Toltec ruled from about 900 to 1200. These peoples were excellent builders, and created many impressive temples and elaborately carved statues.

This is the Arenal volcano during a recent eruption. Lava can flow more than 2km (1.5 miles) from the volcano's base.

Land of volcanoes

Along the Pacific coast of Central America are more than 40 volcanoes. Lava from volcanic eruptions helps make the soil fertile, which is good for growing crops such as bananas and coffee. The volcanoes erupt regularly, and can be very dangerous. For example, the Arenal volcano in Costa Rica wiped out a whole town in a 1963 eruption, and has produced frequent lava flows ever since.

A white-nosed coati raids a banana tree in Costa Rica. These Central American mammals eat all kinds of fruit.

Sun and storms

The Caribbean islands have stunning sandy beaches and a hot climate. But their position in the Atlantic Ocean means that they are often hit by tropical storms and hurricanes. Some hurricanes reach wind speeds of 250kph (155mph).

Internet links

For links to websites where you can take virtual tours of Mexico and the Caribbean, and discover ancient Mayan sites on an interactive map, go to www.usborne-quicklinks.com

Linking oceans

The Panama Canal is one of the world's busiest shipping routes. It cuts through the country of Panama and is a short cut for ships sailing between the Atlantic and Pacific oceans. Before the canal opened, ships had to sail around South America, an extra 12,500km (7,800 miles).

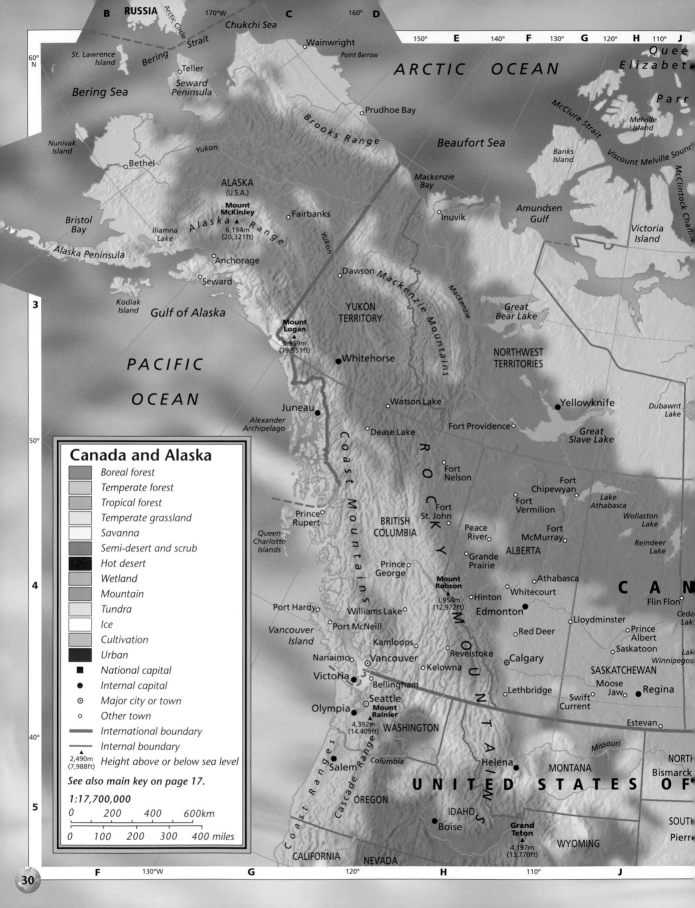

Arctic Circle

Chukchi Sea

60° N

Bering   Strait

Wainwright

Point Barrow

ARCTIC   OCEAN

Quee
Elizabet

St. Lawrence
Island

Teller

Seward
Peninsula

Bering Sea

Prudhoe Bay

Beaufort Sea

Parr

McClure Strait

Melville
Island

Nunivak
Island

Bethel

Yukon

ALASKA
(U.S.A.)

Brooks   Range

Mackenzie
Bay

Inuvik

Banks
Island

Viscount Melville Sound

McClintock Channel

Mount
McKinley
▲
6,194m
(20,321ft)

Fairbanks

Amundsen
Gulf

Victoria
Island

Bristol
Bay

Iliamna
Lake

Alaska   Range

Yukon

Anchorage

Alaska Peninsula

Seward

Kodiak
Island

Gulf of Alaska

Dawson

Mackenzie Mountains

Great
Bear Lake

3

Mount
Logan
▲
5,959m
(19,551ft)

YUKON
TERRITORY

Mackenzie

NORTHWEST
TERRITORIES

PACIFIC

OCEAN

Whitehorse

Watson Lake

Yellowknife

Dubawnt
Lake

Juneau

50°

Alexander
Archipelago

Dease Lake

Fort Providence

Great
Slave Lake

Fort
Nelson

Canada and Alaska

Boreal forest

Temperate forest

Tropical forest

Temperate grassland

Savanna

Semi-desert and scrub

Hot desert

Wetland

Mountain

Tundra

Ice

Cultivation

Urban

■   National capital

●   Internal capital

⊙   Major city or town

○   Other town

Prince
Rupert

Queen
Charlotte
Islands

Coast   Mountains

BRITISH
COLUMBIA

Fort
St. John

Peace
River

Fort
Chipewyan

Fort
Vermilion

Lake
Athabasca

Wollaston
Lake

Fort
McMurray

Reindeer
Lake

ALBERTA

C   A   N

4

Prince
George

Mount
Robson
▲
3,954m
(12,972ft)

R   O   C   K   Y

Grande
Prairie

Hinton

Athabasca

Whitecourt

Flin Flon

Ceda
Lak

Port Hardy

Williams Lake

Edmonton

Lloydminster

Prince
Albert

Vancouver
Island

Port McNeill

Red Deer

Saskatoon

Winnipego

Nanaimo

Kamloops

Vancouver

Revelstoke

Calgary

SASKATCHEWAN

International boundary

Internal boundary

2,490m
(7,988ft)   Height above or below sea level

See also main key on page 17.

1:17,700,000

0   200   400   600km

0   100   200   300   400 miles

Victoria

Bellingham

Seattle

Olympia

Salem

OREGON

Coast   Ranges

Cascade   Range

Columbia

Boise

IDAHO

Kelowna

Lethbridge

Swift
Current

Moose
Jaw

Regina

Estevan

Mount
Rainier
▲
4,392m
(14,409ft)

WASHINGTON

M   O   U   N   T

Helena

MONTANA

Missouri

NORTH

Bismarck

UNITED   STATES   OF

SOUTH

Pierre

Grand
Teton
▲
4,197m
(13,770ft)

WYOMING

CALIFORNIA

NEVADA

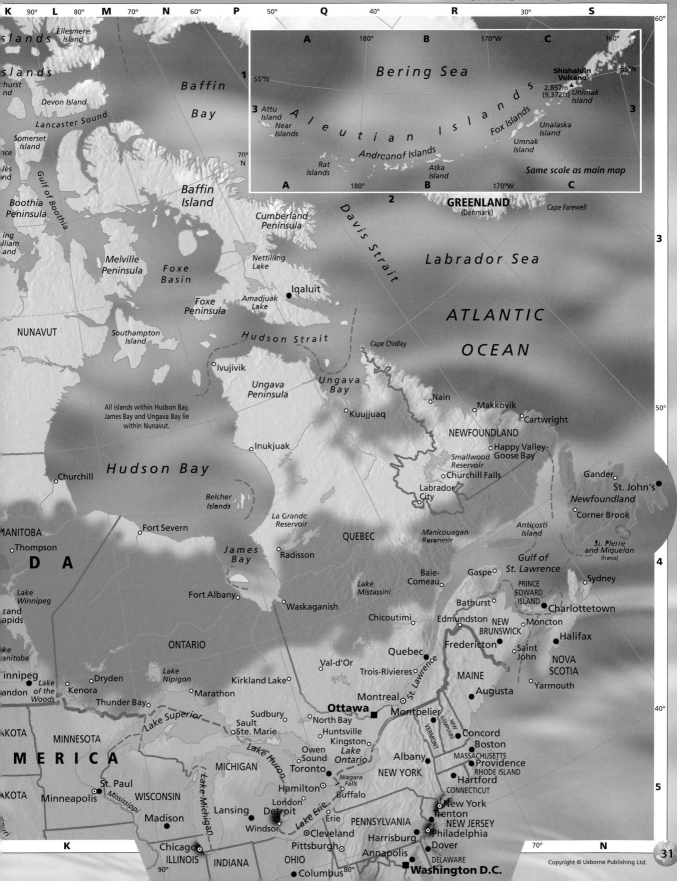

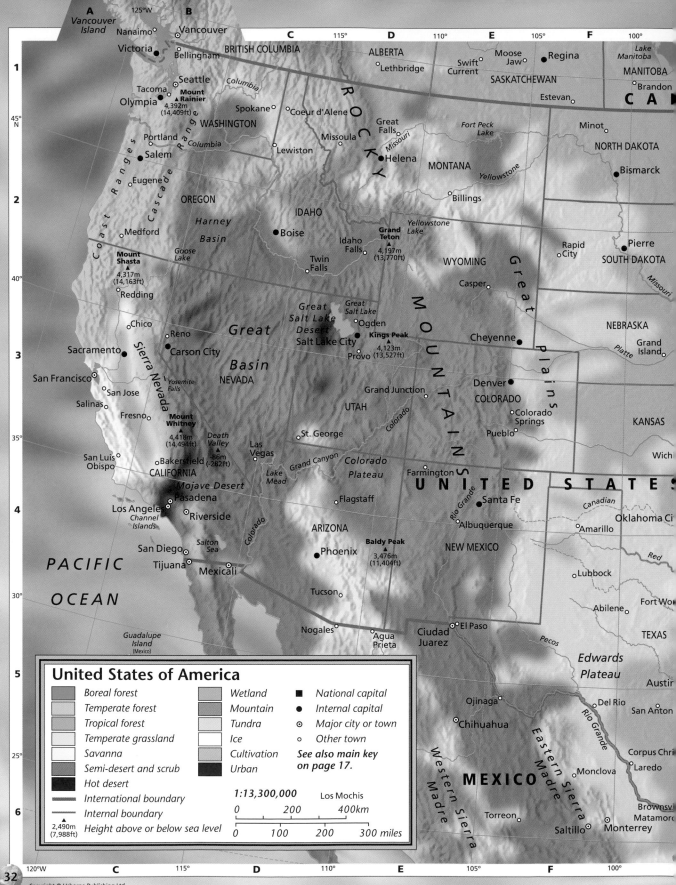

A
125°W
B
C
115°
D
110°
E
105°
F
100°

Vancouver
Island
Nanaimo
Vancouver
Victoria
Bellingham
BRITISH COLUMBIA
ALBERTA
Lethbridge
Swift
Current
Moose
Jaw
Regina
Lake
Manitoba
MANITOBA
Brandon
CAN

1

Seattle
Tacoma
Olympia
Mount
Rainier
4,392m
(14,409ft)
Columbia
Spokane
Coeur d'Alene
SASKATCHEWAN
Estevan
Minot
NORTH DAKOTA
Bismarck

45°
N
Portland
Salem
Eugene
WASHINGTON
Columbia
Lewiston
Missoula
Great
Falls
Helena
Missouri
MONTANA
Fort Peck
Lake
Yellowstone
Billings

2
Medford
OREGON
Harney
Basin
Goose
Lake
IDAHO
Boise
Idaho
Falls
Twin
Falls
Grand
Teton
4,197m
(13,770ft)
Yellowstone
Lake
WYOMING
Casper
Rapid
City
Pierre
SOUTH DAKOTA
Missouri

Mount
Shasta
4,317m
(14,163ft)
Redding
Chico
Reno
Carson City
Great
Salt Lake
Desert
Great
Salt Lake
Ogden
Salt Lake City
Kings Peak
4,123m
(13,527ft)
Provo
Cheyenne
NEBRASKA
Grand
Island

40°

3
Sacramento
San Francisco
San Jose
Salinas
Fresno
Sierra Nevada
Yosemite
Falls
Great
Basin
NEVADA
Grand Junction
Colorado
UTAH
Denver
COLORADO
Colorado
Springs
Pueblo
KANSAS
Wich

35°
San Luis
Obispo
Mount
Whitney
4,418m
(14,494ft)
Death
Valley
-86m
(-282ft)
Las
Vegas
St. George
Grand Canyon
Colorado
Plateau
Farmington
UNITED STATES
Canadian
Oklahoma Ci

4
Bakersfield
CALIFORNIA
Mojave Desert
Pasadena
Los Angeles
Riverside
Channel
Islands
Lake
Mead
Colorado
Flagstaff
Santa Fe
Albuquerque
Rio Grande
Amarillo
Red

San Diego
Tijuana
Mexicali
Salton
Sea
Colorado
ARIZONA
Phoenix
Baldy Peak
3,476m
(11,404ft)
NEW MEXICO
Lubbock
Fort Wo
Abilene
TEXAS

PACIFIC
Tucson

30°
OCEAN
Nogales
Agua
Prieta
Ciudad
Juarez
El Paso
Pecos
Edwards
Plateau
Austir

Guadalupe
Island
(Mexico)

Los Mochis

San Anton

5
Ojinaga
Del Rio
Rio Grande

Chihuahua
Corpus Chri
Laredo

25°
MEXICO
Western Sierra Madre
Eastern Sierra Madre
Monclova
Brownsvi
Matamor

6
Torreon
Saltillo
Monterrey

120°W
C
115°
D
110°
E
105°
F
100°

United States of America

Boreal forest	Wetland	■	National capital
Temperate forest	Mountain	●	Internal capital
Tropical forest	Tundra	⊙	Major city or town
Temperate grassland	Ice	○	Other town
Savanna	Cultivation		
Semi-desert and scrub	Urban	**See also main key**
Hot desert		**on page 17.**

International boundary
Internal boundary
2,490m
(7,988ft) Height above or below sea level

1:13,300,000

0   200   400km
0   100   200   300 miles

95° H 90° J 85° K 80° L 75° M 70° N 65°

Lake Winnipeg

innipeg Kenora Dryden Lake Nipigon ONTARIO

D A Lake of the Woods Marathon Kirkland Lake Cabonga Reservoir Val-d'Or Gouin Reservoir QUEBEC Chicoutimi Bathurst Edmundston NEW BRUNSWICK 1

and Forks Thunder Bay Sault Ste. Marie Sudbury North Bay Ottawa Huntsville Trois-Rivieres Montreal Quebec St. Lawrence MAINE St. Stephen Fredericton Saint John 45° N

argo Duluth MINNESOTA Lake Superior VERMONT Montpelier NEW HAMPSHIRE Portland Augusta Bangor Gulf of Maine 2

Minneapolis St. Paul Green Bay WISCONSIN MICHIGAN Lake Huron Owen Sound Toronto Lake Ontario Kingston Rochester Syracuse NEW YORK Albany Concord MASSACHUSETTS Boston Cape Cod Providence

oux Falls Madison Milwaukee Lake Michigan Grand Rapids Lansing Hamilton Niagara Falls Buffalo Springfield Hartford RHODE ISLAND CONNECTICUT

Sioux City Cedar Rapids Rockford Chicago South Bend Detroit Windsor London Lake Erie Erie Jamestown Newark New York Trenton 40°

Omaha Des Moines IOWA Peoria Fort Wayne Toledo Cleveland PENNSYLVANIA Harrisburg Pittsburgh Philadelphia NEW JERSEY Atlantic City

Lincoln ILLINOIS INDIANA OHIO Columbus Baltimore Dover DELAWARE 3

Kansas City Quincy Springfield Indianapolis Cincinnati WEST VIRGINIA MARYLAND Annapolis Washington D.C.

opeka Jefferson City St. Louis Evansville Ohio Frankfort Lexington Charleston Charlottesville VIRGINIA Richmond Virginia Beach

MISSOURI Cape Girardeau Kentucky Lake KENTUCKY Roanoke 35°

OF Springfield Plateau Ozark Nashville Knoxville Tennessee Greensboro Raleigh Cape Hatteras

Tulsa AMERICA Jonesboro Jackson TENNESSEE Chattanooga Appalachian Mountains NORTH CAROLINA Charlotte ATLANTIC 4

arkansas Little Rock Memphis Tupelo Huntsville Clark Hill Lake Columbia OCEAN

KLAHOMA ARKANSAS Mississippi Greenville Birmingham Tuscaloosa MISSISSIPPI ALABAMA GEORGIA SOUTH CAROLINA Charleston Macon

Texarkana Shreveport Vicksburg Meridian Jackson Montgomery Columbus Albany Savannah

Dallas LOUISIANA Hattiesburg Valdosta Jacksonville

aco Sam Rayburn Reservoir Toledo Bend Reservoir Mobile Pensacola Apalachee Bay Tallahassee Daytona Beach

Beaumont Baton Rouge New Orleans Mississippi Delta Orlando Cape Canaveral

ouston Galveston Mississippi Delta FLORIDA

Gulf of Mexico St. Petersburg Tampa Lake Okeechobee Grand Bahama Abaco THE BAHAMAS Eleuthera 25°

Fort Lauderdale Freeport City Cat Island

The Everglades Miami Nassau

Key West Florida Keys Andros Tropic of Cancer 6

Straits of Florida Long Island Acklins Island

Matanzas Santa Clara 75°

Havana CUBA Ciego de Avila 33

Cienfuegos Camaguey

Pinar del Rio 85° 80°

Hawaiian Islands inset:
160°W Same scale as main map Hawaiian Islands 7 Kauai Oahu Molokai Honolulu Kahului Maui HAWAII (U.S.A.) 4,205m (13,796ft)▲ 20°N 8 PACIFIC OCEAN Hilo 160°W P Hawaii 155°

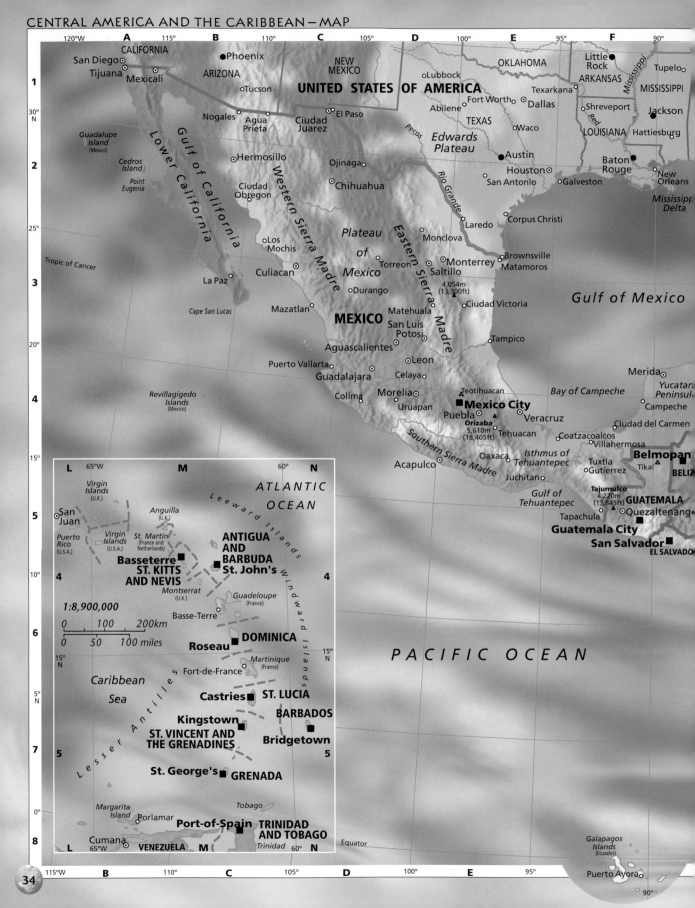

A   115°   B   110°   C   105°   D   100°   E   95°   F   90°

120°W

CALIFORNIA
San Diego
Tijuana
Mexicali
Phoenix
ARIZONA
NEW MEXICO
OKLAHOMA
Little Rock
ARKANSAS
Tupelo
MISSISSIPPI
Jackson

1

30°N
Nogales
Agua Prieta
Ciudad Juarez
El Paso
Lubbock
Abilene
Fort Worth
Waco
TEXAS
Texarkana
Dallas
Shreveport
LOUISIANA
Hattiesburg

UNITED STATES OF AMERICA

Guadalupe Island (Mexico)
Cedros Island
Point Eugenia
Hermosillo
Ciudad Obregon
Ojinaga
Chihuahua
Pecos
Rio Grande
Edwards Plateau
Austin
Houston
San Antonio
Galveston
Baton Rouge
New Orleans

2

25°
Tropic of Cancer
La Paz
Los Mochis
Culiacan
Durango
Plateau of Mexico
Torreon
Saltillo
Monclova
Monterrey
Matamoros
Laredo
Corpus Christi
Brownsville
Mississippi Delta

Gulf of Mexico

3

Cape San Lucas
Mazatlan
4,054m (13,300ft)
Matehuala
San Luis Potosi
Ciudad Victoria
Tampico

20°
Revillagigedo Islands (Mexico)
Aguascalientes
Leon
Merida
Yucatan Peninsula
Campeche
Bay of Campeche

4

Puerto Vallarta
Guadalajara
Celaya
Morelia
Colima
Uruapan
Teotihuacan
Mexico City
Puebla
Veracruz
Orizaba 5,610m (18,405ft)
Tehuacan
Ciudad del Carmen
Villahermosa
Coatzacoalcos
Belmopan
BELIZE

15°
Acapulco
Southern Sierra Madre
Oaxaca
Isthmus of Tehuantepec
Juchitan
Tuxtla Gutierrez
Tikal
Tajumulco 4,220m (13,845ft)
GUATEMALA
Quezaltenang

Gulf of Tehuantepec
Tapachula
Guatemala City
San Salvador
EL SALVADOR

MEXICO

Western Sierra Madre
Eastern Sierra Madre

Lower California
Gulf of California

Inset map (Caribbean):

L   65°W   M   60°   N

ATLANTIC OCEAN

Virgin Islands (U.K.)
San Juan
Puerto Rico (U.S.A.)
Virgin Islands (U.S.A.)
Anguilla (U.K.)
St. Martin (France and Netherlands)
Leeward Islands

ANTIGUA AND BARBUDA
St. John's

4

Basseterre
ST. KITTS AND NEVIS
Montserrat (U.K.)

1:8,900,000

0   100   200km
0   50   100 miles

Guadeloupe (France)
Basse-Terre

Windward Islands

6

Roseau
DOMINICA

15°N

Martinique (France)
Fort-de-France

Caribbean Sea

Castries
ST. LUCIA

5°N

Kingstown
ST. VINCENT AND THE GRENADINES

BARBADOS
Bridgetown

7

St. George's
GRENADA

5

Lesser Antilles

0°
Margarita Island
Porlamar
Tobago
Port-of-Spain
TRINIDAD AND TOBAGO

8

Cumana
VENEZUELA
Trinidad

L   65°W   M   60°   N

PACIFIC OCEAN

Equator

Galapagos Islands (Ecuador)

8

115°W   B   110°   C   105°   D   100°   E   95°

Puerto Ayora
90°

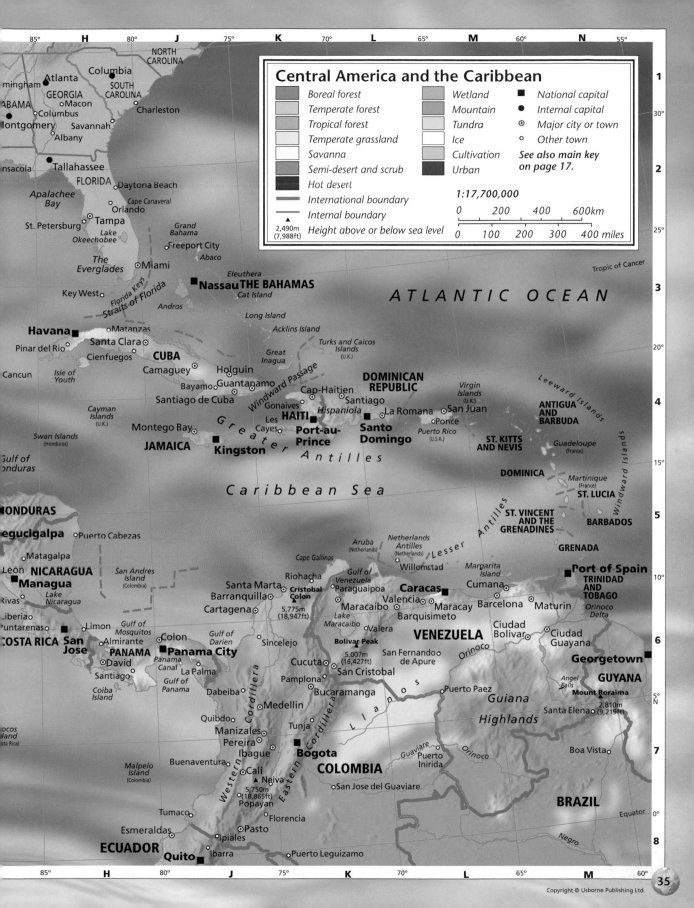

SOUTH AMERICA

South America is made up of 12 independent countries, along with French Guiana, which belongs to France. The continent's biggest and most industrialized country is Brazil, which covers about half of the total land. Brazil is also home to half of South America's population.

This is a guanaco. Guanacos are members of the camel family that live in South America. Guanaco hair is used to make textiles.

Caribbean Sea

Caracas

VENEZUELA

Medellin

Bogota

Orinoco

COLOMBIA

Equator

Quito

ECUADOR

Galapagos
Islands
(Ecuador)

Guayaquil

Mana

PERU

Lima

BOLIVIA

La Paz

Sucre

Tropic of Capricorn

CHILE

PACIFIC

OCEAN

Santiago

Mendoza

ARGENTIN

Cape Horn

Drake Passag

The shading on this map is there to help you see clearly the different countries that make up the continent.

Georgetown
Paramaribo
YANA   Cayenne
SURINAM   FRENCH
GUIANA
(France)

Equator

nazon

°Recife

B R A Z I L

■Brasilia

°Belo Horizonte

Parana

RAGUAY   Sao Paulo   ° Rio de Janeiro

Asuncion

Tropic of Capricorn

°Porto Alegre

ATLANTIC

OCEAN

URUGUAY
■Montevideo
uenos Aires

Falkland Islands
(U.K.)

This is a red-eyed tree frog. These frogs live in rainforests in South and Central America.

Facts

Total land area 17,866,130 sq km (6,898,113 sq miles)
Total population 346 million
Biggest city Sao Paulo, Brazil
Biggest country Brazil 8,547,400 sq km (3,300,151 sq miles)
Smallest country Surinam 163,270 sq km (63,039 sq miles)

Highest mountain Aconcagua, Argentina 6,959m (22,831ft)
Longest river Amazon, mainly in Brazil 6,440km (4,000 miles)
Biggest lake Lake Maracaibo, Venezuela 13,312 sq km (5,140 sq miles)
Highest waterfall Angel Falls, on the Churun River, Venezuela 979m (3,212ft)
Biggest desert Patagonian Desert, Argentina 673,000 sq km (260,000 sq miles)
Biggest island Tierra del Fuego 46,360 sq km (17,900 sq miles)

Main mineral deposits Copper, tin, molybdenum, bauxite, emeralds
Main fuel deposits Oil, coal

South America has a varied and dramatic landscape. In the north there are lush, tropical rainforests, and in central areas are grassy plains, called pampas. In the far south there are glaciers, which are huge, slow-moving masses of ice.

The big picture

The Andes mountain range stretches more than 7,250km (4,500 miles) down the whole length of western South America. It is the longest chain of mountains on Earth.

South America also has the second-longest river in the world, the Amazon. It snakes through the northern half of the continent, from the Andes in Peru to the coast of Brazil, and carries around one-fifth of the world's fresh water.

On this satellite image of South America the Andes mountains are clearly visible in the west. The range contains many active volcanoes.

This flock of large birds, called scarlet ibises, is flying over lush forest in Venezuela.

Icy lands

The southern tip of South America is near Antarctica, which means that the climate is extremely cold. There are glaciers in the mountainous regions, and icebergs in the area's many lakes. South America's most southerly point is Cape Horn. The seas around it are rough and stormy, which can make sailing around Cape Horn very dangerous.

The bluish-white shape in the middle of this image is part of a huge glacier. Melting ice gradually flows into Lake Viedma, shown in the bottom right.

Internet links

For links to websites where you can watch slide shows of Peru's people and places and visit Brazil, Argentina and other South American countries, go to **www.usborne-quicklinks.com**

Water source

On the border of Brazil and Paraguay is a vast expanse of water, about 1,350 sq km (520 sq miles) in size. This is the Itaipu reservoir, a man-made water source which provides water for homes, farms and factories in many areas of Brazil and Paraguay. In the past there had been many droughts, so the reservoir was built to provide a reliable supply of water.

This large blue area is part of the huge Itaipu reservoir, which forms part of the border between Paraguay (left) and Brazil (right).

The river running down the lower part of this image is the Parana River. It flows southward on the eastern side of South America.

This is a mountainous part of the Atacama Desert. In the middle are two snow-capped volcanoes, and on the right are white areas of salt from evaporated salt lakes.

The driest desert

Running down the western coast of Chile is the Atacama Desert, the driest place on Earth. Many areas of the desert go for decades without rain and in some parts rainfall has never been recorded.

Vast areas of the desert are covered in salt, which is all that is left of evaporated saltwater lakes. The rocky landscape looks like the Moon's surface, and NASA vehicles have been tested there in preparation for crossing the Moon's rugged terrain.

One of South America's main features is the Amazon rainforest. This is the largest rainforest in the world, covering an area nearly the size of Europe. The continent also has fascinating cities, both ancient and modern.

Machu Picchu

High in the Andes Mountains of Peru lies the ancient, ruined city of Machu Picchu. It was built by the Incas, the South American people who ruled the western part of the continent from about 1400 to 1530. The city contains the ruins of many stone buildings, such as temples, palaces and storerooms, which were built around large central courtyards.

This is Machu Picchu, in the Andes. The city's buildings were constructed on wide steps cut into the sloping ground.

Amazing Amazon

The Amazon rainforest spreads across northern South America and is home to one-third of all the world's animal species. The rainforest contains over 100 species of snakes, from rare boa constrictors to common green parrot snakes.

Parrot snakes live in trees in the Amazon rainforest. They often open their mouths wide like this to scare off predators.

Here is part of the wealthy, crowded financial district in Santiago, Chile.

City sprawl

South America has many huge cities, such as Sao Paulo in Brazil and Santiago in Chile. The growth of business and industry in these cities has led to the creation of towering skyscrapers, but also causes extra traffic and pollution. The cities are so overcrowded that many people live in poor, run-down suburbs.

Island animals

The Galapagos Islands are a cluster of small, rocky islands that lie in the Pacific Ocean, about 1,000km (600 miles) off the coast of Ecuador.

The islands are home to all kinds of unusual animals, such as giant tortoises. These enormous creatures weigh up to 250kg (550lb), and can live for more than a hundred years. Many tropical birds live on the islands too, including Galapagos penguins and frigate birds.

Fantastic falls

South America's mountainous landscape has led to the formation of many waterfalls, including Angel Falls in Venezuela, which is the world's biggest waterfall. It is 979m (3,212ft) high, more than twice the height of the tallest building in the world.

A male frigate bird puffs out his bright red pouch to attract females. Frigate birds live on many of the Galapagos Islands.

Internet links

For links to websites where you can watch a movie about the Amazon rainforest and take a virtual tour of Machu Picchu, go to **www.usborne-quicklinks.com**

NORTHERN SOUTH AMERICA—MAP

A 85°W   **B** 80°   **C**

Cape Gallinas   Aruba 70°   Netherlands Antilles   65°
Willemstad   Lesser Antilles   **GRENADA**
75°   (Netherlands)   (Netherlands)

1   Liberia   Riohacha   Gulf of   Paraguaipoa   Coro   Tortuga   Margarita   **TRINIDAD AND TOBAGO**
10°   Puntarenas   Santa Marta   Cristobal   Venezuela   Island   Island
   Limon   Barranquilla   Colon   Maracaibo   Maracay   **Caracas**   Cumana   Guiria   **Port-of Spain**
San Jose   Cartagena   5,775m   Lagunillas   Barcelona   Maturin
COSTA   Colon   (18,947ft)   Lake   Barquisimeto   Valencia   Tucupita
RICA   Almirante   Sincelejo   Maracaibo   Valera   Araure   Zaraza   Ciudad   Orinoco
   David   **Panama City**   Magangue   **Bolivar Peak**   Barinas   **VENEZUELA**   Bolivar   Delta

2   Puerto   Santiago   Penonome   Panama   La Palma   Turbo   Caceres   5,007m   San Fernando   Caicara   Ciudad   Angel
  Armuelles   **PANAMA**   Canal   Pamplona   (16,427ft)   de Apure   Guayana   Falls
  Coiba   Gulf of   Dabeiba   Bucaramanga   San Cristobal   Cravo   Puerto   **Mount Roraima**
  Island   Panama   Medellin   Duitama   Norte   Paez   2,810m   (9,219ft)
   Nuqui   Quibdo   Tunja   Guiana   Santa Elena

5° N   Malpelo Island   Pereira   Manizales   **Bogota**   Highlands   Boa Vista
   (Colombia)   Buga   Ibague   Guaviare   Orinoco
  Buenaventura   Cali   **COLOMBIA**   Puerto   Inirida

3   Tumaco   Popayan   5,750m   Neiva   San Jose del Guaviare
   (18,865ft)   Florencia
  Esmeraldas   Cape   Ibarra   Ipiales   Pasto
   San Francisco   **Quito**   Nueva Loja   Puerto Leguizamo   Negro

0° Equator   Santo Domingo de los Colorados   Quevedo   La Chorrera   Japura
  Manta   Ambato   6,310m   (20,702ft)   Montalvo
   ECUADOR   Babahoyo
4   La Libertad   Guayaquil   Amazon   Amazon
  Gulf of   Cuenca   Iquitos
  Guayaquil   Tumbes   Machala   Leticia
  Talara   Loja   Maranon   Atalaia do Norte
5° S   Sullana   Zumba   **S e l v a s**
  Piura   Chulucanas   Yurimaguas   Ucayali   Jurua
  Cape Negro   Chiclayo   Moyobamba   Purus   Madeira

5   Pacasmayo   Cajamarca   **PERU**   Cruzeiro do Sul   Porto Velho
  Trujillo   Huacrachuco   Pucallpa
  Chimbote   **Mount Huascaran**   Huanuco   Rio Branco   Riberalta

10°   6,746m   (22,132ft)   Cerro de Pasco   Cobija
  PACIFIC   La Oroya   Puerto   Maldonado
  OCEAN   Huancayo   Magdalena
6   **Lima**   Quillabamba   Machu Picchu   Rurrenabaque
  Mala   Ayacucho   Cusco   Trinidad
  Chincha Alta   Ica   Sicuani
15°   Nazca   **Mount Coropuna**   Juliaca   Lake Titicaca   Concepcion
  Chala   6,425m   (21,079ft)   Puno   **La Paz**   **BOLIVIA**   Cochabamba
7   Mollendo   Arequipa   **Mount Illimani**   Oruro   Santa   San Jose de
   6,402m   (21,004ft)   Cruz   Chiquitos
  Gulf of Arica   Lake   Challapata
   Arica   Poopo   **Sucre**
  CHILE   Potosi   Camiri   Charagua

20°

Galapagos Islands inset:

N   90°W   **P**
Same scale as main map
9   Galapagos Islands   **9**
   (Ecuador)
0° Equator   San Salvador   **0°**
Fernandina   Santa Cruz
Isabela   Puerto   San Cristobal
10   Ayora   **10**
PACIFIC OCEAN
N   90°W   **P**

42

A 85°W   **B** 80°   **C** 75°   **D** 70°   **E** 65°   **F**

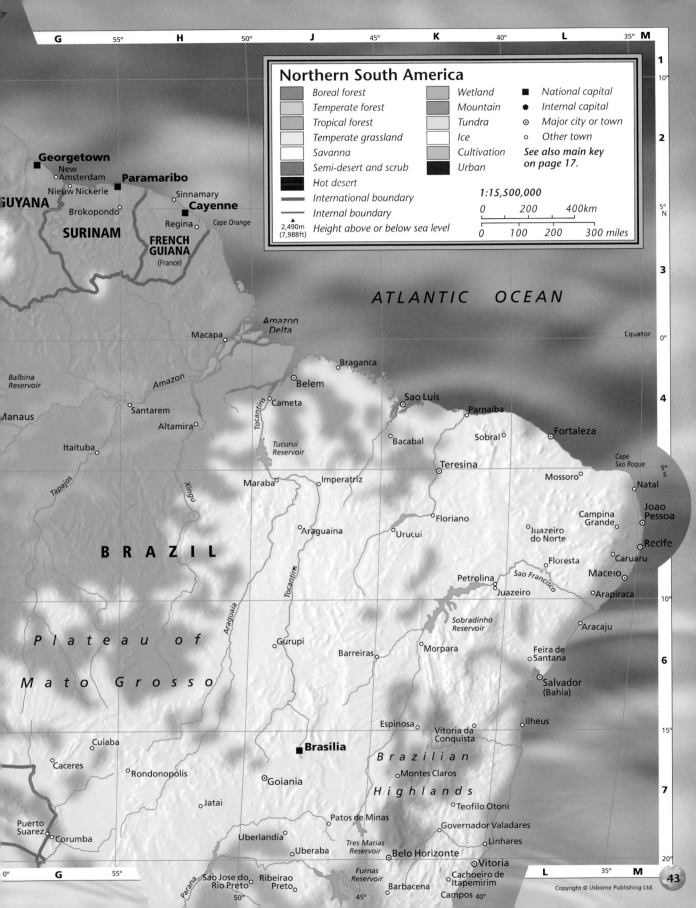

Northern South America

Boreal forest
Temperate forest
Tropical forest
Temperate grassland
Savanna
Semi-desert and scrub
Hot desert
International boundary
Internal boundary
▲ 2,490m (7,988ft) Height above or below sea level

Wetland
Mountain
Tundra
Ice
Cultivation
Urban

■ National capital
● Internal capital
⊙ Major city or town
○ Other town

See also main key on page 17.

1:15,500,000

0   200   400km
0   100   200   300 miles

ATLANTIC OCEAN

Georgetown
New Amsterdam
Nieuw Nickerie
GUYANA
Brokopondo
SURINAM
Paramaribo
Sinnamary
Cayenne
Regina
FRENCH GUIANA
(France)
Cape Orange

Equator

Macapa
Amazon Delta
Braganca
Belem
Balbina Reservoir
Amazon
Manaus
Santarem
Altamira
Itaituba
Cameta
Tocantins
Tucurui Reservoir
Sao Luis
Parnaiba
Bacabal
Sobral
Fortaleza
Cape Sao Roque
Teresina
Mossoro
Natal

Tapajos
Xingu
Maraba
Imperatriz
Floriano
Urucui
Juazeiro do Norte
Campina Grande
Joao Pessoa
Recife
Caruaru

B R A Z I L
Araguaina
Floresta
Maceio
Petrolina
Sao Francisco
Juazeiro
Arapiraca

Araguaia
Tocantins
Gurupi
Barreiras
Morpara
Sobradinho Reservoir
Aracaju

P l a t e a u   o f
Espinosa
Feira de Santana
Salvador
(Bahia)

M a t o   G r o s s o
Vitoria da Conquista
Ilheus

Cuiaba
Caceres
Rondonopolis
Brasilia
B r a z i l i a n
Montes Claros
Goiania
H i g h l a n d s

Jatai
Teofilo Otoni
Patos de Minas
Governador Valadares
Puerto Suarez
Corumba
Uberlandia
Tres Marias Reservoir
Linhares
Uberaba
Belo Horizonte
Vitoria
Sao Jose do Rio Preto
Ribeirao Preto
Furnas Reservoir
Cachoeiro de Itapemirim
Parana
Barbacena
Campos

43

Copyright © Usborne Publishing Ltd.

SOUTHERN SOUTH AMERICA—MAP

1
10°
S
2
15°
3
20°
4
25°
5
30°
6

D 70°W
65°
60°
55°
50°
45°
40°

L
K
J
H
G
F
E

Sobradinho
Reservoir

Morpara

Feira de Santana
Ilheus
Vitoria da
Conquista

Espinosa
Montes Claros
Teofilo Otoni
Linhares

Barreiras
Governador
Valadares
Vitoria
Cachoeiro
de Itapemirim
Campos

Patos de Minas
Belo Horizonte
Barbacena
Juiz
de Fora
Macae
Nova Iguacu
Rio de Janeiro
Tropic of Capricorn

B r a z i l i a n   H i g h l a n d s

Brasilia
Goiania
Uberaba
Furnas
Reservoir
Tres Marias
Reservoir
Pocos de
Caldas
Mount
Agulhas
Negras
2,787m
(9,144ft)
Sao Paulo

Ribeirao
Preto
Araraquara
Campinas

Gurupi
Uberlandia
Sao Jose do Rio Preto
Presidente
Prudente
Marilia
Itapetininga
Curitiba
Paranagua
Itajai
Florianopolis
Criciuma

B R A Z I L

Tocantins

Araguaia

P l a t e a u   o f

M a t o   G r o s s o

Jatai

Campo Grande
Dourados
Ponta Pora
Londrina
Cascavel
Foz do Iguacu
Iguacu
Falls
Eldorado
Guarapuava
Passo Fundo
Santa Maria
Caxias do Sul
Porto Alegre
Patos
Lagoon
Rio Grande

Rondonopolis

Cuiaba

Caceres

Corumba

Puerto Suarez
Pedro Juan
Caballero
Concepcion
Ciudad
del
Este
Posadas
Mirim
Lake

Paraguay
PARAGUAY
Asuncion
Villarrica
Encarnacion
Uruguaiana
Rivera
Bage
Pelotas
Melo
URUGUAY
Durazno
Minas

San Jose de
Chiquitos

Concepcion
Santa Cruz
Camiri
Formosa
Reconquista
Concordia
Salto
Tacuarembo
Paysandu
Gualeguaychu

Parana

BOLIVIA
Sucre
Charagua
Tarija
Tartagal
San Salvador
de Jujuy
San Miguel de Tucuman
Corrientes
Santiago del Estero
Salado
Santa Fe
San Nicolas
de los Arroyos
Buenos
Aires

Cochabamba
Oruro
Challapata
Potosi
Jyuni
Tupiza
Salta
Catamarca
La Rioja
San Francisco
Venado
Tuerto
Chacabuco

Mount
Illimani
6,402m
(21,004ft)
La Paz
Lake
Titicaca
Lake
Poopo
Ollague
Uyuni
San Pedro de Atacama
Mount
Ojos del Salado
6,908m
(22,664ft)
Cordoba
Rio Cuarto
Villa Maria
Rufino
Merlo
San Luis
Villa Mercedes

PERU
Juliaca
Puno
Iquique
Calama
Antofagasta
San Juan
Mendoza
San Rafael
Aconcagua
6,959m
(22,831ft)

Rio Branco
Cobja
Puerto
Maldonado
Riberalta
Rurrenabaque
Magdalena
Trinidad

C H I L E
Taltal
Chanara
Copia
Valle
Coquimbo
Ovalle
Illapel
Valparaiso
Santiago
Rancagua
San Fernando

Tropic of

A n d e s

G r a n   C h a c o

Pilcomayo

Rosario

44

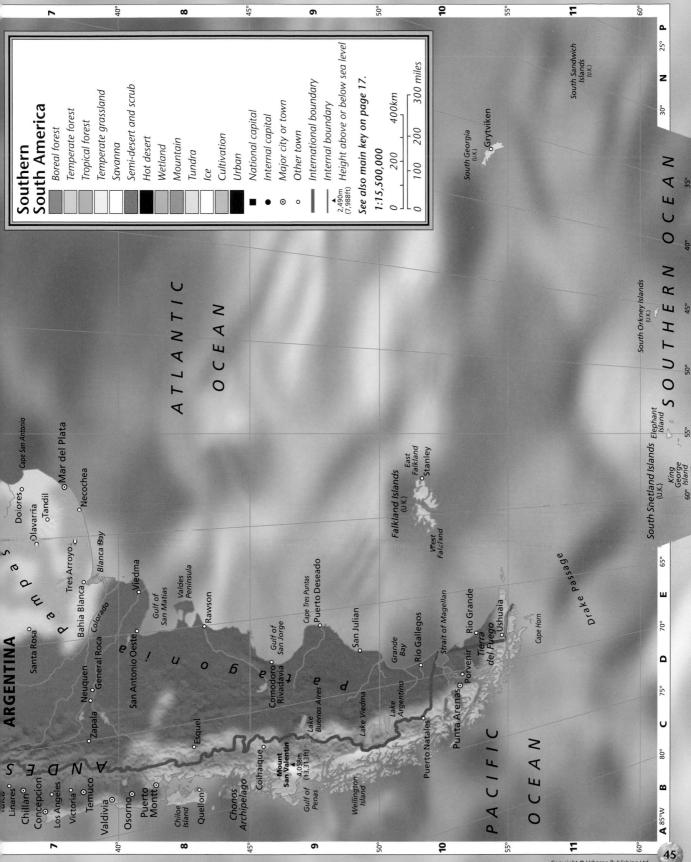

AUSTRALASIA AND OCEANIA

Australasia is made up of Australia, New Zealand and Papua New Guinea. Oceania is a collection of over 20,000 islands stretching out into the Pacific Ocean.

Northern Mariana Islands
(U.S.A.)

International Date Line

Guam (U.S.A.)

MARSHALL ISLANDS

Koror ■

Palikir ■

■ Majuro

PALAU

FEDERATED STATES OF MICRONESIA

■ Bairiki

Equator

■ Yaren

NAURU

KIRIBATI

INDIAN

PAPUA NEW GUINEA

New Guinea

SOLOMON ISLANDS

TUVALU
Funafuti ■

OCEAN

Arafura Sea

Port Moresby ■

Honiara ■

SAMOA

Wallis and Futuna (France)

Coral Sea Islands Territory (Australia)

VANUATU

FIJI

Apia

Coral Sea

Port-Vila ■

■ Suva

TONGA

New Caledonia (France)

Nukualofa ■

Noumea

Tropic of Capricorn

AUSTRALIA

Brisbane

Darling

Perth

Adelaide

Murray

Sydney

Canberra

NEW ZEALAND

Auckland

Melbourne

North Island

Tasmania

Tasman Sea

Wellington

Christchurch

South Island

International Date Line

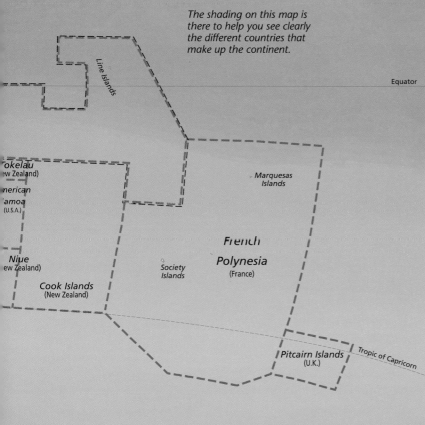

This small island belongs to Papua New Guinea.

PACIFIC OCEAN

The shading on this map is there to help you see clearly the different countries that make up the continent.

Line Islands

Equator

Tokelau
(New Zealand)

American
Samoa
(U.S.A.)

Marquesas
Islands

Niue
(New Zealand)

Society
Islands

French
Polynesia
(France)

Cook Islands
(New Zealand)

Pitcairn Islands
(U.K.)

Tropic of Capricorn

Facts

Total land area 8,564,400 sq km (3,306,715 sq miles)

Total population 31 million

Biggest city Sydney, Australia

Biggest country Australia 7,686,850 sq km (2,967,124 sq miles)

Smallest country Nauru 21 sq km (8 sq miles)

Highest mountain Mount Wilhelm, Papua New Guinea 4,509m (14,793ft)

Longest river Murray/Darling River, Australia 3,718km (2,310 miles)

Biggest lake Lake Eyre, Australia 9,000 sq km (3,470 sq miles)

Highest waterfall Sutherland Falls, on the Arthur River, New Zealand 580m (1,904ft)

Biggest desert Great Victoria Desert, Australia 388,500 sq km (150,000 sq miles)

Biggest island New Guinea 800,000 sq km (309,000 sq miles) (Australia is counted as a continental land mass and not as an island.)

Main mineral deposits Iron, nickel, precious stones, lead, bauxite

Main fuel deposits Oil, coal, uranium

The Moorish idol fish is found in shallow waters throughout the Pacific. It has very bold stripes and a long, distinctive snout.

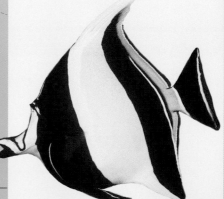

47

Australasia and Oceania's climate is generally very hot. New Zealand and Papua New Guinea are both lush, while Australia is mostly barren. The tiny tropical islands that make up Oceania are surrounded by vast areas of open sea.

This image shows a section of the Southern Alps of South Island, New Zealand. The two turquoise patches are Lake Pukaki and Lake Tekapo.

In this satellite view of Australasia and Oceania, areas of vegetation are green and desert areas are yellow.

Milky waters

New Zealand has two main islands, North Island and South Island, and several smaller ones. On South Island there is a mountain range called the Southern Alps, which has some dramatic milky-turquoise lakes. Their cloudy appearance is caused by rock dust, which is collected, finely ground and then deposited in the lake by glaciers. The rock dust is so fine, it stays suspended in the water, instead of sinking.

Land of bushfires

Most of Australia is hot, dry desert and the country suffers badly from bushfires almost every year. The fires are usually caused by lightning striking dry vegetation. Some species of trees found in Australia have adapted to cope with the constant outbreaks of fire. Eucalyptus trees can withstand fire, and some types of banksia trees actually need fire to open their seed pods.

Internet links

For links to websites with photo galleries, video clips and tours of Australasia and Oceania, go to **www.usborne-quicklinks.com**

These are the Palau Rock Islands of Micronesia, Oceania. There are over 200 rock islands in total. Each one is made of limestone rock and covered with thick forest.

Tropical islands

Lots of the small islands in the South Pacific are volcanoes. Coral reefs (dense colonies of tentacled sea animals) often grow in shallow waters around the islands. They form barriers which trap water between the reef and the island's coast. The trapped water is known as a lagoon.

Many of the volcanoes are inactive, and are slowly sinking back into the sea. Sometimes, a volcano sinks entirely into the sea, leaving behind a shallow lagoon surrounded by a coral reef. This is called an atoll.

This is Bora Bora Island, a volcanic island in the South Pacific. Vegetation is green, deep water is black and shallow water is pale blue.

The coral reef is the thin, white line around the edge.

This is Lake Eyre in Australia. It wasn't completely dry when this picture was taken – dry areas are pale pink and wet areas are dark pink.

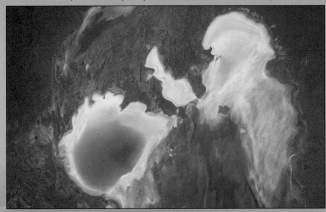

A vanishing lake

Australia's largest salt lake, Lake Eyre, is in the dry, central part of the country. Most of the year it is virtually dry, and you can see a glistening sheet of white salt on the lake bed. When the lake fills, it spreads out over 9,500 sq km (3,670 sq miles), but this usually only happens about once every eight years. The lake has two main sections, Lake Eyre North and Lake Eyre South, which are joined by a channel called the Goyder Channel.

Australasia and Oceania's attractions include a group of huge stone carvings, a strange tree formation and animals equipped with their own baby-carriers.

Great Barrier Reef

Around the coast of Queensland, Australia, lies the Great Barrier Reef, an enormous coral reef structure. It is made up of over 2,800 coral reefs, covering 345,000 sq km (133,200 sq miles) and is home to more than 1,500 species of fish.

Coral reefs are very fragile. They are found in clear, shallow waters with a constant, warm temperature. Global warming might make the sea too hot for coral reefs to survive, and the Great Barrier Reef could die out.

Easter Island

Easter Island is a remote island, far east of Australia, famous for its large stone carvings of human figures with large heads. The carvings are thought to be between 400 and 1,000 years old, and are believed to represent the spirits of important chiefs and ancestors of the island. A Dutch navigator named Jacob Roggeveen gave Easter Island its name when he first visited it on Easter day in 1722.

These sculptures on Easter Island were carved out of volcanic rock. They are about 4m (13ft) tall, and some are partly buried.

Internet links

For links to websites where you can dive into the Great Barrier Reef and explore Easter Island, go to **www.usborne-quicklinks.com**

The Olgas

In Uluru National Park, in Australia's Northern Territory, there is a group of 36 enormous rocks known as the Olgas. The rocks are a type of sandstone, which means they were formed by loose sand that has become hardened and folded by the Earth's movements to produce layered rocks. The rocks were gradually eroded by wind and rain into the rounded hills we see today. The sand grains that make up the sandstone are mostly made of a pink mineral called feldspar.

These rounded rocks are the Olgas. The aboriginals, who were the first people to settle in Australia, named the site "Kata Tjunta" meaning "many heads".

This is a tree kangaroo, a type of animal only found in Queensland, Australia, and Papua New Guinea. Tree kangaroos can leap great distances from tree to tree.

The seven-in-one tree

On the island of Rarotonga, in the Cook Islands, there is a group of seven coconut trees which have grown naturally in a perfect circle. A legend tells that the seven trees grew from one seed, so they are known as the "seven-in-one tree", but they probably grew from seven separate seeds.

Marsupials

Australasia and Oceania are home to lots of unusual animals, including a group of mammals called marsupials. As soon as marsupials are born, they crawl into a pouch of skin on their mother's tummy. They stay inside the pouch for the first few months of their lives. Kangaroos, koalas, wombats and possums are all marsupials.

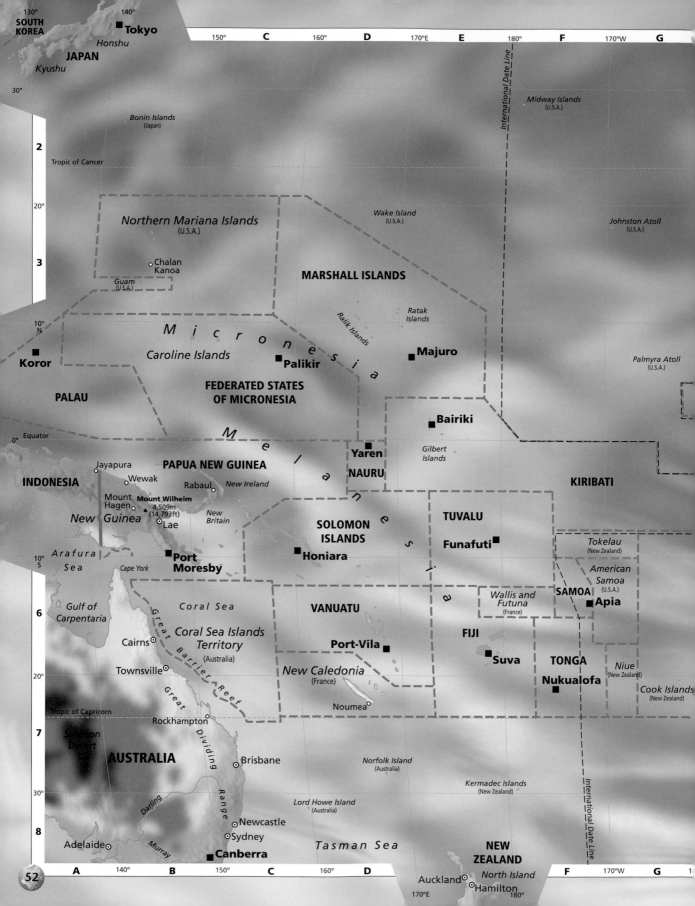

SOUTH
KOREA
■ Tokyo
JAPAN
Honshu

Kyushu

150°   C   160°   D   170°E   E   180°   F   170°W   G

30°

Bonin Islands
(Japan)

2

Tropic of Cancer

International Date Line

Midway Islands
(U.S.A.)

20°

Northern Mariana Islands
(U.S.A.)

Wake Island
(U.S.A.)

Johnston Atoll
(U.S.A.)

3

○ Chalan
Kanoa

MARSHALL ISLANDS

Guam
(U.S.A.)

10°
N

M i c r o n e s i a

Ralik Islands

Ratak
Islands

■ Koror

Caroline Islands

■ Majuro

Palmyra Atoll
(U.S.A.)

PALAU

■ Palikir

FEDERATED STATES
OF MICRONESIA

M e *l* a *n*

■ Bairiki

Equator

0°

Gilbert
Islands

Jayapura ○

PAPUA NEW GUINEA

■ Yaren

KIRIBATI

INDONESIA

○ Wewak

Rabaul ○

New Ireland

NAURU

New Guinea

Mount
Hagen ○

Mount Wilhelm
▲ 4,509m
(14,793ft)
○ Lae

New
Britain

TUVALU

Tokelau
(New Zealand)

Arafura
Sea

SOLOMON
ISLANDS

■ Funafuti

American
Samoa
(U.S.A.)

10°
S

■ Port
Moresby

Cape York

■ Honiara

e
s
i

Wallis and
Futuna
(France)

SAMOA

■ Apia

Gulf of
Carpentaria

Cairns ○

Coral Sea

VANUATU

a

FIJI

6

Coral Sea Islands
Territory
(Australia)

Port-Vila ■

■ Suva

TONGA

Niue
(New Zealand)

Townsville ○

Great

New Caledonia
(France)

20°

Barrier

■ Nukualofa

Cook Islands
(New Zealand)

Tropic of Capricorn

Reef

Noumea ○

Rockhampton ○

7

Simpson
Desert

Great

Brisbane ○

Norfolk Island
(Australia)

AUSTRALIA

Dividing

Kermadec Islands
(New Zealand)

30°

Darling

Range

Lord Howe Island
(Australia)

8

○ Newcastle

Adelaide ○

Murray

○ Sydney

■ Canberra

Tasman Sea

NEW
ZEALAND

International Date Line

A   140°   B   150°   C   160°   D   170°E   F   170°W   G

Auckland ○   *North Island*

170°E   ○ Hamilton   180°

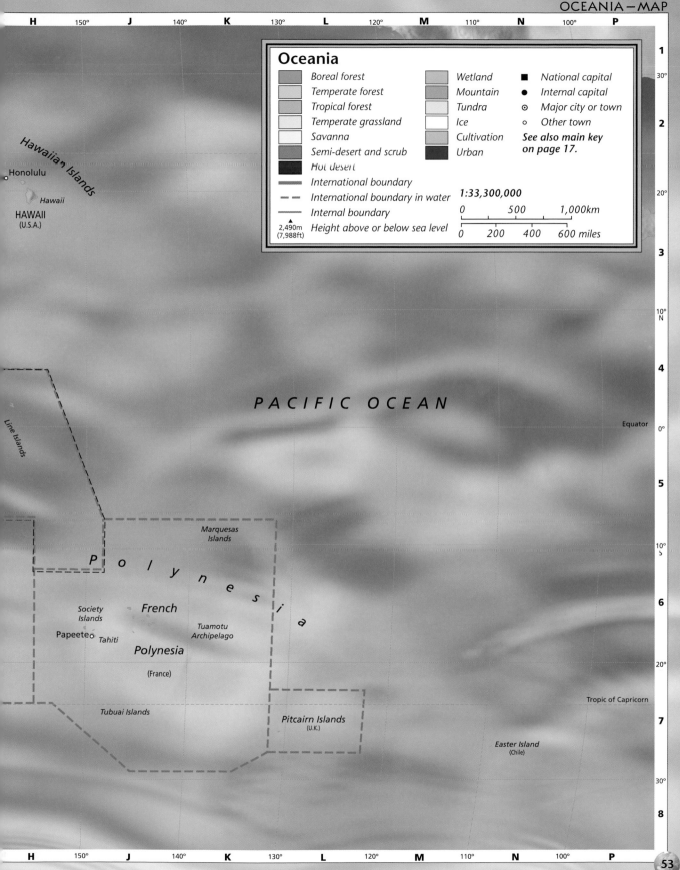

Oceania

Boreal forest	Wetland	■ National capital
Temperate forest	Mountain	● Internal capital
Tropical forest	Tundra	⊙ Major city or town
Temperate grassland	Ice	○ Other town
Savanna	Cultivation	
Semi-desert and scrub	Urban	See also main key on page 17.
Hot desert		

International boundary
International boundary in water
Internal boundary
▲ 2,490m (7,988ft) Height above or below sea level

1:33,300,000

0   500   1,000km
0   200   400   600 miles

Honolulu
Hawaiian Islands
Hawaii
HAWAII (U.S.A.)

PACIFIC OCEAN

Equator

Line Islands

Marquesas Islands

Polynesia

Society Islands
French
Tuamotu Archipelago
Papeete Tahiti
Polynesia
(France)

Tubuai Islands

Pitcairn Islands (U.K.)

Easter Island (Chile)

Tropic of Capricorn

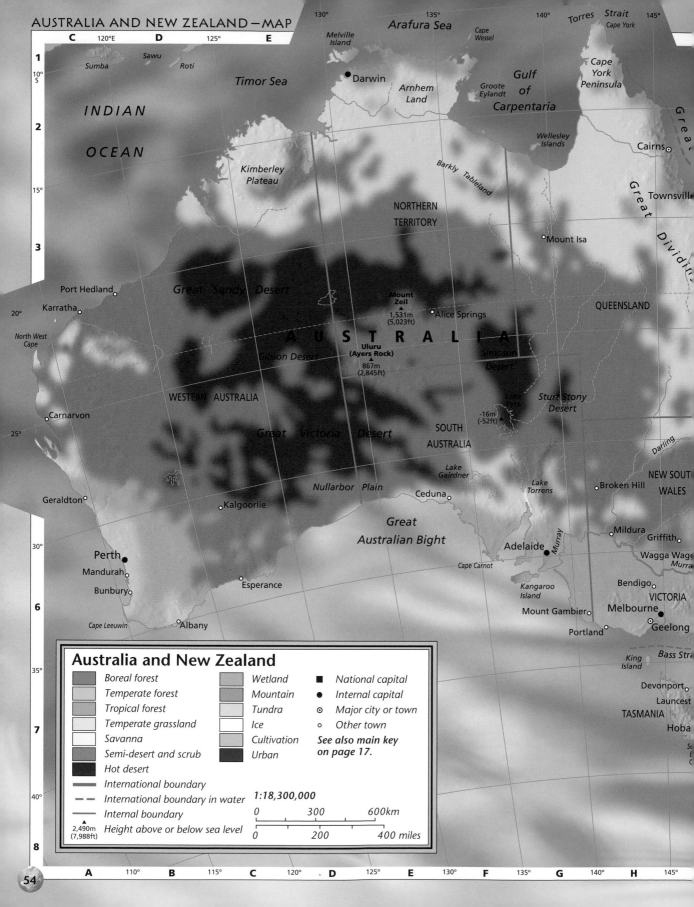

Arafura Sea

Torres Strait

Cape Wessel

Cape York

INDIAN OCEAN

Timor Sea

Melville Island

Darwin

Arnhem Land

Gulf of Carpentaria

Groote Eylandt

Cape York Peninsula

Wellesley Islands

Great Dividing

Cairns

Kimberley Plateau

Barkly Tableland

NORTHERN TERRITORY

Townsville

Port Hedland

Karratha

Great Sandy Desert

Mount Zeil
1,531m
(5,023ft)

Alice Springs

Mount Isa

QUEENSLAND

North West Cape

A U S T R A L I A

Uluru
(Ayers Rock)
867m
(2,845ft)

Simpson Desert

Carnarvon

Gibson Desert

WESTERN AUSTRALIA

Lake Eyre
-16m
(-52ft)

Sturt Stony Desert

Great Victoria Desert

SOUTH AUSTRALIA

Darling

Geraldton

Kalgoorlie

Nullarbor Plain

Lake Gairdner

Ceduna

Lake Torrens

Broken Hill

NEW SOUTH WALES

Mildura

Griffith

Great Australian Bight

Adelaide

Murray

Wagga Wagga

Perth

Mandurah

Bunbury

Esperance

Cape Carnot

Kangaroo Island

Bendigo

VICTORIA

Cape Leeuwin

Albany

Mount Gambier

Melbourne

Geelong

Portland

King Island

Bass Strait

Devonport

Launceston

TASMANIA

Hoba

Australia and New Zealand

- Boreal forest
- Temperate forest
- Tropical forest
- Temperate grassland
- Savanna
- Semi-desert and scrub
- Hot desert
- Wetland
- Mountain
- Tundra
- Ice
- Cultivation
- Urban

■ National capital
● Internal capital
⊙ Major city or town
○ Other town

See also main key on page 17.

── International boundary
--- International boundary in water
── Internal boundary
▲ 2,490m (7,988ft) Height above or below sea level

1:18,300,000

0   300   600km

0   200   400 miles

A 110°   B 115°   C 120°   D 125°   E 130°   F 135°   G 140°   H 145°

Coral Sea

Rennell
Island

SOLOMON ISLANDS   Santa Cruz
Islands

TUVALU

10°
S

1

*Coral Sea
Islands
Territory*
(Australia)

VANUATU   Banks Islands

2

Espiritu
Santo
○ Luganville

Malakula

15°

Chesterfield
Islands

Efate ■ **Port-Vila**

FIJI

Vanua Levu

New Caledonia
(France)

Lautoka
○

Viti Levu   ■ **Suva**

○ Mackay

Barrier Reef

3

○ khampton

○ Gladstone

○ Bundaberg

Range

Fraser Island

○ Gympie

Noumea
○

*Loyalty
Islands*

20°

Toowoomba ○

● Brisbane
◎ Gold Coast

PACIFIC OCEAN

4

○ Moree

Great Dividing Range

○ Grafton

○ Armidale

25°

Norfolk Island
○ (Australia)

○ Dubbo

○ Port Macquarie

*Lord Howe
Island*
(Australia)

5

○ Newcastle

● Sydney
○ Wollongong

Kermadec Islands
(New Zealand)

30°

● **Canberra**
**AUSTRALIAN CAPITAL
TERRITORY**

**Mount
osciuszko**
▲
229m
,313ft)

6

Tasman Sea

North Cape

● Whangarei

*Flinders
Island*

◎ **Auckland**

North Island

35°

Hamilton ◎

○ Rotorua
*Lake
Taupo*

East Cape

New Plymouth ○

○ Napier

7

*Cape
Farewell*

Nelson ○

Cook Strait

■ **Wellington**

South Island

**NEW
ZEALAND**

**Aoraki
(Mount Cook)**
▲
3,754m
(12,316ft)

◎ Christchurch

Sutherland Falls

40°

Cape Providence

◎ Dunedin

Chatham Islands
(New Zealand)

Invercargill ○

Stewart Island   *South West Cape*

8

ASIA

Asia is the largest continent and has over 40 countries, including Russia, the biggest country in the world. As well as large land masses, it has thousands of islands and inlets, giving it over 160,000km (100,000 miles) of coastline. Turkey and Russia are partly in Europe and partly in Asia, but both are shown in full on the map on the right.

The shading on this map is there to help you see clearly the different countries that make up the continent.

This is a type of Chinese boat called a junk, sailing in the sea off Singapore.

ARCTIC OCEAN

Franz Josef Land

Novaya Zemlya

Barents Sea

Kara Sea

■ Moscow

Ob

Yenisey

R U S

Volga

Black Sea

■ Ankara

TURKEY

GEORGIA

Caspian Sea

■ Astana

KAZAKHSTAN

CYPRUS

ARMENIA

AZERBAIJAN

Aral Sea

UZBEKISTAN

LEBANON
Beirut ■

SYRIA
■ Damascus

TURKMENISTAN

Ashgabat ■

Tashkent ■

■ Bishkek

KYRGYZSTAN

Jerusalem ■
ISRAEL

■ Amman
JORDAN

■ Baghdad

■ Tehran

Dushanbe ■

TAJIKISTAN

IRAQ

IRAN

Tropic of Cancer

KUWAIT

Kabul ■
AFGHANISTAN

■ Islamabad

SAUDI
ARABIA

BAHRAIN
QATAR

Riyadh ■

Doha ■

■ Abu Dhabi

PAKISTAN

Indus

■ New Delhi

NEPAL
Kathmandu ■

UNITED ARAB
EMIRATES

■ Muscat

■ Sana

OMAN

Arabian Sea

Ganges

Thimph
BANGLADES

YEMEN

INDIA

Socotra (Yemen)

Bay of Bengal

INDIAN OCEAN

Equator

Sri Jayewardenepura Kotte ■

SRI LANKA

■ Colombo

MALDIVES
■ Male

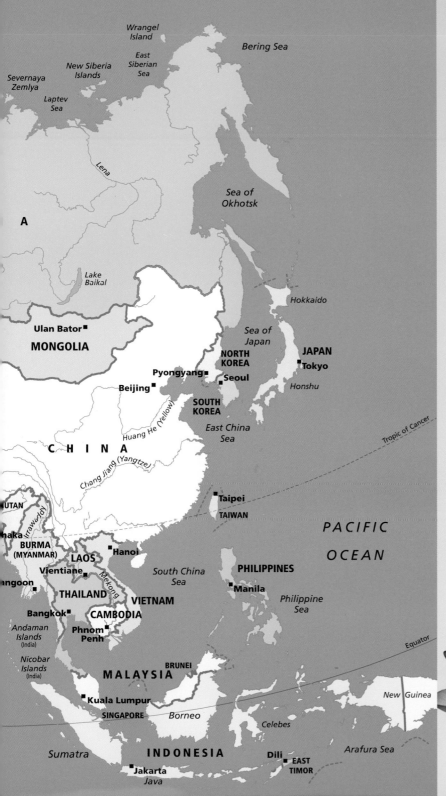

Wrangel
Island

Bering Sea

East
Siberian
Sea

New Siberia
Islands

Severnaya
Zemlya

Laptev
Sea

Lena

Sea of
Okhotsk

A

Lake
Baikal

Hokkaido

Ulan Bator■

Sea of
Japan

MONGOLIA

NORTH
KOREA

JAPAN
■Tokyo

Pyongyang■

Seoul

Honshu

Beijing■

SOUTH
KOREA

Huang He (Yellow)

East China
Sea

Tropic of Cancer

C H I N A

Chang Jiang (Yangtze)

■Taipei

PACIFIC

TAIWAN

ÜTAN

Irrawaddy

OCEAN

haka

BURMA
(MYANMAR)

■Hanoi

LAOS

South China
Sea

PHILIPPINES

Vientiane■

Mekong

■Manila

angoon

THAILAND

VIETNAM

Philippine
Sea

Bangkok■

CAMBODIA

Andaman
Islands
(India)

Phnom
Penh■

Nicobar
Islands
(India)

BRUNEI

Equator

MALAYSIA

New Guinea

■Kuala Lumpur

SINGAPORE

Borneo

Celebes

Sumatra

INDONESIA

Dili
■EAST
TIMOR

Arafura Sea

■Jakarta

Java

Facts

Total land area 44,537,920 sq km
(17,196,090 sq miles)
Total population 3.8 billion
(including all of Russia)
Biggest city Tokyo, Japan
Biggest country Russia *Total area:
17,075,200 sq km (6,592,735 sq
miles) Area of Asiatic Russia:
12,780,800 sq km (4,934,667 sq miles)*
Smallest country Maldives *300 sq km
(116 sq miles)*

Highest mountain Mount Everest,
Nepal/China border *8,850m (29,035ft)*
Longest river Chang Jiang (Yangtze),
China *6,380km (3,964 miles)*
Biggest lake Caspian Sea, western
Asia *370,999 sq km (143,243 sq miles)*
Highest waterfall Jog Falls, on the
Sharavati River, India *253m (830ft)*
Biggest desert Arabian Desert, in and
around Saudi Arabia *2,230,000 sq km
(900,000 sq miles)*
Biggest island Borneo *751,100 sq km
(290,000 sq miles)*

Main mineral deposits Zinc, mica, tin,
chromium, iron, nickel
Main fuel deposits Oil, coal,
uranium, natural gas

*These are lotus flowers, a type of
water lily. In China they are
associated with purity and for
Buddhists they are sacred.*

Asia is made up of all kinds of rugged terrain. In the far north are vast, frozen plains, and farther south are dry deserts. Asia also has enormous mountain ranges, including the Himalayas, the world's highest range. Most of Asia's population lives in the far south, which is hot and humid, with lush rainforests.

The white areas in the middle of this satellite image of Asia are mountain ranges, which include the Himalayas.

Empty land

Southern Saudi Arabia has a sandy desert that covers an area about the size of France. It is called Rub al Khali, and is often nicknamed the Empty Quarter as it has hardly any plants or animals and no permanent human settlements. Strong winds blow the sand into mounds that can be more than 330m (1,000ft) high, taller than the Eiffel Tower in Paris.

This view of Rub al Khali in Saudi Arabia shows how the wind has blown sand into long, high ridges.

This photograph shows a section of the Great Wall of China, which winds across northern China. The wall can be seen from space as a long, thin line.

This satellite image shows several volcanoes in Kamchatka, Russia. Red areas indicate snow. The pale streaks down the craters' sides are mudflows of ash and melting snow.

Russian wilderness

Kamchatka, in the far east of Russia, is one of the world's most remote areas. Its one main town is accessible only by air or sea. Much of the land is mountainous, with more than 300 volcanoes. Some of these are active, and they regularly eject boiling rivers of mud and great plumes of steam from their rocky craters.

Internet links

For links to websites where you can take a virtual tour of the Great Wall of China and see the River Ganges from space, go to **www.usborne-quicklinks.com**

A sacred river

The River Ganges begins in the Himalayas and flows through India and Bangladesh to the Indian Ocean. The river is regarded as holy by followers of the Hindu religion. Every day thousands of Hindus bathe in the Ganges, which they believe washes away their sins. People often worship the river by throwing flowers into it or floating oil lamps on its surface.

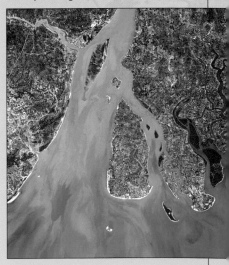

Here is the Ganges Delta in India, where the River Ganges flows into the Bay of Bengal (bottom).

uch of central and southern Asia is densely populated, so there are many large cities, including Tokyo, the world's most populous city. There are beautiful natural areas too, such as the forests and mountain ranges of China.

A panda climbs a tree in China. Pandas are good climbers, and often rest or sleep high in trees.

Pandas of China

Wild pandas live in the mountainous forests of China. Pandas depend on the bamboo that grows there, as their diet consists almost exclusively of bamboo shoots. But forests are being cut down, so pandas are losing their habitat and food source. There may be as few as 1,000 wild pandas left.

A floating market

Near Bangkok, in Thailand, there is a famous floating market which is held on a canal. Farmers go there daily with fresh fruit and vegetables piled high on narrow boats. Customers weave their way along the busy canal in similar boats, looking for bargains. They must come early, though, as the market begins at about 8 a.m., and everything is sold by 11 a.m.

These women have brought fruit and vegetables to sell at Bangkok's floating market.

Enormous department stores with glaring neon signs line a street in central Tokyo.

Japanese capital

One of Asia's most vibrant cities is Tokyo, the capital of Japan. This big, sprawling city has been rebuilt twice, first in the 1920s when an earthquake destroyed vast areas, and then after the Second World War, when bombs devastated the city. Modern Tokyo is a mixture of a few old streets and many new, towering skyscrapers.

Forbidden City

In the middle of the city of Beijing, in China, is an ancient, walled city. For hundreds of years it was the palace of China's kings, or emperors. It was known as the Forbidden City because no one but the emperor, his family and guests was allowed in its grounds.

China no longer has a royal family, and the Forbidden City is a popular tourist attraction. The city has 800 buildings, including huge temples and elaborate arches, decorated with ornate carvings and grand bronze statues.

Internet links

For links to websites where you can see panoramic movies of China's Forbidden City and take a tour of Tokyo, go to
www.usborne-quicklinks.com

This bronze tortoise stands in Beijing's Forbidden City. According to ancient Chinese beliefs, tortoises were divine animals, and tortoise statues were said to bring good luck.

The countries of western Asia are full of important cultural and historical sights, such as places of worship and the remains of ancient civilizations. The Asian part of Russia stretches far across the continent. It is dominated by the region of Siberia, where the climate is so harsh that most of the land is uninhabited.

This museum in Jerusalem, Israel, houses ancient manuscripts known as the Dead Sea Scrolls.

The Dead Sea

The Dead Sea, in Israel, gets its name because it is so salty that nothing can live in it. However, many people swim in the sea, as its water contains health-giving minerals.

The Dead Sea is also famous for the Dead Sea Scrolls. These are 2,000-year-old Jewish handwritten papers that were discovered in caves by the sea. The scrolls cover mainly religious topics, and have helped historians to learn what life was like in ancient times.

Homes of rock

The region of Cappadocia, near Ankara in central Turkey, has a strange landscape of rocky cones, made of soft volcanic rock. Many hundreds of years ago, people carved caves in the rock, creating whole towns and villages that included houses, stables and even churches. They also built an amazing network of underground tunnels that linked the houses.

These rocky peaks in Cappadocia, Turkey, were carved out to create rock houses. Today, they are crumbling away.

Holy places

Many different religions are followed in Asia, and their various places of worship and study, such as Muslim mosques and Hindu temples, are found in towns and cities all over the continent. Many of these buildings are intricately decorated, for example with huge domes covered in thousands of patterned tiles.

This elaborate, domed building in Esfahan, Iran, is a school for Muslim students.

This is the Trans-Siberian Express in Siberia. The train runs from Moscow to Vladivostok, stopping at other stations on the way.

Russian train trip

Crossing the enormous country of Russia is the Trans-Siberian rail line. This is the longest rail line in the world, running more than 9,000km (5,600 miles) between Moscow in the west and Vladivostok in the east. The line passes through the plains of Siberia, which freeze over in winter. The fastest train trip along the line takes about seven days.

Reindeers

Siberia is home to many reindeers. They have thick fur that keeps them warm in winter, and also have such a good sense of smell that they can sniff out plants to eat that are buried deep under the snow.

Internet links

For links to websites where you can find sightseeing guides to the countries of Asia and climb a Buddhist temple, go to
www.usborne-quicklinks.com

These reindeers are being driven by Siberian herders through western Siberia. Reindeers can easily pull heavy, loaded sleds.

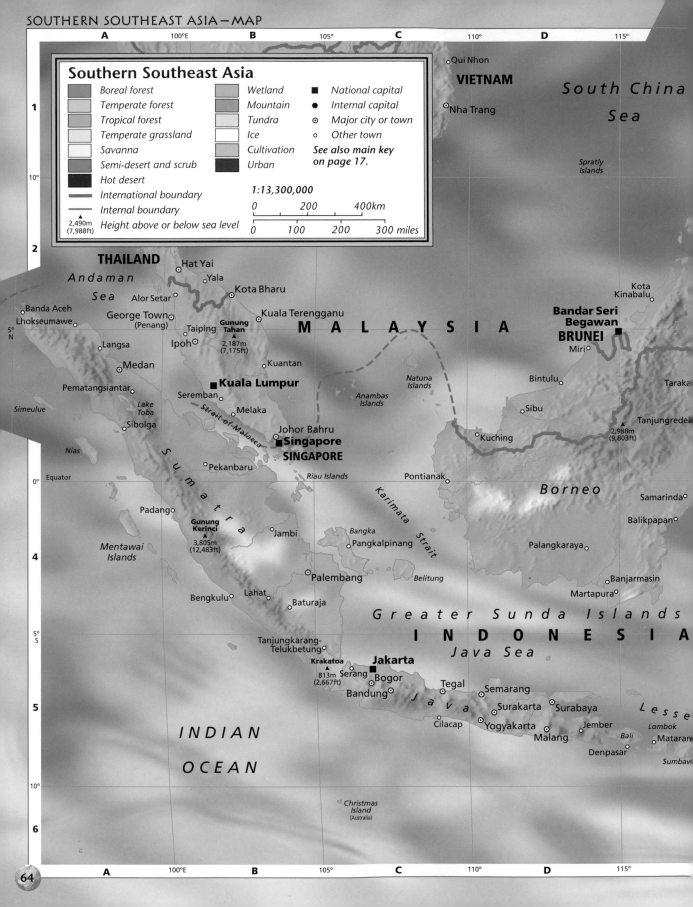

Southern Southeast Asia

▨	Boreal forest	▨	Wetland	■	National capital	
▨	Temperate forest	▨	Mountain	●	Internal capital	
▨	Tropical forest	▨	Tundra	⊙	Major city or town	
▨	Temperate grassland	▫	Ice	○	Other town	
▨	Savanna	▨	Cultivation			
▨	Semi-desert and scrub	■	Urban	*See also main key on page 17.*		
▨	Hot desert					

── International boundary

── Internal boundary

▲ 2,490m (7,988ft) Height above or below sea level

1:13,300,000

0   200   400km

0   100   200   300 miles

VIETNAM

Qui Nhon

Nha Trang

South China Sea

Spratly Islands

Kota Kinabalu

Bandar Seri Begawan
BRUNEI
Miri

THAILAND

Andaman Sea

Hat Yai
Yala
Alor Setar
Kota Bharu
Kuala Terengganu

Banda Aceh
Lhokseumawe
George Town (Penang)
Taiping
Gunung Tahan ▲ 2,187m (7,175ft)
Ipoh

M A L A Y S I A

Langsa
Kuantan

Medan

Pematangsiantar

Kuala Lumpur
Seremban

Bintulu

Taraka

Sibu

Lake Toba

Melaka

Simeulue

Sibolga

Johor Bahru
Singapore
SINGAPORE

Natuna Islands

Anambas Islands

Tanjungrede ▲ 2,988m (9,803ft)

Nias

Pekanbaru

S
u
m
a
t
r
a

Strait of Malacca

Riau Islands

Pontianak

Kuching

B o r n e o

Samarinda

Equator

Padang

Balikpapan

Gunung Kerinci ▲ 3,805m (12,483ft)

Jambi

Bangka

Palangkaraya

Pangkalpinang

Mentawai Islands

Palembang

Belitung

Banjarmasin

Bengkulu
Lahat
Baturaja

Martapura

Karimata Strait

G r e a t e r   S u n d a   I s l a n d s

I N D O N E S I A

Java Sea

Tanjungkarang-Telukbetung

Jakarta

L e s s e

Krakatoa ▲ 813m (2,667ft)
Serang
Bogor

Bandung

Tegal

Semarang

Surakarta
Surabaya

Lombok

J a v a

Mataram

INDIAN OCEAN

Cilacap
Yogyakarta

Jember

Bali

Malang

Denpasar

Sumbav

Christmas Island (Australia)

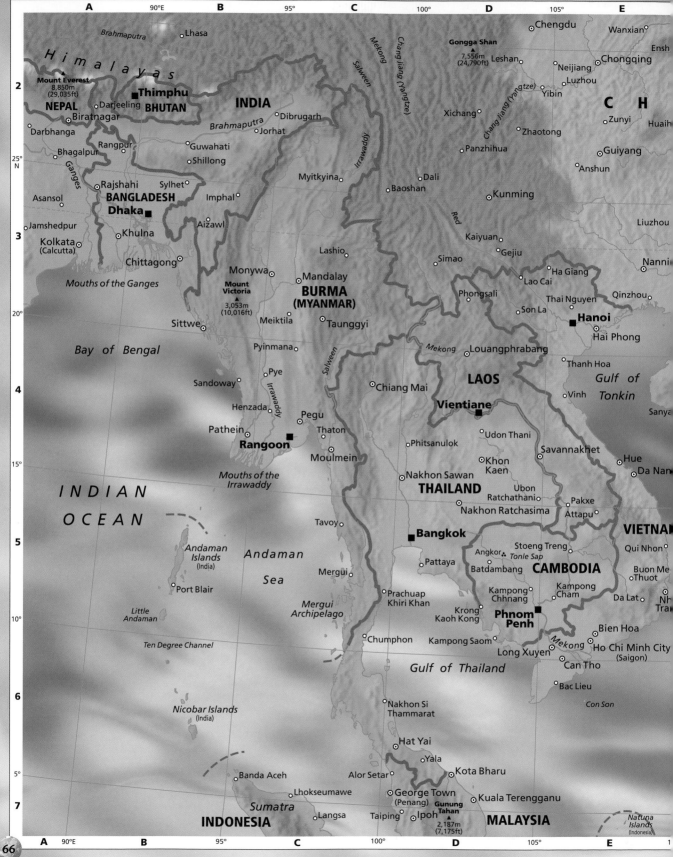

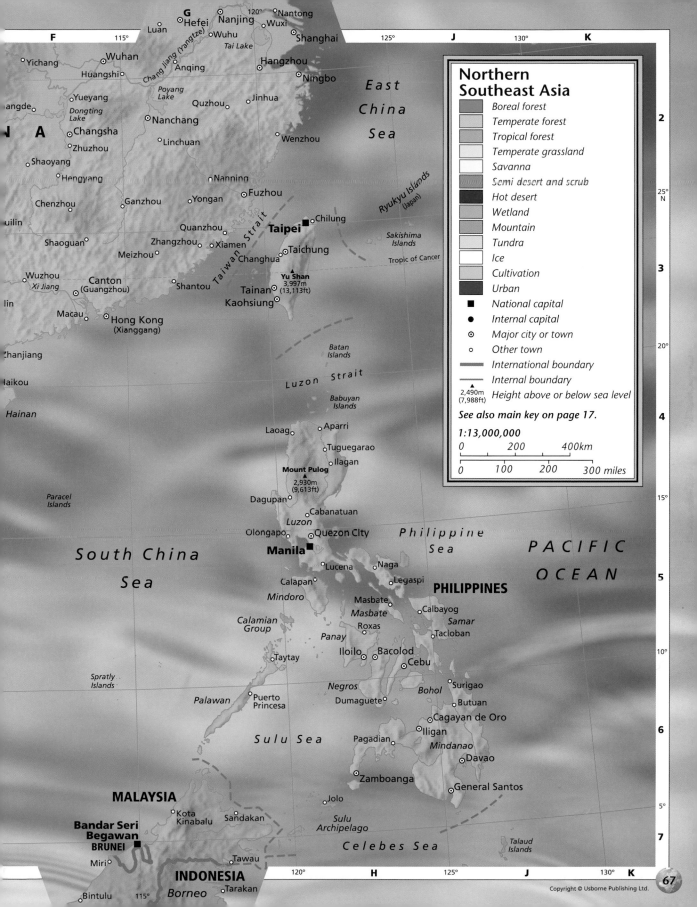

KAZAKHSTAN
Almaty
Yining
Karamay
Dzungarian Basin
Altay
Bulgan
Ulan Bator
MONGOLIA
Kuytun
Shihezi
Urumqi
Lake Issyk
KYRGYZSTAN
Pik Pobedy
7,439m
(24,406ft)
Aksu
Tien Shan
Turpan
Korla
Bosten Lake
-154m
(-505ft)
Turpan Depression
Hami
Altai Mountains
Erenho
Gobi Desert
Lop Lake
Mogao Caves
Yumen
The Great Wall of China
5,547m
(18,199ft)
Baotou
Hohhot
Wuhai
Yinchuan
Altun Mountains
Kunlun Mountains
Qaidam Basin
Golmud
Qinghai Lake
Xining
Lanzhou
Huang He (Yellow)
Taiyu
CHINA
Plateau of Tibet
Siling Lake
TIBET
Yushu
Baoji
Mount Li
(Terracotta Ar
Xian
Himalayas
Nam Lake
Brahmaputra
Lhasa
Salween
Chang Jiang (Yangtze)
Mekong
Shiyan
Xiangfa
NEPAL
Kathmandu
Mount Everest
8,850m
(29,035ft)
Darjeeling
Thimphu
BHUTAN
Gongga Shan
7,556m
(24,790ft)
Chengdu
Yichang
Darbhanga
Patna
Biratnagar
Ganges
Bhagalpur
Rangpur
Brahmaputra
Dibrugarh
Guwahati
Shillong
Leshan
Luzhou
Chang Jiang (Yangtze)
Chongqing
Changde
Huaihua
Hengya
INDIA
Ranchi
Asansol
Rajshahi
Sylhet
BANGLADESH
Dhaka
Imphal
Aizawl
Myitkyina
Xichang
Panzhihua
Dali
Zunyi
Guiyang
Irrawaddy
Kolkata
(Calcutta)
Khulna
Chittagong
Kunming
Guilin
Liuzhou
Cuttack
Tropic of Cancer
Mouths of the Ganges
Monywa
Mandalay
Lashio
Simao
Gejiu
Red
Wuzhou
Nanning
Yulin
Bay of Bengal
Mount Victoria
3,053m
(10,016ft)
BURMA
(MYANMAR)
Taunggyi
Lao Cai
Phongsalí
Son La
Thai Nguyen
Hanoi
Hai Phong
Zhanjiang
Sittwe
INDIAN OCEAN
Sandoway
Pye
Irrawaddy
Salween
Pyinmana
Mekong
Louangphrabang
Thanh Hoa
Gulf of Tonkin
Haikou
Chiang Mai
LAOS
VIETNAM
Hainan
Henzada
Pegu
Rangoon
THAILAND
Vientiane
Udon Thani
Vinh
Sanya
Pathein
Moulmein
Mouths of the Irrawaddy

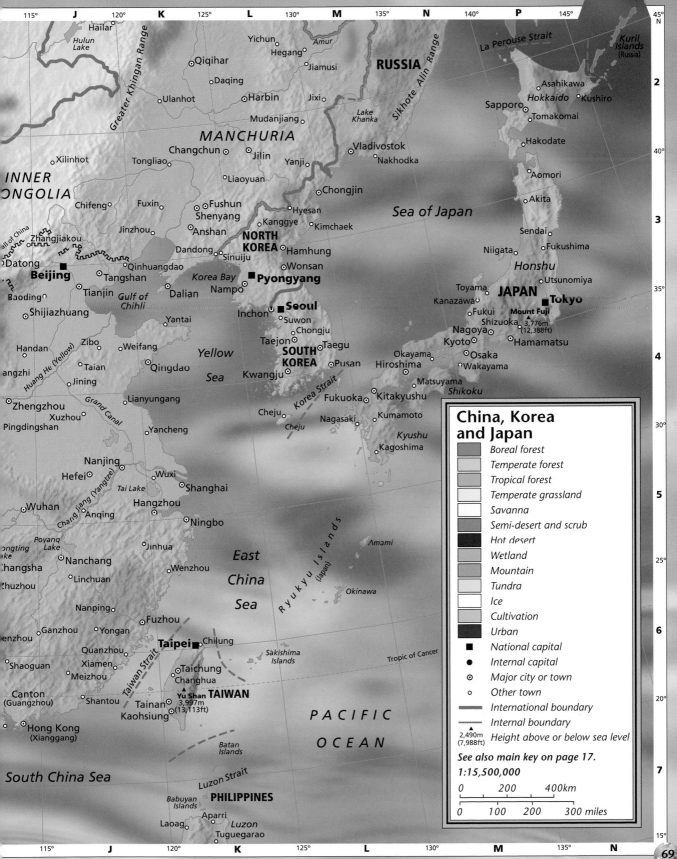

Q

45°
N

115° J 120° K 125° L 130° M 135° N 140° P 145°

Hailar

Hulun Lake

Qiqihar

Yichun

Hegang

Amur

Jiamusi

RUSSIA

La Perouse Strait

Kuril Islands (Russia)

2

Daqing

Ulanhot

Harbin

Jixi

Sikhote Alin Range

Asahikawa

Kushiro

Hokkaido

Sapporo

Tomakomai

Greater Khingan Range

Xilinhot

INNER MONGOLIA

Chifeng

Tongliao

MANCHURIA

Changchun

Jilin

Yanji

Liaoyuan

Lake Khanka

Vladivostok

Nakhodka

Chongjin

Hakodate

Aomori

40°

Akita

Sea of Japan

3

Fuxin

Fushun

Shenyang

Anshan

Hyesan

Kanggye

Kimchaek

Sendai

Fukushima

Honshu

35°

Jinzhou

Wall of China

Zhangjiakou

NORTH KOREA

Dandong

Sinuiju

Hamhung

Niigata

Datong

Qinhuangdao

Wonsan

Utsunomiya

■**Beijing**

Tangshan

Korea Bay

Pyongyang■

Nampo

Toyama

Kanazawa

JAPAN

Tokyo■

Baoding

Tianjin

Gulf of Chihli

Dalian

Yantai

●**Seoul**

Inchon

Suwon

Chongju

Fukui

Shizuoka

Mount Fuji ▲ 3,776m (12,388ft)

Shijiazhuang

Handan

Zibo

Weifang

Yellow

Taejon

SOUTH KOREA

Taegu

Nagoya

Kyoto

Osaka

Hamamatsu

4

angzhi

Taian

Qingdao

Sea

Pusan

Okayama

Hiroshima

Wakayama

Huang He (Yellow)

Jining

Kwangju

Korea Strait

Matsuyama

Shikoku

Zhengzhou

Grand Canal

Lianyungang

Xuzhou

Yancheng

Cheju

Cheju

Fukuoka

Kitakyushu

Nagasaki

Kumamoto

Kyushu

Kagoshima

30°

Pingdingshan

Nanjing

Hefei

Chang Jiang (Yangtze)

Wuxi

Tai Lake

Shanghai

5

Wuhan

Anqing

Hangzhou

Ningbo

Poyang Lake

ongting Lake

Nanchang

Linchuan

Jinhua

Wenzhou

East China Sea

Amami

25°

hangsha

huzhou

Nanping

Ryukyu Islands (Japan)

Okinawa

Fuzhou

Ganzhou

Yongan

enzhou

Taipei■

Chilung

Sakishima Islands

Tropic of Cancer

6

Quanzhou

Xiamen

Taichung

Changhua

20°

Shaoguan

Meizhou

Yu Shan 3,997m (13,113ft) ▲

Tainan

TAIWAN

PACIFIC

Canton (Guangzhou)

Shantou

Kaohsiung

Taiwan Strait

OCEAN

Hong Kong (Xianggang)

Batan Islands

South China Sea

Luzon Strait

PHILIPPINES

7

Babuyan Islands

Aparri

Laoag

Luzon

Tuguegarao

15°

115° J 120° K 125° L 130° M 135° N

China, Korea and Japan

▬	*Boreal forest*
▬	*Temperate forest*
▬	*Tropical forest*
▬	*Temperate grassland*
▢	*Savanna*
▬	*Semi-desert and scrub*
▬	*Hot desert*
▬	*Wetland*
▬	*Mountain*
▢	*Tundra*
▢	*Ice*
▬	*Cultivation*
▬	*Urban*
■	*National capital*
●	*Internal capital*
⊙	*Major city or town*
○	*Other town*
▬▬	*International boundary*
▬	*Internal boundary*
▲ 2,490m (7,988ft)	*Height above or below sea level*

See also main key on page 17.

1:15,500,000

0   200   400km

0   100   200   300 miles

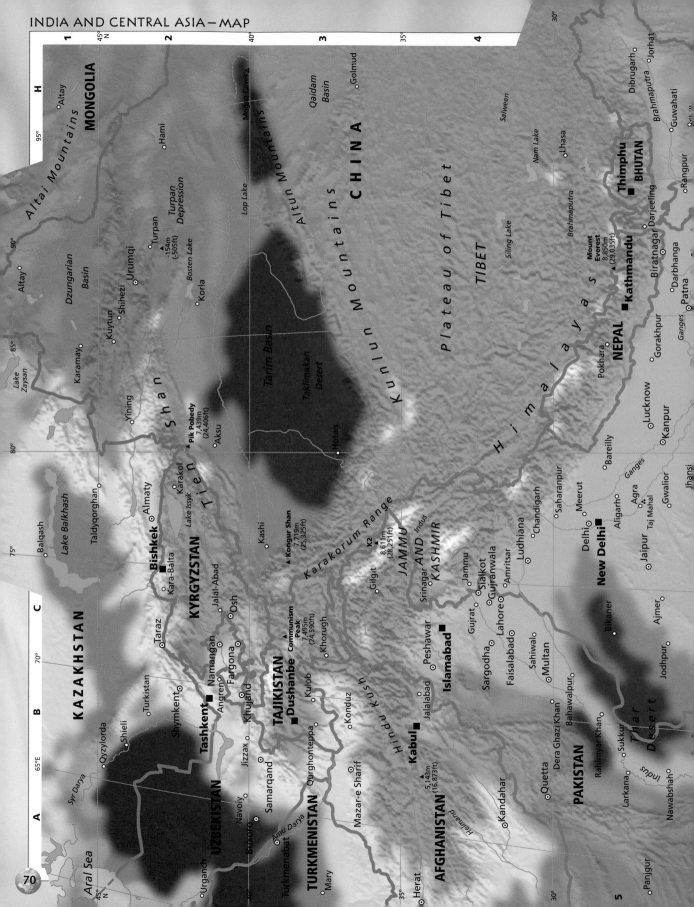

1 45° N

2 40°

3 35°

4 30°

H

MONGOLIA

Altay

Altai Mountains

Hami

CHINA

Mogao Caves

Qaidam Basin

Golmud

Saltween

95°

Turpan
-154m
(-505ft)

Turpan Depression

Urumqi

Bosten Lake

Lop Lake

Altun Mountains

Nam Lake

Lhasa

90°

Altay

Shihezi

Korla

TIBET

Brahmaputra

Thimphu
BHUTAN

Dibrugarh

Jorhat

Dzungarian Basin

Kuytun

Karamay

Plateau of Tibet

Mount Everest
8,850m
(29,035ft)

Brahmaputra

Darjeeling

Rangpur

Guwahati

85°

Lake Zaysan

Karamay

Kunlun Mountains

Siling Lake

Kathmandu

Biratnagar

Darbhanga

Patna

Tarim Basin

NEPAL

Pokhara

Gorakhpur

Ganges

80°

Yining

Tien Shan

Taklimakan Desert

Hotan

Himalayas

Lucknow

Kanpur

Pik Pobedy
7,439m
(24,406ft)

Aksu

Lake Issyk

Karakol

Karakol

KAZAKHSTAN

Bishkek

Almaty

Kashi

Kongur Shan
7,719m
(25,325ft)

K2
8,611m
(28,251ft)

Bareilly

75°

Balqash

Lake Balkhash

Taldyqorghan

Kara-Balta

KYRGYZSTAN

Jalal-Abad

Karakorum Range

Indus

JAMMU
AND
KASHMIR

Saharanpur

Meerut

Aligarh

Taj Mahal

C

Taraz

Osh

Gilgit

Srinagar

Jammu

Chandigarh

Delhi

New Delhi

Jaipur

Agra

Gwalior

Jhansi

70°

Shymkent

Namangan

Communism Peak
7,495m
(24,590ft)

Khorough

Peshawar

Sialkot

Gujranwala

Ludhiana

Amritsar

Bikaner

Ajmer

Turkistan

Angren

Fargona

Kulob

Islamabad

Gujrat

Lahore

Sahiwal

Jodhpur

B

Tashkent

Khujand

TAJIKISTAN

Dushanbe

Konduz

Jalalabad

Sargodha

Faisalabad

Multan

Thar Desert

65° E

Jizzax

Qurghonteppa

Hindu Kush

Kabul

Dera Ghazi Khan

Bahawalpur

Sukkur

Samarqand

5,143m
(16,873ft)

Rahimyar Khan

Indus

UZBEKISTAN

Bukoro

Mazar-e Sharif

AFGHANISTAN

Quetta

PAKISTAN

Larkana

Nawabshah

A

Navoiy

Qyzylorda

Shieli

TURKMENISTAN

Kandahar

Panjgur

Syr Darya

Turkmenabat

Mary

Amu Darya

Helmand

Herat

Aral Sea

Urganch

35°

30°

5

45° N

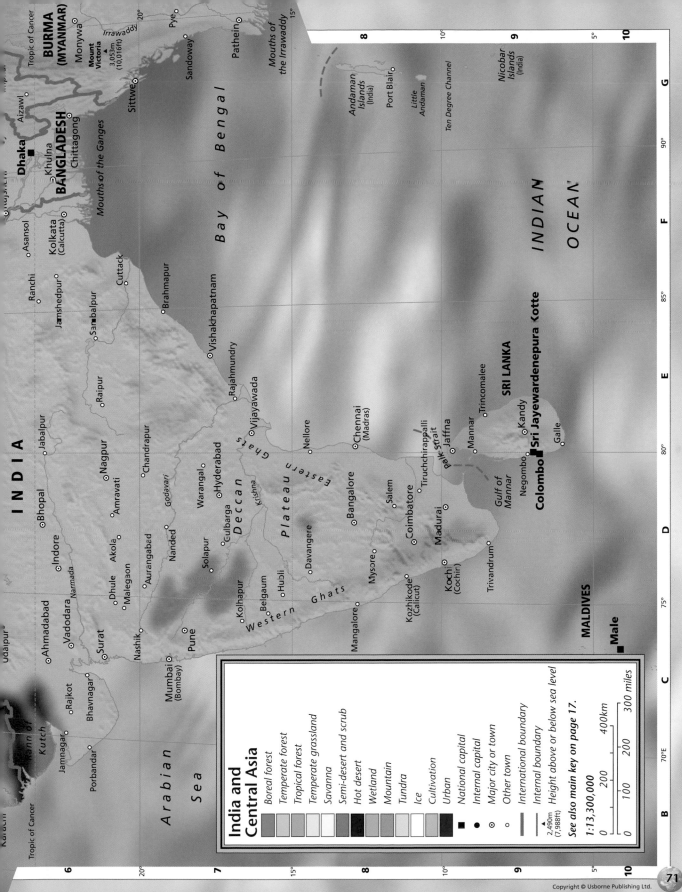

India and Central Asia

Boreal forest
Temperate forest
Tropical forest
Temperate grassland
Savanna
Semi-desert and scrub
Hot desert
Wetland
Mountain
Tundra
Ice
Cultivation
Urban

■ National capital
● Internal capital
⊙ Major city or town
○ Other town
— International boundary
— Internal boundary
▲ 2,490m (7,988ft) Height above or below sea level

See also main key on page 17.

1:13,300,000

0   100   200   300   400km
0   100   200   300 miles

BURMA (MYANMAR)
Monywa
Mount Victoria 3,053m (10,016ft)
Pye
Tropic of Cancer
Irrawaddy
Mouths of the Irrawaddy
Sandoway
Pathein
Sittwe
Aizawl

BANGLADESH
Dhaka
Khulna
Chittagong
Mouths of the Ganges

Asansol
Kolkata (Calcutta)
Ranchi
Jamshedpur
Sambalpur
Cuttack
Brahmapur
Vishakhapatnam
Rajahmundry
Vijayawada

Bay of Bengal

Andaman Islands (India)
Port Blair
Little Andaman
Ten Degree Channel
Nicobar Islands (India)

INDIAN OCEAN

INDIA
Udaipur
Ahmadabad
Rajkot
Bhavnagar
Jamnagar
Porbandar
Rann of Kutch
Tropic of Cancer

Arabian Sea

Vadodara
Surat
Indore
Bhopal
Jabalpur
Nashik
Dhule
Malegaon
Akola
Amravati
Nagpur
Chandrapur
Nanded
Aurangabad
Solapur
Gulbarga
Hyderabad
Warangal
Godavari
Krishna
Narmada

Mumbai (Bombay)
Pune
Kolhapur
Belgaum
Hubli
Mangalore

Deccan Plateau
Eastern Ghats
Western Ghats

Davangere
Bangalore
Mysore
Salem
Coimbatore
Kozhikode (Calicut)
Koch (Cochin)
Trivandrum
Madurai
Tiruchirappalli
Nellore
Chennai (Madras)

Jaffna
Mannar
Trincomalee
Kandy
SRI LANKA
Negombo
Colombo
Sri Jayewardenepura Kotte
Galle
Palk Strait
Gulf of Mannar

MALDIVES
■ **Male**

Copyright © Usborne Publishing Ltd.

71

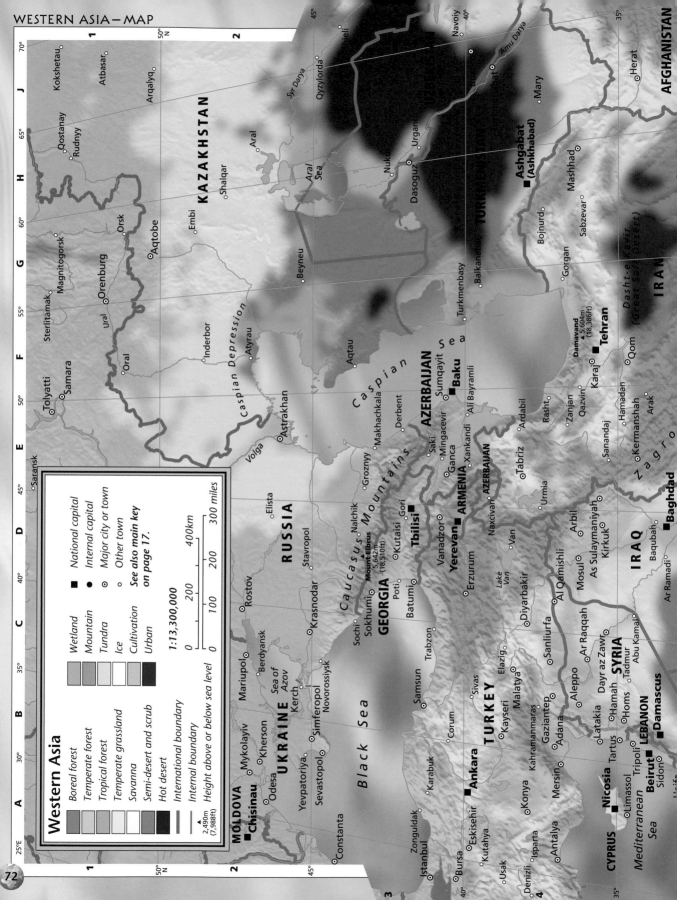

Western Asia

Boreal forest	Wetland
Temperate forest	Mountain
Tropical forest	Tundra
Temperate grassland	Ice
Savanna	Cultivation
Semi-desert and scrub	Urban
Hot desert	

■ National capital
● Internal capital
◉ Major city or town
○ Other town

See also main key on page 17.

1:13,300,000

0	100	200	300 miles
0	200	400km	

— International boundary
— Internal boundary

▲ 2,490m
(7,988ft) Height above or below sea level

AFGHANISTAN
Herat
Mashhad
Sabzevar
Bojnurd
Gorgan
Balkanabat
Turkmenbasy
IRAN
Dasht-e Kavir (Great Salt Desert)
Damavand ▲ 5,604m (18,386ft)
Tehran ■
Karaj ◉
Qom
Qazvin
Zanjan
Hamadan
Kermanshah
Arak
Zagros
Sanandaj
As Sulaymaniyah
Arbil
Kirkuk
Baghdad ■
Baqubah
Ar Ramadi
IRAQ
Mosul
Al Qamishli
Ar Raqqah
Dayr az Zawr
Abu Kamal
SYRIA
Tadmur
Damascus ■
Homs
Hamah
Aleppo
Sanliurfa
Diyarbakir
Lake Van
Van
Urmia
Tabriz
Ardabil
Rasht
Ashgabat (Ashkhabad) ■
TURKMENISTAN
Mary
Dasoguz
Urganch
Nukus
Aral Sea
Shalqar
Aral
KAZAKHSTAN
Qostanay
Rudnyy
Kokshetau
Atbasar
Arqalyq
Embi
Aqtobe
Orsk
Orenburg
Inderbor
Atyrau
Beyneu
Aqtau
Caspian Depression
Ural
Oral
Sterlitamak
Magnitogorsk
Tolyatti
Samara
Saransk
RUSSIA
Astrakhan
Volga
Elista
Stavropol
Rostov
Krasnodar
Elbrus
Mount Elbrus 5,642m (18,510ft)
Caucasus Mountains
Nalchik
Grozny
Makhachkala
Derbent
Sumqayit
Baku ■
Ali Bayramli
Mingacevir
Ganca
Saki
Xankandi
Naxcivan
AZERBAIJAN
ARMENIA
Yerevan ■
Vanadzor
Gori
Tbilisi ■
Kutaisi
GEORGIA
Sukhumi
Poti
Batumi
Sochi
Novorossiysk
Sevastopol
Simferopol
Yevpatoriya
Kerch
UKRAINE
Kherson
Mykolayiv
Odesa
Chisinau ■
MOLDOVA
Mariupol
Berdyansk
Sea of Azov
Black Sea
Constanta
Istanbul
Zonguldak
Karabuk
Samsun
Trabzon
Erzurum
Sivas
Corum
Ankara ■
Kayseri
Malatya
Kahramanmaras
Gaziantep
Adana
Mersin
Konya
Eskisehir
Kutahya
Denizli
Isparta
Antalya
Usak
Bursa
TURKEY
Elazig
Latakia
Tartus
Tripoli
Beirut ■
Sidon
LEBANON
Nicosia ■
CYPRUS
Limassol
Mediterranean Sea
Caspian Sea

25°E 30° 35° 40° 45° 50° 55° 60° 65° 70°
50°N
45°
35°

72

UNITED
KINGDOM
London ■

North
Sea

*Norwegian
Sea*

Arctic Circle

Svalbard
(Norway)

A
20°

B

ARCTIC

Paris ■

BELGIUM

NETHERLANDS

NORWAY

40°

*Franz Josef
Land*

C

60°

D
80°

E

LUXEMBOURG

FRANCE

DENMARK

Oslo ■

SWEDEN

North Cape

*Barents
Sea*

*Novaya
Zemlya*

GERMANY

Berlin ■

*Baltic
Sea*

Stockholm ■

FINLAND

○ Murmansk

*Kola
Peninsula*

*Kara
Sea*

3

CZECH
REPUBLIC

AUSTRIA

POLAND

LITHUANIA

ESTONIA

Helsinki ■

*Lake
Ladoga*

○ St. Petersburg

○ Arkhangelsk

○ Vorkuta

○ Norilsk

Warsaw ■

LATVIA

Vilnius ■

*Lake
Onega*

○ Ukhta

Budapest ■

SLOVAKIA

Minsk ■

HUNGARY

BELARUS

○ Lviv

○ Cherepovets

Ural Mountains

Ob

○ Novyy Urengoy

ROMANIA

Kiev ■

MOLDOVA

UKRAINE

Moscow ■

○ Ryazan

○ Nizhniy Novgorod

West Siberian

Chisinau ■

○ Kharkiv

Volga

○ Voronezh

○ Kazan

Perm ○

Plain

○ Surgut

Ob

○ Odesa

○ Dnipropetrovsk

○ Samara

○ Yekaterinburg

Yenisey

○ Simferopol

*Black
Sea*

○ Rostov

○ Volgograd

Oral ○

○ Orenburg

○ Chelyabinsk

Irtysh

○ Omsk

R U S

40°
N

Ankara ■

Krasnodar ○

Mount Elbrus
▲ 5,642m
(18,510ft)

○ Astrakhan

○ Aqtobe

○ Tomsk

○ Krasnoyars

TURKEY

Volga

Astrakhan

○ Atyrau

KAZAKHSTAN

○ Novosibirsk

○ Abaka

○ Adana

GEORGIA

Tbilisi ■

Astana ■

Pavlodar ○

○ Barnaul

○ Aleppo

ARMENIA

Yerevan ■

*Caspian
Sea*

○ Aqtau

○ Qaraghandy

Uskemen ○

Kyzyl

SYRIA

AZERBAIJAN

Baku ■

○ Altay

○ Mosul

○ Tabriz

*Aral
Sea*

○ Nukus

○ Qyzylorda

○ Balqash

*Lake
Balkhash*

Alta

4

Baghdad ■

IRAQ

Damavand
▲ 5,604m
(18,386ft)

Tehran ○

Dasoguz ○

UZBEKISTAN

TURKMENISTAN

○ Shymkent

Almaty ○

○ Urumqi

**Ashgabat
(Ashkhabad)** ■

Tashkent ■

Bishkek ■

○ Ahvaz

○ Esfahan

Turkmenabat ○

Samarqand ○

KYRGYZSTAN

Tien Shan

○ Aksu

Kuwait City ■

○ Mashhad

○ Osh

Dushanbe ■

KUWAIT

TAJIKISTAN

**SAUDI
ARABIA**

Persian Gulf (The Gulf)

○ Herat

○ Mazar-e Sharif

Riyadh ■

Manama ■

○ Shiraz

AFGHANISTAN

K2
▲ 8,611m
(28,251ft)

○ Hotan

Taklimakan Desert

QATAR

Bandar-e
Abbas ○

○ Zahedan

Kabul ■

Doha ■

IRAN

○ Kandahar

Islamabad ■

Abu Dhabi ■

○ Srinagar

Plateau of Tibet

PAKISTAN

Indus

○ Lahore

INDIA

C

60°E

D

80°

E

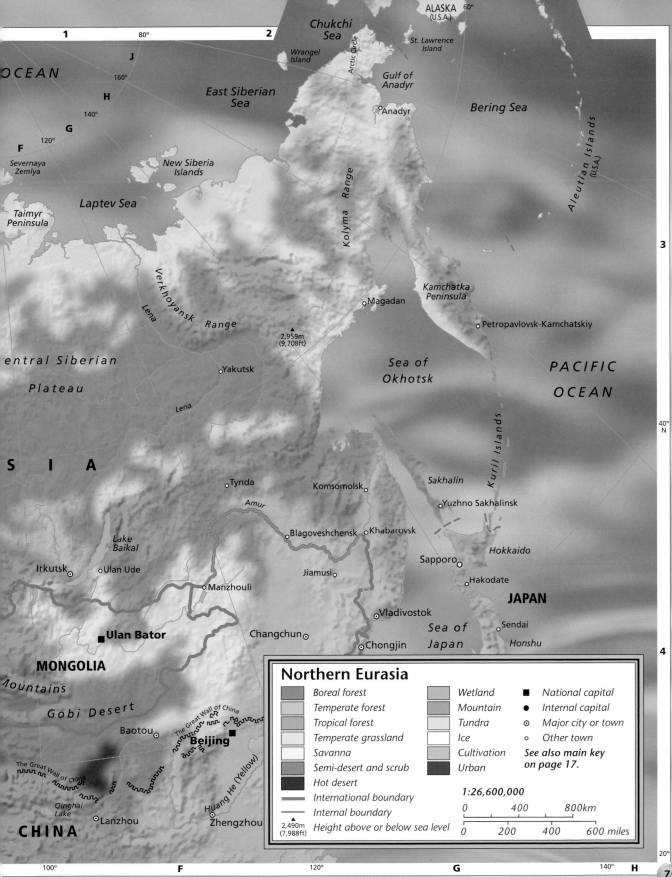

ALASKA (U.S.A.) 60°

Chukchi Sea

Wrangel Island

East Siberian Sea

St. Lawrence Island

Gulf of Anadyr

Bering Sea

•Anadyr

Aleutian Islands (U.S.A.)

OCEAN

J

160°

H

140°

G

120°

F

Severnaya Zemlya

New Siberia Islands

Taimyr Peninsula

Laptev Sea

Kolyma Range

3

Verkhoyansk Range

Lena

Central Siberian Plateau

Lena

2,959m (9,708ft) ▲

•Yakutsk

•Magadan

Kamchatka Peninsula

•Petropavlovsk-Kamchatskiy

Sea of Okhotsk

PACIFIC OCEAN

40° N

S I A

Kuril Islands

•Tynda

Komsomolsk○

Amur

Blagoveshchensk○

○Khabarovsk

Jiamusi○

Sakhalin

•Yuzhno Sakhalinsk

Hokkaido

Sapporo○

○Hakodate

Lake Baikal

Irkutsk◉

○Ulan Ude

○Manzhouli

JAPAN

•Vladivostok

Sea of Japan

○Sendai

Honshu

Changchun○

◉Chongjin

4

■Ulan Bator

MONGOLIA

Mountains

Gobi Desert

Baotou○

The Great Wall of China

■Beijing

The Great Wall of China

Qinghai Lake

○Lanzhou

Huang He (Yellow)

Zhengzhou○

CHINA

Northern Eurasia

▭ Boreal forest	▭ Wetland
▭ Temperate forest	▭ Mountain
▭ Tropical forest	▭ Tundra
▭ Temperate grassland	▭ Ice
▭ Savanna	▭ Cultivation
▭ Semi-desert and scrub	▭ Urban
▭ Hot desert	

── International boundary
── Internal boundary

2,490m (7,988ft) ▲ Height above or below sea level

■ National capital
● Internal capital
◉ Major city or town
○ Other town

See also main key on page 17.

1:26,600,000

0   400   800km

0   200   400   600 miles

20°

1   80°   2

100°   F   120°   G   140°   H

EUROPE

Europe is a small continent, packed with over 40 countries and more than 700 million people. Russia is an enormous country, spanning two continents. Its western part is in Europe, while its eastern part is in Asia. The European part of Russia is larger than any other country in Europe.

The shading on this map is there to help you see clearly the different countries that make up the continent.

Arctic Circle

ARCTIC OCEAN

Reykjavik
ICELAND

Norwegian Sea

Faroe Islands (Denmark)

SWEDEN

Shetland Islands

NORWAY

Oslo

Orkney Islands

Stockholm

North Sea

DENMARK

Baltic Sea

IRELAND
Dublin

Copenhagen

UNITED KINGDOM

Amsterdam

The Hague
NETHERLANDS

Berlin

POLAN

London

Brussels

GERMANY

BELGIUM

LUXEMBOURG
Luxembourg

Prague

CZECH REPUBLIC

Paris

Rhine

Vienna

Bratislava

Bay of Biscay

FRANCE

Bern
SWITZERLAND

Vaduz

LIECHTENSTEIN

AUSTRIA

Budapest

SLOVENIA
Ljubljana

HUNGAR

Zagreb

ATLANTIC

CROATIA

MONACO

SAN MARINO

BOSNIA AND HERZEGOVINA
Sarajevo

OCEAN

ANDORRA

Andorra la Vella

ITALY

MONTENEGR
Podgorica

PORTUGAL

Corsica

Rome

VATICAN CITY

ALBAN
Tira

Lisbon

Madrid

SPAIN

Sardinia

Balearic Islands

Mediterranean Sea

Sicily

MALTA
Valletta

Barents Sea

Arctic Circle

⊙ Murmansk

⊙ Arkhangelsk

FINLAND

elsinki

⊙ St. Petersburg

R U S S I A

■ Tallinn
ESTONIA

Nizhniy Novgorod ⊙   ⊙ Kazan

Riga LATVIA

■ Moscow

LITHUANIA
Vilnius ■

SSIA

Volga

■ Minsk

BELARUS

Warsaw

■ Kiev

Dnieper

Volgograd ⊙

UKRAINE

LOVAKIA

MOLDOVA

■ Chisinau

ROMANIA

elgrade

■ Bucharest

BIA Danube

Black Sea

SOVO
Pristina ■ Sofia

BULGARIA

■ Skopje

MACEDONIA

TURKEY

GREECE

■ Athens

Crete

Facts

Total land area 10,205,720 sq km
(3,940,428 sq miles) (including
European Russia)
Total population 727 million
(including all of Russia)
Biggest city Moscow, Russia
Biggest country Russia *Total area:
17,075,200 sq km (6,592,735 sq
miles) Area of European Russia:
4,294,400 sq km (1,658,068 sq miles)*
Smallest country Vatican City *0.44
sq km (0.17 sq miles)*

Highest mountain Elbrus, Russia
5,642m (18,510ft)
Longest river Volga *3,700km
(2,298 miles)*
Biggest lake Lake Ladoga, Russia
17,700 sq km (6,834 sq miles)
Highest waterfall Utigard, on the
Jostedal Glacier, Norway *800m
(2,625ft)*
Biggest desert No deserts in Europe
Biggest island Great Britain *234,410
sq km (90,506 sq miles)*

Main mineral deposits Bauxite, zinc,
iron, potash, fluorspar
Main fuel deposits Oil, coal, natural
gas, peat, uranium

*A cow in Devon, in the
south of England*

77

Europe has lots of islands and many of its countries are largely surrounded by sea. The Alps, one of Europe's principal mountain ranges, lies in the west, and is the source of many of its major rivers, including the Rhine and the Rhone.

Europe by night

Satellite pictures taken at night show how much light is being generated in different areas. Highly populated areas, such as Europe, where there are many big cities, light up brightly at night. This is because when many people live in one area, the combined lights of all the buildings at night are so bright they show up as a dot.

This is a satellite image of Mount Vesuvius, a volcano in southern Italy. The black dot in the middle is the crater.

Mount Vesuvius

Mount Vesuvius is a volcano near the city of Naples in southern Italy. It is famous for its eruption in AD79, which buried the towns of Pompeii and Herculaneum in around 30m (100ft) of ash, mud and stones. The towns remained buried until the 18th century when they were rediscovered.

Vesuvius is monitored very carefully today, as it is close to the city of Naples and more than two million people live nearby. It has had over 50 minor eruptions since the one in AD79.

This satellite image of Europe was taken at night, but the land and water have been falsely-shaded, so you can see their outlines clearly. Each blue dot represents a highly populated area that is lit up.

Internet links

For links to websites where you can explore the Rhine and other rivers of Europe, go to
www.usborne-quicklinks.com

This area of the Alps is in Switzerland. Over 70% of Switzerland is mountainous.

The Rhine River

The Rhine River carries more traffic than any other river in the world. It is 1,320km (820 miles) long and winds through the west of Europe, flowing from the Alps in Switzerland, along the Swiss-Austrian border, through Germany and France to the Netherlands. Many cities lie along its banks, including Strasbourg, in France, and Cologne, in Germany.

This is a section of the Rhine River running through west Germany. The river is black, vegetation is blue and buildings are brown. The patchwork of rectangles to the east of the river is farmland.

Norwegian fjords

Norway's dramatic coastline is a mixture of steep mountains and long, thin inlets of water, called fjords. The fjords were formed by glaciers. When glacier ice builds up at the top of a mountain, it becomes heavy and starts to slide down the slopes, carving out a deep channel in the rock. When the glacier melts, the water fills the channel, making a fjord.

The satellite image below shows an area of Norway's coastline. The long, thin blue strips are inlets of water, called fjords.

Eastern Europe stretches as far as the Ural Mountains, which separate European Russia from Asian Russia. Northern Europe is made up of Iceland and the Scandinavian countries, including Norway and Sweden.

Onion-shaped domes

Early Russian churches have an easily recognizable style, with high walls, very few doors and windows, and steeply-sloped roofs topped with onion-shaped domes. This style became popular during the 11th century. Many of these early churches were built from wood, as it was a building material widely available from Russia's dense forests.

This is the Church of the Intercession on Kizhi Island in northern Russia. It was built almost entirely from wood in 1764.

This is a Viking helmet. It was discovered in a grave in Uppland, Sweden.

Viking lands

During the 9th to the 11th centuries, the Vikings, a group of master ship builders and sea traders from Scandinavia, dominated northern Europe. Viking heritage can still be seen today. The Vikings carved stories and pictures into large stones, called rune stones. Many of these stones have survived and give clues to how they lived. The Viking Ship Museum in Oslo, Norway, has three well-preserved Viking ships, and in Sweden, a Viking festival is held each year in a reconstructed Viking village.

In this dramatic image of Budapest you can see the Chain Bridge, which links Buda and Pest across the Danube River.

Internet links

For a link to a website where you can print out a Viking map game, go to **www.usborne-quicklinks.com**

Danube River

The Danube River flows from the west to the east of Europe, through many major cities, including Bratislava, the capital of Slovakia, and Budapest, the capital of Hungary. The river splits Budapest into two parts, Buda and Pest. The Royal Palace is in Buda, on the west bank, while Hungary's parliament building is in Pest, on the east bank.

Atlantic puffins

One type of bird common throughout northern Europe is the Atlantic puffin. Atlantic puffins are sea birds that live in the cold waters around the coasts of the North Atlantic Ocean.

Atlantic puffins are very skilled at diving underwater to catch fish to eat. They only come ashore once a year to nest on rocky cliff tops and grassy islands. Iceland has the largest puffin population in the world at around nine million.

These are Atlantic puffins. They are about 18cm (10in) tall and have yellow, orange and blue beaks, which is why they are also known as sea parrots.

The west of Europe stretches as far as Portugal on the Atlantic coast, while southern Europe reaches down to the many small islands in the Mediterranean Sea, where the climate is famously sunny, warm and dry.

Sights of London

There are many famous sights in London, from the huge clock tower of Big Ben, to Buckingham Palace, the official residency of the Queen.

One of the city's most recent additions is the London Eye, the world's largest Ferris wheel, which was constructed to mark the millennium. The top of the wheel is 135m (443ft) high, giving an impressive view of the city.

The London Eye sits on the south bank of the River Thames. Big Ben sits on the opposite bank.

Internet links

For a link to a website where you can send virtual postcards of famous landmarks in Europe, go to **www.usborne-quicklinks.com**

Eiffel Tower

The Eiffel Tower in Paris, France, was opened in 1889, and has since had over 200 million visitors. It was built for an international exhibition celebrating the scientific and engineering achievements of the time. The iron structure is around 300m (980ft) tall and has three levels with many shops and restaurants.

There are over 350 electric lamps fitted to the outside of the Eiffel Tower, lighting it up dramatically at night.

The Leaning Tower

One of Italy's most famous sights is the Leaning Tower of Pisa. The 55m (180ft) tall bell tower is part of Pisa Cathedral. Building work began on it in 1173, and the tower started to lean while it was being built. It leans because the ground beneath it is a mixture of sand and clay, which are easily compressed. The huge weight of the tower compressed the ground more in some areas than others, so the tower began to lean.

This marble statue of a discus thrower is a copy of a bronze statue from 5th-century Greece. The statue, housed in the National Museum in Rome, Italy, is a symbol of the Olympic games.

Home of the Olympics

Athletes from all over the world compete in the Olympic games every four years. The first Olympic games were held in celebration of the Greek God Zeus in Olympia, Greece, in 776BC. Today, some of the foundations, steps and pillars of the original stadium, which seated around 30,000 spectactors, remain. The start and finish lines of the running track, and the judges' seats, have also survived.

Mikkeli

25° *Paijanne* 30°
Lake

Hameenlinna
Pihlaja
Lake

20°E Turku Lahti FINLAND
Kouvola
Espoo Lappeenranta
Helsinki Kotka *Saimaa*
Lake

Aland
Islands

Vyborg

Baltic Sea Gulf of Finland

C 35° D 40° E

Lake
Onega

Konosha

Hiiumaa Tallinn Zelenogorsk
St. Petersburg

Haapsalu Kohtla-
Jarve Kingisepp Volkhov *White*
Lake Vologda

Kuressaare Narva Gatchina Pushkin Tikhvin Cherepovets
Pskov

Saaremaa Parnu ESTONIA Kirishi

2 Ventspils *Gulf* Tartu Novgorod Borovichi *Rybinsk* Rybinsk
of *Reservoir* Kostroma
Riga Voru *Lake*
Jurmala Cesis *Lake* *Ilmen* Vyshniy Volochek *Volga* Yaroslavl Kineshma *Volga*
Pskov
Riga Aluksne Pskov Valdai Tver *Gorki*
Jelgava LATVIA Opochka Hills Semen
Ivanovo *Reservoir*
Jekabpils 343m
Siauliai Ludza Velikiye (1,125ft) Rzhev Sergiyev
Panevezys Daugavpils Luki Posad Vladimir Nizhniy
55° LITHUANIA Zelenograd Oka Novgor
N Navapolatsk Podolsk Moscow
Kaunas Polatsk Murom
Marijampole Obninsk Kolomna Arzamas
Vitsyebsk Smolensk Kaluga Serpukhov
Alytus Vilnius *Dnieper* Ryazan
Maladzyechna Oka
Hrodna Lida Orsha Roslavl Tula Saransk
Barysaw
Minsk Zhodzina Mahilyow Bryansk 293m
3 Baranavichy BELARUS (961ft) Yelets Michurinsk Penza
Slutsk Babruysk Klintsy Orel Kamenka
Salihorsk Zhlobin *Desna* Lipetsk Tambov
Pinsk *Pripet* Svyetlahorsk Kursk
Marshes Homyel Staryy Voronezh
Mazyr Rechytsa *Pripet* Oskol
Lutsk Chernihiv Sumy Kamyshi
Rivne Korosten *Kievske* Central Russian Uplands
Shepetivka *Reservoir* Lubny
50° Zhytomyr Kharkiv
417m Kiev *Dnieper*
(1,368ft) Bila Tserkva Poltava Slovyansk Lysychansk
Khmelnytskyy Kremenchukske Kramatorsk Volgograd
Vinnytsya *Reservoir* Dnipropetrovsk Luhansk
Kamyanets-Podilskyy Cherkasy Kremenchuk Horlivka *Donets*
Uman UKRAINE Kirovohrad Oleksandriya Donetsk
4 Botosani Balti Dniprodzerzhynsk Zaporizhzhya Novocherkassk *Don*
Rabnita Yuzhnoukrayinsk Kryvyy Rih *Tsimlyansk*
Iasi MOLDOVA Nikopol Mariupol *Reservoir* Volgodonsk
Chisinau *Dniester* Mykolayiv *Kakhovske* Melitopol Rostov
Tighina Tiraspol *Dnieper* *Reservoir*
ROMANIA Bilhorod Odesa Kherson Berdyansk
Dnistrovskyy
Galati *Black Sea* *Sea of Azov*
45° Braila
Tulcea *Mouths of*
the Danube

North European Plain
Western Dvina

B 30°E C 35° D 40° E 45°

84

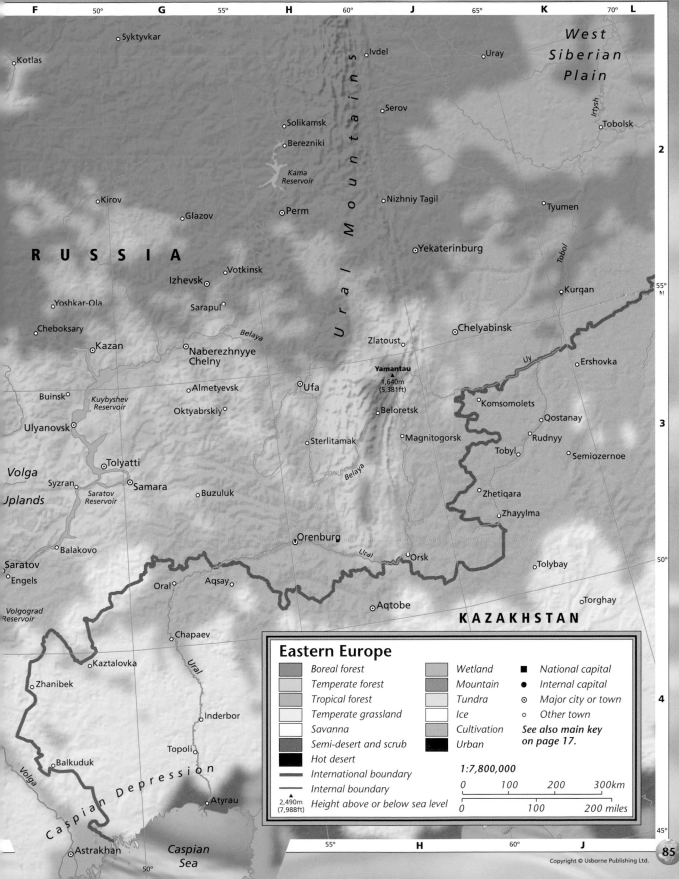

F 50° G 55° H 60° J 65° K 70° L

West Siberian Plain

Kotlas

Syktyvkar

Ivdel

Uray

Irtysh

Tobolsk

Solikamsk

Serov

Berezniki

Kama Reservoir

Kirov

Glazov

Perm

Nizhniy Tagil

Tyumen

Tobol

Yekaterinburg

R U S S I A

Yoshkar-Ola

Izhevsk

Votkinsk

Kurgan

55° N

Sarapul

Belaya

Zlatoust

Chelyabinsk

Cheboksary

Kazan

Naberezhnyye Chelny

Ufa

Yamantau 1,640m (5,381ft)

UY

Ershovka

Buinsk

Kuybyshev Reservoir

Almetyevsk

Beloretsk

Komsomolets

3

Ulyanovsk

Oktyabrskiy

Qostanay

Rudnyy

Volga Uplands

Tolyatti

Sterlitamak

Magnitogorsk

Tobyl

Semiozernoe

Syzran

Samara

Buzuluk

Belaya

Zhetiqara

Saratov Reservoir

Zhayylma

Balakovo

Orenburg

Ural

Orsk

Tolybay

50°

Saratov

Engels

Oral

Aqsay

Aqtobe

Torghay

Volgograd Reservoir

K A Z A K H S T A N

Chapaev

Kaztalovka

Ural

4

Zhanibek

Inderbor

Topoli

Balkuduk

Volga

C a s p i a n   D e p r e s s i o n

Atyrau

Caspian Sea

Astrakhan

50°

55° H 60° J

45°

Eastern Europe

▮ Boreal forest	▮ Wetland	▪ National capital	
▮ Temperate forest	▮ Mountain	● Internal capital	
▮ Tropical forest	▮ Tundra	⊙ Major city or town	
▮ Temperate grassland	▮ Ice	○ Other town	
▮ Savanna	▮ Cultivation	**See also main key on page 17.**	
▮ Semi-desert and scrub	▮ Urban		
▮ Hot desert			

— International boundary

— Internal boundary

▲ 2,490m (7,988ft) Height above or below sea level

1:7,800,000

0   100   200   300km

0   100   200 miles

1 68°N 2 64° 3 60° 4

M
40°

Barents Sea

Kola Peninsula

White Sea

RUSSIA

Arctic Circle

Lake Onega

Lake Vyg

Tikhvin

Borovichi

Severomorsk

Belomorsk

Lake Top

Petrozavodsk

Volkhov

Lake Ilmen

L
36°

Murmansk

Monchegorsk

▲1,191m
(3,907ft)

Apatity

Lake Seg

Lake Ladoga

St. Petersburg

Pushkin

Gatchina

Novgorod

K
32°

Kandalaksha

Lake Kuyto

Kostomuksha

Medvezhyegorsk

Vyborg

Kingisepp

Kirishi

Lake Pya

Lieksa

Zelenogorsk

Narva

Lake Peipus

Kirkenes

Lake Inari

Lokan Reservoir

Kuusamo

Kuhmo

Pielis Lake

Kuopio

Varkaus

Hauki Lake

Pihlaja Lake

Saimaa Lake

Kouvola

Kotka

ESTONIA

Vadso

Utsjoki

Sevettijarvi

Kaamanen

Sodankyla

Kiuruvesi

Jyvaskyla

Puula Lake

Paljanne Lake

Lappeenranta

Kohtla-Jarve

Tallinn

Vaaso

Alta

Lapland

Rovaniemi

Oulu Lake

Kajaani

Saarjarvi

Mikkeli

Lahti

Helsinki

Espoo

Haapsalu

Hammerfest

North Cape

Soroya

Hammerfest

Tromso

Kiruna

Stora Lule Lake

Boden

Skelleftea

Storavan Lake

Umea

Sundsvall

Hudiksvall

Gavle

Uppsala

Eskilstuna

Stockholm

Sodertalje

Norrkoping

G
20°

Kebnekaise
▲2,114m
(6,935ft)

Narvik

Svolvaer

Bodo

Moi Rana

Ostersund

Indals

Stor Lake

Namsos

Steinkjer

Trondheim

Oppdal

Lillehammer

Honefoss

Oslo

Drammen

Karlstad

Orebro

Lake Vaner

Lidkoping

NORWAY

SWEDEN

Galdhopiggen
▲2,469m
(8,100ft)

Bergen

Odda

Stavanger

Kristiansand

Arendal

Larvik

Fredrikstad

Norwegian Sea

Vestfjorden

Lofoten

Vesteralen

FINLAND

Oulu

Raahe

Kokkola

Tornio

Pori

Rauma

Turku

Tampere

Hameenlinna

Kurikka

Nasi Lake

Alavus

Aland Islands

Gulf of Bothnia

Baltic Sea

Hiiumaa

Gulf of Finland

Kotka

ICELAND inset map:

A 4°W 0° B 4°E C 8° D

ICELAND

Isafjordhur

Siglufjordhur

Seydhisfjordhur

Langanes

Vatnajokull

Hvannadalshnukur
▲2,119m
(6,952ft)

Reykjavik

Keflavik

Faxafloi

Arctic Circle

ATLANTIC OCEAN

Same scale as main map

N P Q

20°W 16° 20°

64°N

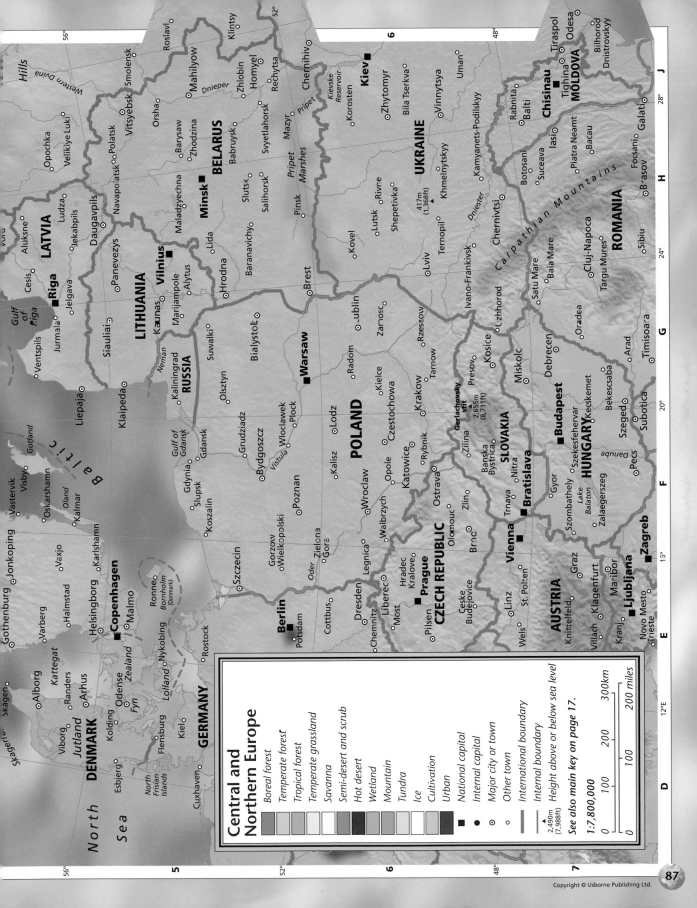

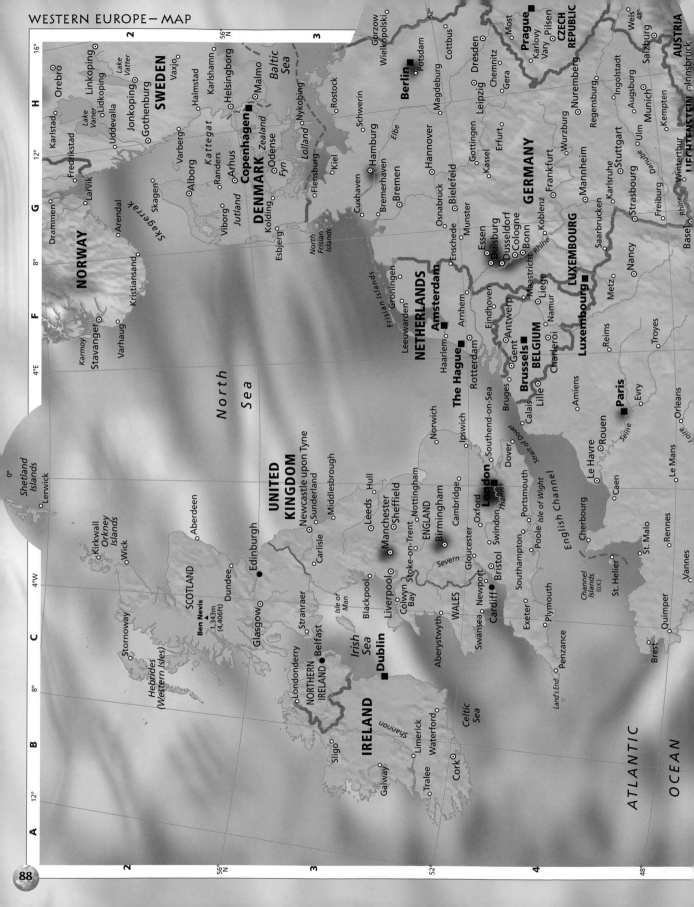

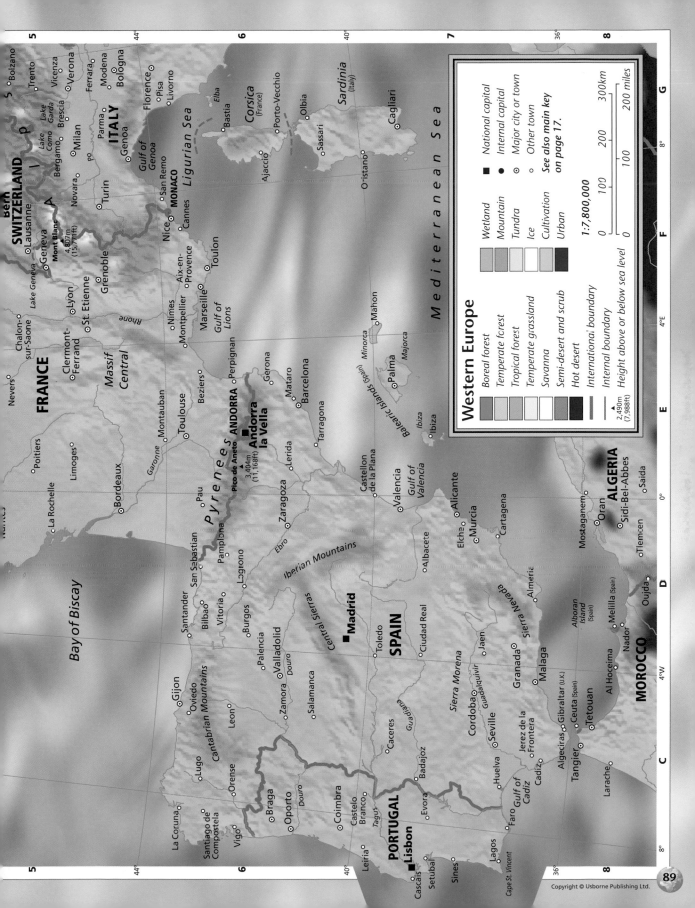

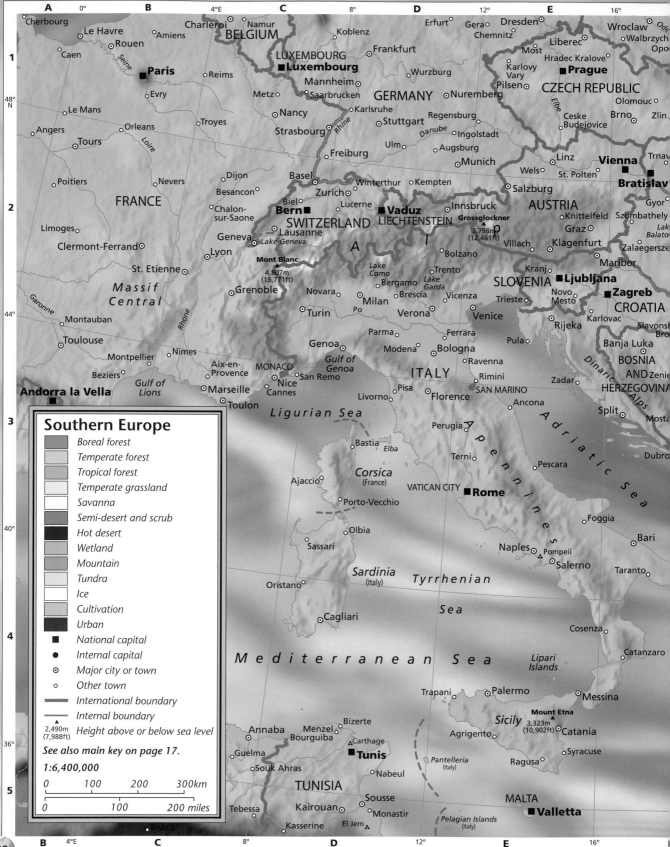

| | A | 0° | B | 4°E | C | 8° | D | 12° | E | 16° |

BELGIUM
Cherbourg
Le Havre
Rouen
Amiens
Charleroi
Namur
Koblenz
Frankfurt
Erfurt
Gera
Dresden
Wroclaw
Walbrzych
Opo
LUXEMBOURG
■ Luxembourg
Most
Chemnitz
Liberec
Hradec Kralove
Caen
■ Paris
Reims
Wurzburg
Karlovy
Vary
Pilsen
■ Prague
CZECH REPUBLIC
48°N
Evry
Metz
Saarbrucken
Mannheim
Nuremberg
GERMANY
Olomouc
Le Mans
Nancy
Karlsruhe
Regensburg
Ceske
Budejovice
Brno
Zlin
Angers
Orleans
Troyes
Strasbourg
Stuttgart
Ingolstadt
Danube
Linz
Vienna
Trnav
Tours
Loire
Freiburg
Ulm
Augsburg
Wels
St. Polten
Bratislav
FRANCE
Poitiers
Nevers
Dijon
Basel
Winterthur
Kempten
Munich
Salzburg
Gyor
Besancon
Zurich
Innsbruck
Szombathely
2
Limoges
Chalon-sur-Saone
Biel
Bern ■
Lucerne
Vaduz ■
LIECHTENSTEIN
Grossglockner
3,798m
(12,461ft)
AUSTRIA
Knittelfeld
Graz
Lake
Balato
Clermont-Ferrand
Geneva
Lausanne
SWITZERLAND
Bolzano
Villach
Klagenfurt
Zalaegersze
Lyon
Lake Geneva
Trento
A
Maribor
Mont Blanc
4,807m
(15,771ft)
Lake
Como
Bergamo
Lake
Garda
SLOVENIA
Ljubljana ■
Zagreb ■
44°
Massif
Central
Grenoble
Novara
Milan
Brescia
Vicenza
Po
Verona
Trieste
Novo
Mesto
CROATIA
Garonne
Turin
Rijeka
Karlovac
Slavons
Bro
Montauban
Parma
Modena
Ferrara
Bologna
Pula
Banja Luka
BOSNIA
Toulouse
Genoa
Ravenna
ITALY
Zadar
AND
Zenic
Montpellier
Nimes
Gulf of
Genoa
Rimini
Dinaric
HERZEGOVINA
Beziers
Aix-en-Provence
MONACO
San Remo
Ancona
Split
Alps
Andorra la Vella ■
Gulf of
Lions
Marseille
Nice
Cannes
Livorno
Pisa
Florence
SAN MARINO
Adriatic
Toulon
Ligurian Sea
Perugia
Apennines
Dubro
3
Bastia
Elba
Terni
Pescara
Ajaccio
Corsica
(France)
VATICAN CITY
Rome ■
Sea
Porto-Vecchio
Foggia
40°
Olbia
Naples
Bari
Sassari
Pompeii
Salerno
Taranto
Sardinia
(Italy)
Tyrrhenian
Oristano
Cosenza
4
Cagliari
Sea
Catanzaro
Mediterranean Sea
Lipari
Islands
Trapani
Palermo
Messina
Sicily
Mount Etna
3,323m
(10,902ft)
Catania
Annaba
Menzel
Bourguiba
Bizerte
Agrigento
Syracuse
36°
Guelma
Carthage
Pantelleria
(Italy)
Ragusa
Tunis ■
Souk Ahras
Nabeul
MALTA
5
TUNISIA
Sousse
Valletta ■
Tebessa
Kairouan
Monastir
Pelagian Islands
(Italy)
Kasserine
El Jem
Biskra

| | B | 4°E | C | 8° | D | 12° | E | 16° |

Southern Europe

- Boreal forest
- Temperate forest
- Tropical forest
- Temperate grassland
- Savanna
- Semi-desert and scrub
- Hot desert
- Wetland
- Mountain
- Tundra
- Ice
- Cultivation
- Urban
- ■ National capital
- ● Internal capital
- ⊙ Major city or town
- ○ Other town
- International boundary
- Internal boundary
- ▲ 2,490m
(7,988ft) Height above or below sea level

See also main key on page 17.

1:6,400,000

0   100   200   300km

0   100   200 miles

Kielce
Czestochowa
Zamosc
Lutsk
Rivne
Zhytomyr
Kiev
Lubny
Poltava

Katowice
Rybnik
Krakow
Tarnow
Rzeszow
Shepetivka
Bila Tserkva
Cherkasy
Kremenchukske Reservoir
Kremenchuk
Slovyansk
Kramatorsk

Ostrava
POLAND
Vistula
Lviv
417m (1,368ft)
UKRAINE
Dnipropetrovsk
48° N

Zilina
Gerlachovsky stit
2,655m (8,711ft)
Presov
Ivano-Frankivsk
Ternopil
Khmelnytskyy
Vinnytsya
Uman
Oleksandriya
Kirovohrad
Dniprodzerzhynsk
Dnieper
Zaporizhzhya

Banska Bystrica
Kosice
Uzhhorod
Dniester
Kamyanets-Podilskyy
Kryvyy Rih
Nikopol

SLOVAKIA
Miskolc
Chernivtsi
Carpathian Mountains
Botosani
Suceava
Balti
MOLDOVA
Rabnita
Yuzhnoukrayinsk
Kakhovske Reservoir
Berdyansk
Melitopol
2

Budapest
Debrecen
Satu Mare
Baia Mare
Iasi
Piatra Neamt
Chisinau
Tighina
Tiraspol
Mykolayiv
Kherson
Sea of Azov

Szekesfehervar
HUNGARY
Oradea
Cluj-Napoca
Targu Mures
Bacau
Odesa
Dzhankoy
Kerch

Kecskemet
Bekescsaba
Arad
ROMANIA
Sibiu
Mount Moldoveanu 2,544m (8,346ft)
Focsani
Bilhorod-Dnistrovskyy
Crimea
Feodosiya

Szeged
Danube
Timisoara
Transylvanian Alps
Brasov
Galati
Braila
Yevpatoria
Simferopol

Pecs
Subotica
Osijek
Novi Sad
Ramnicu Valcea
Buzau
Tulcea
Mouths of the Danube
Sevastopol
44°

Tuzla
Belgrade
Kragujevac
Drobeta-Turnu Severin
Pitesti
Ploiesti
Bucharest
Constanta

SERBIA
Craiova
Danube
Ruse
Black Sea

Sarajevo
Kraljevo
Nis
Vratsa
Dobrich
Varna

MONTENEGRO
Leskovac
Pleven
BULGARIA
Shumen

Niksic
KOSOVO
Vranje
Sliven
Stara Zagora
Burgas
Zonguldak
Karabuk
Corum
3

Podgorica
Pristina
Kumanovo
Sofia
Plovdiv

Tetovo
Blagoevgrad
Edirne
Istanbul
Adapazari
Lecce
Shkoder
Skopje
MACEDONIA
Prilep
Serres
Tekirdag
Bursa
Eskisehir
Kirikkale

Durres
Tirana
Bitola
Kavala
Istanbul
Sea of Marmara
Ankara

Elbasan
ALBANIA
Korce
Thessaloniki
Thasos
Canakkale
Kutahya
Lake Tuz

Vlore
Mount Olympus 2,917m (9,570ft)
Limnos
Balikesir
TURKEY
Aksaray
4

Corfu
Pindus Mountains
Ioannina
Larisa
Volos
Aegean Sea
Lesvos
Akhisar
Usak
Konya

Corfu
Preveza
GREECE
Lamia
Euboea
Skyros
Chios
Izmir
Manisa
Odemis
Isparta
Beysehir Lake
Karaman

Kefallonia
Chalkida
Ephesus
Aydin
Denizli
Taurus Mountains

Patra
Peiraias
Athens
Cyclades
Antalya
Alanya

Ionian Sea
Pyrgos
Dodecanese
Gulf of Antalya

Kalamata
Rhodes
Rhodes
Kyrenia
Nicosia

Kythira
Karpathos
CYPRUS
Larnaca

Chania
Crete
Irakleio
Paphos
Limassol

Ierapetra

AFRICA

Africa is the second-biggest continent in the world, and has 53 countries. These range from the vast, dry Sudan, to small, tropical islands such as the Seychelles. More than a quarter of Africa's countries are landlocked, with no access to the sea except through other countries.

Here is a group of Masai people from East Africa, silhouetted against a sunset over the flat grasslands of Africa.

Madeira
(Portugal)

Canary Islands
(Spain)

Tropic of Cancer

Rabat
Algiers
Tunis
MOROCCO
TUNISIA
Tripoli
Laayoune
ALGERIA
LIBYA
WESTERN
SAHARA
(Morocco)
MAURITANIA
Nouakchott
MALI
NIGER
CHAD
CAPE VERDE
Praia
Dakar
SENEGAL
Niger
Niamey
THE GAMBIA
Banjul
Bamako
Ouagadougou
Ndjamena
Bissau
BURKINA FASO
NIGERIA
GUINEA-BISSAU
GUINEA
BENIN
Abuja
CENTRAL
AFRICAN
REPUBLIC
Conakry
IVORY
COAST
TOGO
Freetown
GHANA
Porto-Novo
SIERRA LEONE
Yamoussoukro
Lome
CAMEROON
Bangui
Monrovia
LIBERIA
Accra
Malabo
Yaounde
EQUATORIAL
GUINEA
Congo
Equator
Libreville
SAO TOME
AND PRINCIPE
GABON
CONGO

ATLANTIC
Brazzaville
Kinshasa

OCEAN
Luanda

ANGOLA

NAMIBIA

Tropic of Capricorn
Windhoek

Orange

Cape Town

The shading on this map is there to help you see clearly the different countries that make up the continent.

Cairo

EGYPT

Tropic of Cancer

Nile

Khartoum

ERITREA
Asmara

SUDAN

DJIBOUTI Djibouti

Addis Ababa   SOMALIA

ETHIOPIA

Mogadishu

UGANDA
Kampala   KENYA

:ONGO   Kigali   Nairobi

(DEM.   RWANDA
BURUNDI
REP.)   Bujumbura

Dodoma

Victoria
SEYCHELLES

TANZANIA   Dar es Salaam

Equator

INDIAN

MALAWI   Moroni
COMOROS

ZAMBIA   Lilongwe
Lusaka

OCEAN

Zambezi

Harare   MOZAMBIQUE
ZIMBABWE

Antananarivo

OTSWANA

MADAGASCAR   MAURITIUS
Port Louis

aborone

Reunion
(France)   Tropic of Capricorn

Pretoria   Maputo

Mbabane SWAZILAND
Lobamba

oemfontein   Maseru
LESOTHO

;OUTH
AFRICA

Facts

Total land area 30,311,690 sq km (11,703,343 sq miles)
Total population 794 million
Biggest city Lagos, Nigeria
Biggest country Sudan *2,505,810 sq km (967,493 sq miles)*
Smallest country Seychelles *455 sq km (176 sq miles)*

Highest mountain Kilimanjaro, Tanzania *5,895m (19,340ft)*
Longest river Nile, running from Burundi to Egypt *6,671km (4,145 miles)*
Biggest lake Lake Victoria, between Tanzania, Kenya and Uganda *69,215 sq km (26,724 sq miles)*
Highest waterfall Tugela Falls, on the Tugela River, South Africa *610m (2,000ft)*
Biggest desert Sahara, North Africa *9,100,000 sq km (3,500,000 sq miles)*
Biggest island Madagascar *587,040 sq km (226,656 sq miles)*

Main mineral deposits Gold, copper, diamonds, iron ore, manganese, bauxite
Main fuel deposits Coal, uranium, natural gas

This greater flamingo is from the Transvaal National Park, South Africa.

93

Africa is home to the world's longest river, the Nile, and its largest desert, the Sahara. In southern Africa there are two more large deserts, the Kalahari and the Namib. Africa also has enormous rainforests in central areas, near the Equator.

A convoy of camels moves across the Sahara Desert in North Africa. The strange swirls of sand are formed by strong winds.

Desert weather

Temperatures in the Sahara Desert can rise as high as 55°C (131°F) during the day, but often fall below freezing point at night. Strong winds blow across the desert and whip up mini whirlwinds called dust devils. These suck up sand and hurl it high into the air.

This satellite image clearly shows the vast Sahara Desert in North Africa. It covers an area about the size of the U.S.A.

Moroccan mountain life

The Atlas Mountains dominate the country of Morocco, north of the Sahara Desert. High in the mountains are villages which are home to groups of African people called Berbers. Berbers have lived in Morocco for thousands of years and today still follow their traditional way of life, herding sheep and goats.

This image shows the curves and folds of the Atlas Mountains in Morocco. They were formed by earthquakes and other movements of the Earth.

Internet links

For links to websites where you can
explore the extreme landscapes of Africa
and spend 24 hours in the Namib, go to
www.usborne-quicklinks.com

River in the desert

The River Nile winds its way
through eastern Africa, from
Burundi all the way to the
Mediterranean Sea. It is
almost the only water source
in this dry, arid part of Africa,
so major cities, such as Cairo
in Egypt, have grown up near it.
The soil near the Nile's banks
is fertile enough to farm on,
especially near the coast where
the river splits into many streams.

Wild forests

The large, dense rainforests of central
Africa are home to more than half of
Africa's wild animals, including
chimpanzees, gorillas and elephants.
Many of these animals have never
come into contact with humans.

*The dense rainforest of central Africa is pink in this
satellite image. Running across the middle of the
picture is the large Congo River. It splits into many
smaller rivers, creating a huge swampy area.*

*The dark blue water
in the lower right
of this satellite image
is the Red Sea. The
triangular piece
of land jutting into
it is part of Egypt.*

*This is the River
Nile, running
through Egypt.
As the river reaches
the sea, it splits
into many streams
that create an
expanse of fertile,
swampy land.
This is the large
green area at the
top of the image.*

One of Africa's most populous countries is Egypt, which has busy cities such as its capital, Cairo, as well as the remains of ancient civilizations. Africa also has many areas of natural beauty, such as the vast wildlife parks in the south and east of the continent.

Pyramids and the Sphinx

One of the ancient wonders of the world is found at Giza, in Egypt – the group of three Great Pyramids. These stone structures were built by the ancient Egyptians as tombs for their pharaohs, or kings. The biggest pyramid is about 140m (480ft) high, and probably took 20 years to build. You can see a picture of the pyramids on page 1 of this atlas.

In front of the pyramids stands the Great Sphinx, an enormous statue of a lion with a man's head. It was probably carved as a monument to a pharaoh, though no one is sure which one. Some historians believe there are secret rooms and tunnels underneath the Sphinx.

This is the Great Sphinx of Egypt. It was carved out of soft limestone which has crumbled over the years. Part of the Sphinx's nose is now missing.

Cape Town

At Africa's southern tip, in the country of South Africa, is the city of Cape Town. It is famous for its elegant buildings, sandy beaches and busy waterfront. The city is right next to Table Mountain, which gets its name from its distinctive flat top. Thick clouds often cover the mountain and are nicknamed the Table Cloth.

This is Cape Town, with Table Mountain behind.

A panther chameleon clings to a branch. It can wrap its tail around the branch too, for extra grip. Panther chameleons live only in Madagascar.

On safari

Wild animals such as lions, elephants, buffaloes and zebras live on the grasslands of eastern and southern Africa. The land is divided into many specially protected wildlife parks that tourists can visit on safari trips.

These parks are some of the last remaining places where cheetahs live. These big cats were once found all over Africa but are now endangered. Cheetahs are the world's fastest land animals, able to run at a speed of 115kph (70mph).

Wildlife island

Madagascar is a large island in the Indian Ocean, off Africa's southeastern coast. It has thick, steamy rainforests which are home to many animals not found anywhere else in the world. These include rare chameleons and over 50 species of monkey-like animals called lemurs.

Internet links

For links to websites where you can see the Sphinx, explore an Egyptian pyramid and go on a photo safari, go to **www.usborne-quicklinks.com**

A cheetah in Kenya, eastern Africa, hisses and spits fiercely to scare away enemies.

A 0° B 5°E

Saida
Djelfa
Atlas Mountains
Ghardaia
Touggourt
El Oued
Ouargla
Batna
Biskra
Tebessa
Gafsa
Tozeur
Chott
el Jerid
Gabes
Tataouine
Tataouine

Annaba
Menzel
Bourguiba
Bizerte
Carthage
Tunis
Kairouan
Sousse
Monastir
El Jem
Sfax
Kerkenah
Islands
Gulf of Gabes
Jerba

Sicily
(Italy)
Catania
Syracuse
Pantelleria
(Italy)
Pelagian
Islands
(Italy)

GREECE Athe

MALTA
Valletta

Mediterranea

TUNISIA

Tripoli
Al Khums
Leptis Magna
Misratah
Gharyan
Surt
Gulf of
Sidra
Benghazi
Cyrene
Al Bayda
Darnah
Tubruq
Ajdabiya

30°N

Tademait
Plateau
Great
Eastern Erg
Ghadamis

ALGERIA

3

25°

Illizi
Sabha
Murzuq

LIBYA

Libya

Ghat
Ahaggar
Mountains
Mount Tahat
2,918m
(9,573ft)
Tropic of Cancer

4

Tamanrasset

Al Jaw

20°

Djado
Plateau

Tibesti
Mountains

Emi Koussi
3,415m
(11,204ft)

MALI S A H A R A

5

Agadez
NIGER
Faya-Largeau

Bodele
Depression

15°
Ennedi
Plateau

Tahoua

CHAD

Dosso
Sokoto
Maradi
Zinder
Mao
S A H E L
Abeche

6
Birnin-Kebbi
Katsina
Lake Chad
Mount Ma
3,088
(10,13

Kandi
Gusau
Kano
Maiduguri
Ndjamena
Mongo

Zaria
Potiskum
Am Timan

10°
Kaduna
NIGERIA
Kainji
Reservoir
Maroua

7
Saki
Minna
Jos
Kumo
Bongor
Nya
Bida
Niger
Abuja
CAMEROON
Birao

B 5°E C 10° D 15° E 20° F

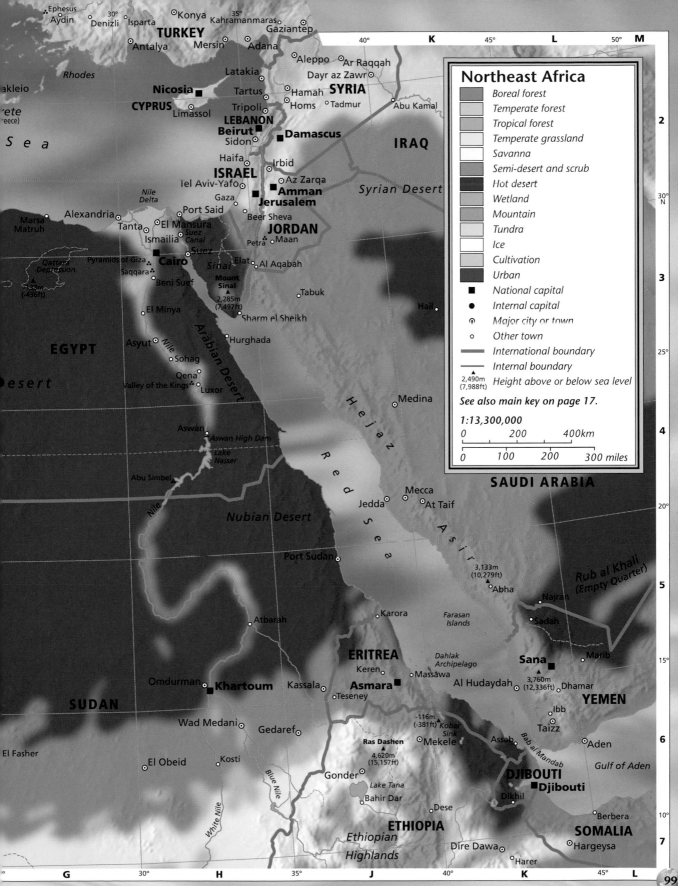

Northeast Africa

Key:
- Boreal forest
- Temperate forest
- Tropical forest
- Temperate grassland
- Savanna
- Semi-desert and scrub
- Hot desert
- Wetland
- Mountain
- Tundra
- Ice
- Cultivation
- Urban

- ■ National capital
- ● Internal capital
- ⊙ Major city or town
- ○ Other town
- ── International boundary
- ── Internal boundary
- ▲ 2,490m (7,988ft) Height above or below sea level

See also main key on page 17.

1:13,300,000

0   200   400km
0   100   200   300 miles

TURKEY
Ephesus
Aydin   30°   Konya   35°   Kahramanmaras
Denizli   Isparta   Gaziantep
Antalya   Mersin   Adana
                        Aleppo   Ar Raqqah
Rhodes   Latakia   Dayr az Zawr
akleio   Nicosia   Tartus   Hamah   SYRIA
CYPRUS   Tripoli   Homs   Tadmur   Abu Kamal
rete   Limassol
eece)   LEBANON   Beirut   Damascus   IRAQ
            Sidon   Az Zarqa
Sea   Haifa   Irbid   Syrian Desert
            ISRAEL   Amman
            Iel Aviv-Yafo   Jerusalem
Alexandria   Gaza   JORDAN   30°
            Port Said   Beer Sheva   N
Nile   Tanta   El Mansura   Petra   Maan
Delta   Ismailia   Suez
Marsa   Suez Canal
Matruh   Pyramids of Giza   Suez   Sinai   Elat
            Saqqara   Cairo   Al Aqabah   Tabuk
Qattara   Beni Suef   Mount Sinai   Hail
Depression   2,285m (7,497ft)
-155m (-436ft)   El Minya   Sharm el Sheikh   25°
EGYPT   Asyut   Nile   Hurghada
            Sohag
Desert   Qena   Arabian Desert   Medina
        Valley of the Kings   Luxor   Hejaz
        Aswan
        Aswan High Dam   Red Sea   Mecca   SAUDI ARABIA
        Lake Nasser   Jedda   At Taif   20°
Abu Simbel   Nile   Rub al Khali (Empty Quarter)
        Nubian Desert   Port Sudan   3,133m (10,279ft)   Najran
                        Abha   Sadah
        Atbarah   Karora   Farasan Islands   Marib
SUDAN   ERITREA   Dahlak   Sana   15°
Omdurman   Kassala   Keren   Archipelago   3,760m (12,336ft)   Dhamar
    Khartoum   Massawa   Al Hudaydah   YEMEN
            Teseney   Asmara   Ibb
El Fasher   Wad Medani   Gedaref   -116m (-381ft)   Kobar   Taizz   Aden
        Kosti   Sink   Assab   Gulf of Aden
El Obeid   Ras Dashen   Mekele   Bab al Mandab   Berbera
                4,620m (15,157ft)   DJIBOUTI   Djibouti
            Gonder   Lake Tana   Dikhil   SOMALIA
                Bahir Dar   Dese   Hargeysa
            ETHIOPIA
            Ethiopian   Dire Dawa
            Highlands   Harer

Copyright © Usborne Publishing Ltd.   99

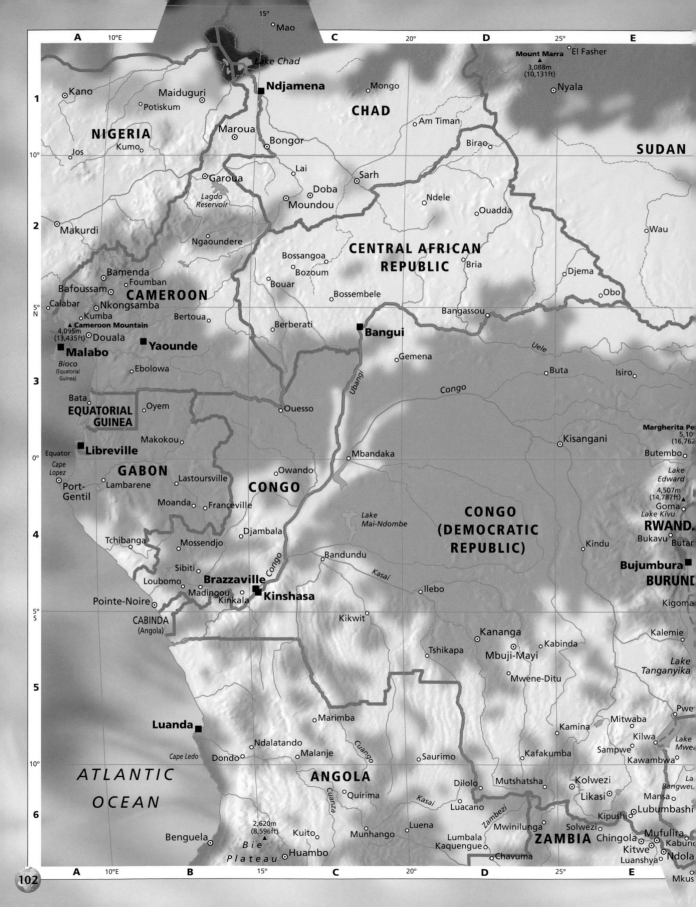

A | 10°E | B | C | 20° | D | 25° | E

15°
Mao

Lake Chad

Mount Marra
3,088m
(10,131ft)
El Fasher

1
Kano
Maiduguri
Potiskum
■ **Ndjamena**
Mongo
CHAD
Nyala

NIGERIA
Jos
Kumo
Maroua
Bongor
Am Timan
Birao
SUDAN

10°
Garoua
Lai
Sarh
Ndele
Ouadda

Doba
Moundou
Wau

2
Makurdi
*Lagdo
Reservoir*
Ngaoundere
**CENTRAL AFRICAN
REPUBLIC**
Bossangoa
Bozoum
Bria
Djema

Bamenda
Foumban
Bouar
Obo

Bafoussam
CAMEROON
Bossembele

5°
N
Calabar
Nkongsamba
Bertoua
Berberati
Bangassou

Kumba
▲ **Cameroon Mountain**
4,095m
(13,435ft)
■ Douala
■ **Bangui**
Uele

Malabo
Yaounde
Gemena
Buta
Isiro

*Bioco
(Equatorial
Guinea)*
Ebolowa
Ubangi
Congo

3
Bata
Oyem
Margherita Pe
5,10
(16,762

**EQUATORIAL
GUINEA**
Makokou
Mbandaka
Kisangani
Butembo

Equator
■ **Libreville**
*Cape
Lopez*
Owando
GABON
Lastoursville
CONGO
*Lake
Mai-Ndombe*
*Lake
Edward*
4,507m
(14,787ft) ▲
Goma
Lake Kivu

0°
Port-
Gentil
Lambarene
Moanda
Franceville
**CONGO
(DEMOCRATIC
REPUBLIC)**
Kindu
Bukavu
RWAND
Butar

4
Tchibanga
Mossendjo
Djambala
Bandundu
Kasai

Sibiti
Congo
Ilebo
Bujumbura ■
BURUND

Loubomo
Brazzaville ■
Madingou
Kinkala
Kikwit
Kigoma

Pointe-Noire
Kinshasa ■

5°
S
CABINDA
(Angola)
Kananga
Kalemie

Tshikapa
Kabinda

Mbuji-Mayi
*Lake
Tanganyika*

5
Mwene-Ditu
Pwe

Luanda ■
Marimba
Kamina
Mitwaba
Kilwa
*Lake
Mwe*

Ndalatando
Malanje
Kafakumba
Sampwe
Kawambwa

10°
Cape Ledo
Dondo
Cuango
Saurimo
Kolwezi
*La
Bangwe*

ANGOLA
Dilolo
Mutshatsha
Likasi
Mansa

ATLANTIC
Quirima
Kasai
Luacano
Kipushi
Lubumbashi

6
OCEAN
2,620m
(8,596ft)
Luena
Lumbala
Kaquengue
Mwinilunga
Solwezi
ZAMBIA
Chingola
Mufulira
Kabundo

Benguela
*Bie
Plateau*
Kuito
Munhango
Zambezi
Chavuma
Kitwe
Ndola
Luanshya

Huambo

A | 10°E | B | 15° | C | 20° | D | 25° | E

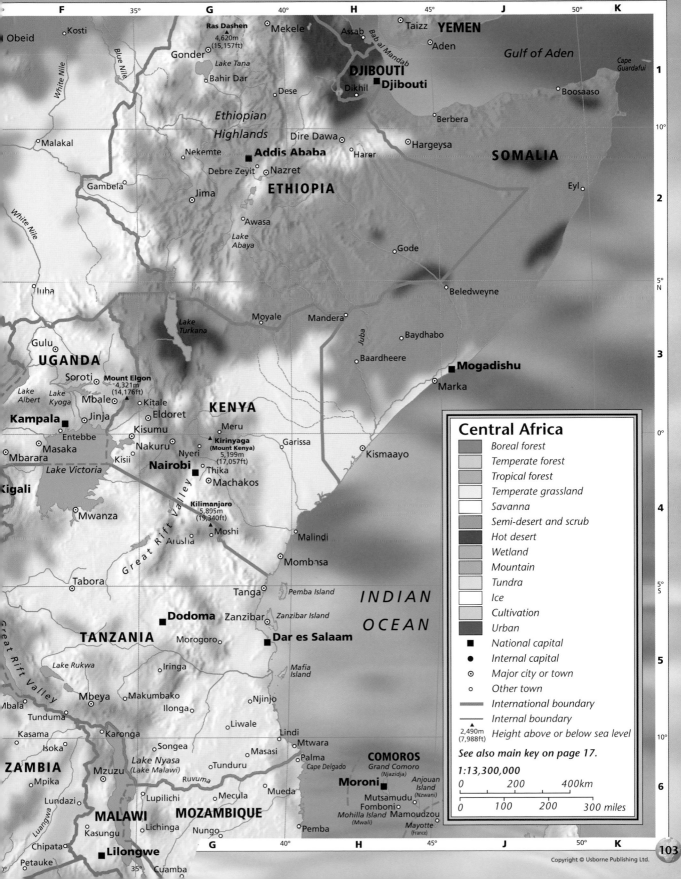

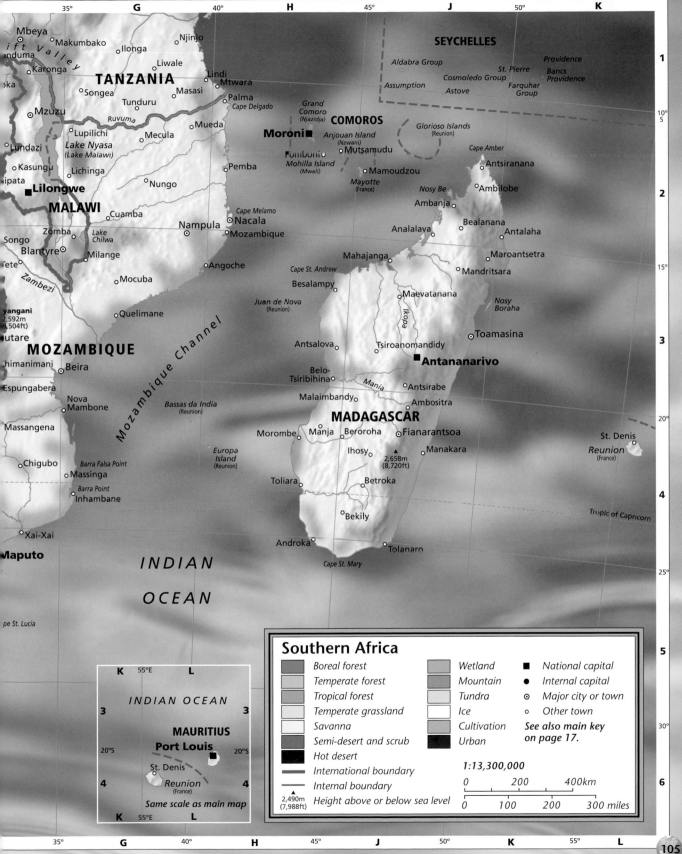

Mbeya
Makumbako
Njinjo
Ilonga
Liwale
nduma
Karonga
Rift Valley
TANZANIA
Lindi
Mtwara
ka
Songea
Tunduru
Masasi
Palma
Cape Delgado
Mzuzu
Lupilichi
Mecula
Mueda
Lundazi
Lichinga
Lake Nyasa
(Lake Malawi)
Pemba
ipata
Kasungu
Nungo
Lilongwe
MALAWI
Cuamba
Cape Melamo
Nacala
Nampula
Mozambique
Zomba
Lake
Chilwa
Songo
Milange
Blantyre
Milange
Angoche
Tete
Zambezi
Mocuba
yangani
2,592m
8,504ft)
Quelimane
utare
MOZAMBIQUE
Besalampy
himanimani
Beira
Espungabera
Nova
Mambone
Bassas da India
(Reunion)
Massangena
Europa
Island
(Reunion)
Chigubo
Barra Falsa Point
Massinga
Barra Point
Inhambane
Xai-Xai
Maputo
pe St. Lucia

SEYCHELLES
Aldabra Group
Providence
St. Pierre
Bancs
Assumption
Cosmoledo Group
Providence
Astove
Farquhar
Group
Grand
Comoro
(Njazidja)
COMOROS
Glorioso Islands
(Reunion)
Moroni
Anjouan Island
(Nzwani)
Cape Amber
ombonio
Mutsamudu
Antsiranana
Mohilla Island
(Mwali)
Mamoudzou
Nosy Be
Ambilobe
Mayotte
(France)
Ambanja
Analalava
Bealanana
Antalaha
Mahajanga
Maroantsetra
Mandritsara
Cape St. Andrew
Juan de Nova
(Reunion)
Maevatanana
Nosy
Boraha
Ikopa
Antsalova
Tsiroanomandidy
Toamasina
Belo-
Tsiribihina
Antananarivo
Mania
Antsirabe
Malaimbandy
Ambositra
MADAGASCAR
Morombe
Manja
Beroroha
Fianarantsoa
St. Denis
Ihosy
Manakara
Reunion
(France)
2,658m
(8,720ft)
Toliara
Betroka
Tropic of Capricorn
Bekily
Androka
Tolanaro
Cape St. Mary

INDIAN

OCEAN

35° *G* *40°* *H* *45°* *J* *50°* *K* *55°* *L*

1
10°
S
2
15°
3
20°
4
25°
5
30°
6

Southern Africa

▮ Boreal forest		▮ Wetland	■ National capital
▮ Temperate forest		▮ Mountain	● Internal capital
▮ Tropical forest		▮ Tundra	⊙ Major city or town
▮ Temperate grassland		▢ Ice	○ Other town
▮ Savanna		▮ Cultivation	*See also main key*
▮ Semi-desert and scrub		▮ Urban	*on page 17.*
■ Hot desert			

—— International boundary

—— Internal boundary

▲ 2,490m
(7,988ft) Height above or below sea level

1:13,300,000

0   200   400km
0   100   200   300 miles

INDIAN OCEAN

K   55°E   L
3 | 3
MAURITIUS
Port Louis
20°S | 20°S
St. Denis
4   *Reunion*   4
(France)
K   55°E   L
Same scale as main map

105

THE ARCTIC AND ANTARCTICA

The Arctic and Antarctica are the world's coldest places. The Arctic is the area around the North Pole, including the Arctic Ocean and the most northerly parts of Europe, North America and Asia. Antarctica is a huge continent at the South Pole.

Frozen island

Within the Arctic is Greenland, the world's largest island. Most Greenlanders live along the rocky coast, as the main body of land is covered in thick ice for most of the year.

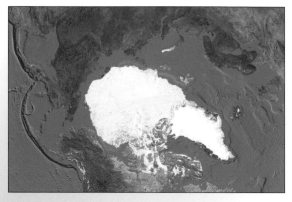

The large white area in this satellite image is ice, covering the Arctic Ocean and Greenland. At the top left of the image is the edge of Russia and at the top right is part of Europe.

This is the entrance to Sweden's Arctic ice hotel. The hotel is open in winter, then melts in the spring when the weather gets milder. The next winter, it is built all over again.

Internet links

For links to websites where you can explore the Arctic, watch video clips about life in Antarctica and meet animals that live at the opposite ends of the Earth, go to
www.usborne-quicklinks.com

A hotel of ice

Every winter, a hotel made entirely of ice is built in the far north of Sweden. Each piece of furniture is sculpted from ice, and even the beds are made of ice blocks. Guests sleep in special thermal sleeping bags with animal skins piled on top for extra warmth.

Icy continent

A huge, jagged sheet of ice permanently covers almost all of Antarctica, and spreads out over nearby seas as well. Scientists think that the area in the far west of the continent may be made up of many islands, but it is hard to tell because they are so far beneath the ice.

Mountains run down the middle of Antarctica, and in the west there are volcanoes. Amazingly, one volcano heats the sea near it so much that it is warm enough to swim in.

The darkest shading on this satellite image of Antarctica indicates ice that is over 3km (2 miles) deep.

These penguins are on the coast of Antarctica. They live in the ocean but come onto land to breed.

Life in Antarctica

The temperature in Antarctica can fall as low as -80°C (-112°F) in winter. It is too cold for people to live there, though scientists visit to study the area. No plants grow in the ice, and the only land animals are tiny mites. But many animals live in the seas around Antarctica, including penguins, seals, whales and fish.

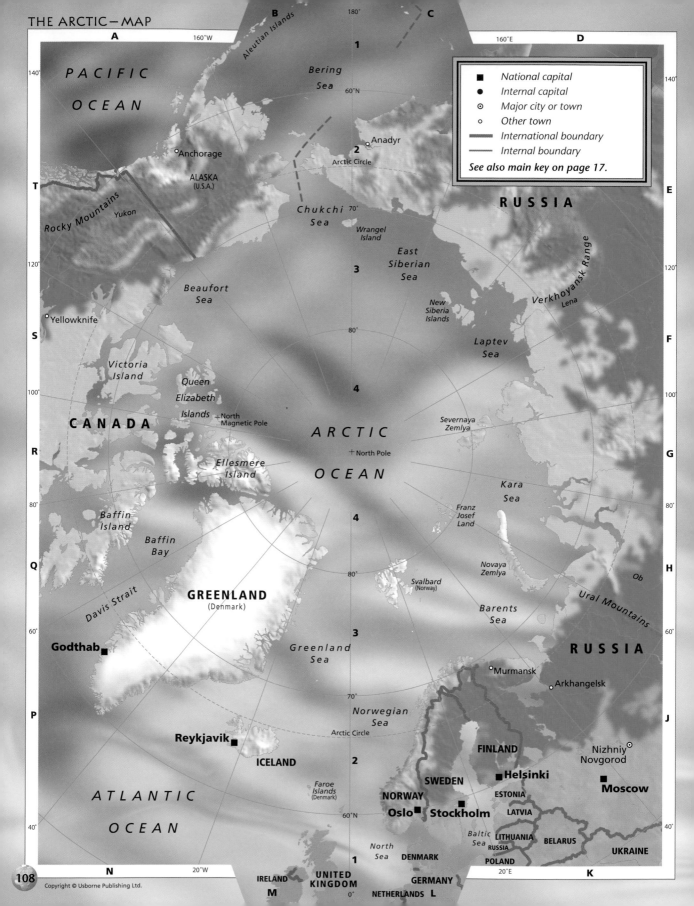

PACIFIC
OCEAN

Aleutian Islands

Bering
Sea

Anadyr

ALASKA
(U.S.A.)

Arctic Circle

Anchorage

RUSSIA

Rocky Mountains   Yukon

Chukchi
Sea

Wrangel
Island

Verkhoyansk Range

Beaufort
Sea

East
Siberian
Sea

New
Siberia
Islands

Lena

Yellowknife

Laptev
Sea

Victoria
Island

Queen
Elizabeth
Islands

North
Magnetic Pole

ARCTIC

Severnaya
Zemlya

CANADA

Ellesmere
Island

OCEAN

North Pole

Kara
Sea

Baffin
Island

Franz
Josef
Land

Baffin
Bay

Novaya
Zemlya

Ob

Svalbard
(Norway)

Ural Mountains

Davis Strait

GREENLAND
(Denmark)

Barents
Sea

RUSSIA

Godthab

Greenland
Sea

Murmansk

Arkhangelsk

Norwegian
Sea

Arctic Circle

Reykjavik

FINLAND

Nizhniy
Novgorod

ICELAND

SWEDEN

Helsinki

ATLANTIC

Faroe
Islands
(Denmark)

ESTONIA

Moscow

NORWAY

OCEAN

Oslo   Stockholm

LATVIA

Baltic
Sea

LITHUANIA   BELARUS

RUSSIA

North
Sea

DENMARK

LITHUANIA

POLAND

UKRAINE

IRELAND

UNITED
KINGDOM

GERMANY

NETHERLANDS

- National capital
- Internal capital
- Major city or town
- Other town
- International boundary
- Internal boundary

See also main key on page 17.

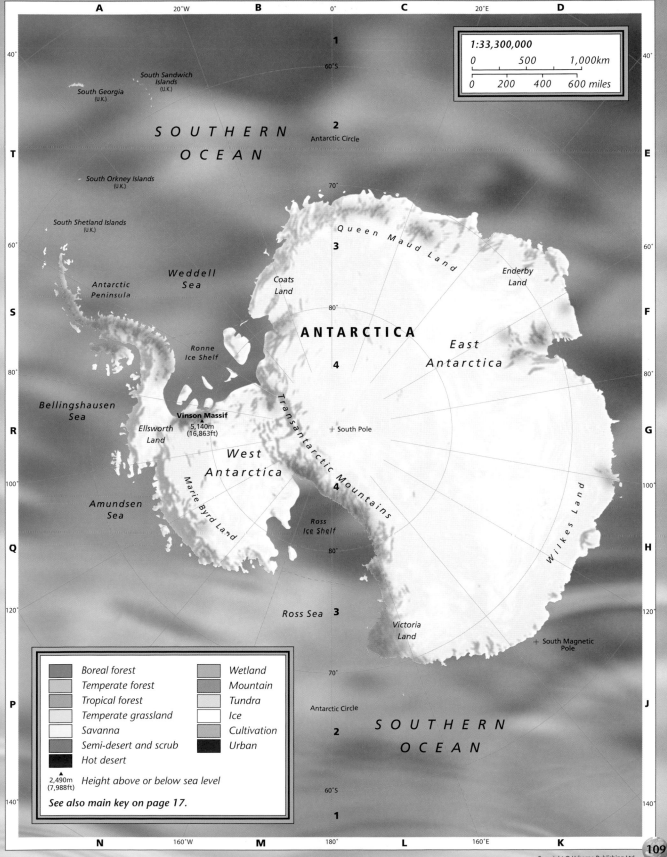

1:33,300,000

| 0 | 500 | 1,000km |
| 0 | 200 | 400 | 600 miles |

A   20°W   B   0°   C   20°E   D

40°

South Sandwich
Islands
(U.K.)

South Georgia
(U.K.)

1

60°S

2

Antarctic Circle

T   E

S O U T H E R N
O C E A N

South Orkney Islands
(U.K.)

70°

South Shetland Islands
(U.K.)

60°

3

Queen Maud Land

Weddell
Sea

Coats
Land

Enderby
Land

Antarctic
Peninsula

S   80°   F

ANTARCTICA

Ronne
Ice Shelf

East
Antarctica

4

Bellingshausen
Sea

Vinson Massif
5,140m
(16,863ft)

+ South Pole

R   G

Ellsworth
Land

West
Antarctica

Transantarctic Mountains

100°

4

Amundsen
Sea

Marie Byrd Land

Wilkes Land

Q   H

Ross
Ice Shelf

80°

120°

Ross Sea   3

Victoria
Land

+ South Magnetic
Pole

P   70°   J

Antarctic Circle

2

S O U T H E R N
O C E A N

60°S

Legend:

Boreal forest	Wetland
Temperate forest	Mountain
Tropical forest	Tundra
Temperate grassland	Ice
Savanna	Cultivation
Semi-desert and scrub	Urban
Hot desert	

2,490m
(7,988ft)   Height above or below sea level

See also main key on page 17.

N   160°W   M   180°   L   160°E   K

1

GEOGRAPHY QUIZ

T est your knowledge of the world's countries, cities, sights and animals with these quiz questions. The answers are on page 129.

The enormous, elaborate church above was designed by a famous Spanish architect named Antonio Gaudí.

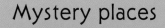

Mystery places

Which famous sights are shown in the photographs on this page? Each has clues to help you.

The marble building on the left is one of the Seven Wonders of the World. It was built by an Indian emperor.

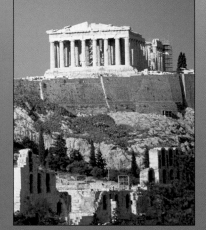

This famous steel bridge crosses the bay of a large North American city. It opened in 1937 and for many years was the longest suspension bridge in the world.

This city skyline is dominated by the tallest freestanding structure in the world. Visitors can go up the tower to a glass-bottomed viewing platform and a revolving restaurant. Can you name the tower and the city?

The ruins above are the remains of some of Europe's most important ancient temples and other public buildings.

Quick quiz

1. Which country's flag consists of a red circle on a white background?

2. When it is noon in Britain, what time is it in Mexico?

3. In which country is the Great Victoria Desert?

4. Which continent is the third-largest in the world?

5. In which country is Brno?

6. What is the world's deepest lake?

7. Name the smallest country in Europe.

8. Which country lies between Nicaragua and Panama?

9. In which country would you pay using naira and kobo as currency?

10. What is Turkey's capital city?

Internet links
For links to websites where you can try test-yourself quizzes and brush up your knowledge of world geography, go to
www.usborne-quicklinks.com

Survival challenge

Could you survive in the world's toughest terrains? Take this test to find out.

1. Which of the following would not be very useful on a trip to Antarctica?
a) A warm hat and gloves
b) An umbrella
c) Sunglasses and sunscreen

2. You are in the Sahara Desert and are short of drinking water. What should you do?
a) Stay active, so you produce sweat to cool yourself down.
b) Put on extra clothes and rest as much as possible.
c) Talk and sing songs to keep yourself alert.

3. When on safari in Africa, which of these spiders should you avoid?
a) Six-eyed crab spiders
b) Button spiders
c) Violin spiders

4. You are walking in the Rocky Mountains and meet a grizzly bear. What should you do?
a) Lie on the ground and play dead.
b) Turn and run away as fast as possible.
c) Back away slowly and calmly.

This grizzly bear is in the Rocky Mountains in Utah, U.S.A. Grizzly bears like to keep well away from humans, but will occasionally attack if they feel threatened.

GAZETTEER OF STATES

Afghanistan

Albania

Algeria

This gazetteer lists the world's 193 independent states, along with key facts about each one. In the lists of languages, the language that is most widely spoken is given first, even if it is not the official language. In the lists of religions, the one followed by the most people is also placed first. Every state has a national flag, which is usually used to represent the country abroad. A few states also have a state flag which they prefer to use instead. The state flags appear here with a dot beside them.

Armenia

Australia

Austria

Andorra

Angola

Antigua and Barbuda

• Argentina

Azerbaijan

Bahamas, The

Bahrain

Bangladesh

AFGHANISTAN (Asia)
Area: 647,500 sq km (249,935 sq miles)
Population: 25,838,797
Capital city: Kabul
Main languages: Dari, Pashto
Main religion: Muslim
Government: transitional
Currency: 1 afghani = 100 puls

ALBANIA (Europe)
Area: 28,750 sq km (11,100 sq miles)
Population: 3,510,484
Capital city: Tirana
Main language: Albanian
Main religions: Muslim, Albanian Orthodox
Government: emerging democracy
Currency: 1 lek = 100 qintars

ALGERIA (Africa)
Area: 2,381,740 sq km (919,589 sq miles)
Population: 31,193,917
Capital city: Algiers
Main languages: Arabic, French, Berber dialects
Main religion: Sunni Muslim
Government: republic
Currency: 1 Algerian dinar = 100 centimes

ANDORRA (Europe)
Area: 468 sq km (181 sq miles)
Population: 67,627
Capital city: Andorra la Vella
Main languages: Catalan, Spanish
Main religion: Roman Catholic
Government: parliamentary democracy
Currency: 1 euro = 100 cents

ANGOLA (Africa)
Area: 1,246,700 sq km (481,351 sq miles)
Population: 10,366,031
Capital city: Luanda
Main languages: Kilongo, Kimbundu, other Bantu languages, Portuguese
Main religions: indigenous, Roman Catholic, Protestant
Government: transitional
Currency: 1 kwanza = 100 lwei

ANTIGUA AND BARBUDA (North America)
Area: 442 sq km (171 sq miles)
Population: 66,970
Capital city: Saint John's
Main languages: Caribbean Creole, English
Main religion: Protestant
Government: constitutional monarchy
Currency: 1 East Caribbean dollar = 100 cents

ARGENTINA (South America)
Area: 2,780,400 sq km (1,073,512 sq miles)
Population: 36,955,182
Capital city: Buenos Aires
Main language: Spanish
Main religion: Roman Catholic
Government: republic
Currency: 1 peso = 100 centavos

ARMENIA (Asia)
Area: 29,800 sq km (11,506 sq miles)
Population: 3,336,100
Capital city: Yerevan
Main language: Armenian
Main religion: Armenian Orthodox
Government: republic
Currency: 1 dram = 100 luma

AUSTRALIA (Australasia/Oceania)
Area: 7,686,850 sq km (2,967,124 sq miles)
Population: 19,357,594
Capital city: Canberra
Main language: English
Main religion: Christian
Government: federal democratic monarchy
Currency: 1 Australian dollar = 100 cents

AUSTRIA (Europe)
Area: 83,858 sq km (32,378 sq miles)
Population: 8,150,835
Capital city: Vienna
Main language: German
Main religion: Roman Catholic
Government: federal republic
Currency: 1 euro = 100 cents

Barbados

Belarus

Belgium

Belize

Benin

Bhutan

• **Bolivia**

AZERBAIJAN (Asia)
Area: 86,600 sq km (33,436 sq miles)
Population: 7,771,092
Capital city: Baku
Main language: Azeri
Main religion: Muslim
Government: republic
Currency: 1 manat = 100 gopiks

BAHAMAS, THE (North America)
Area: 13,940 sq km (5,382 sq miles)
Population: 297,852
Capital city: Nassau
Main languages: Bahamian Creole, English
Main religion: Christian
Government: parliamentary democracy
Currency: 1 Bahamian dollar = 100 cents

BAHRAIN (Asia)
Area: 678 sq km (261 sq miles)
Population: 645,361
Capital city: Manama
Main languages: Arabic, English
Main religion: Muslim
Government: traditional monarchy
Currency: 1 Bahraini dinar = 1,000 fils

BANGLADESH (Asia)
Area: 144,000 sq km (55,598 sq miles)
Population: 131,269,860
Capital city: Dhaka
Main languages: Bengali, English
Main religions: Muslim, Hindu
Government: republic
Currency: 1 taka = 100 poisha

BARBADOS (North America)
Area: 430 sq km (166 sq miles)
Population: 275,330
Capital city: Bridgetown
Main languages: Bajan, English
Main religion: Christian
Government: parliamentary democracy
Currency: 1 Barbadian dollar = 100 cents

BELARUS (Europe)
Area: 207,600 sq km (80,154 sq miles)
Population: 10,350,194
Capital city: Minsk
Main language: Belarusian
Main religion: Eastern Orthodox
Government: republic
Currency: 1 Belarusian ruble = 100 kopecks

BELGIUM (Europe)
Area: 30,510 sq km (11,780 sq miles)
Population: 10,258,762
Capital city: Brussels
Main languages: Dutch, French
Main religions: Roman Catholic, Protestant
Government: constitutional monarchy
Currency: 1 euro = 100 cents

BELIZE (North America)
Area: 22,960 sq km (8,865 sq miles)
Population: 256,062
Capital city: Belmopan
Main languages: Spanish, Belize Creole,
English, Garifuna, Maya

Main religions: Roman Catholic, Protestant
Government: parliamentary democracy
Currency: 1 Belizean dollar = 100 cents

BENIN (Africa)
Area: 112,620 sq km (43,483 sq miles)
Population: 6,590,782
Capital city: Porto-Novo
Main languages: Fon, French, Yoruba
Main religions: indigenous, Christian, Muslim
Government: republic
Currency: 1 CFA* franc = 100 centimes

BHUTAN (Asia)
Area: 47,000 sq km (18,146 sq miles)
Population: 2,049,412
Capital city: Thimphu
Main languages: Dzongkha, Nepali
Main religions: Muslim, Hindu
Government: monarchy
Currency: 1 ngultrum = 100 chetrum

BOLIVIA (South America)
Area: 1,098,580 sq km (424,162 sq miles)
Population: 8,300,463
Capital cities: La Paz, Sucre
Main languages: Spanish, Quechua, Aymara
Main religion: Roman Catholic
Government: republic
Currency: 1 boliviano = 100 centavos

BOSNIA AND HERZEGOVINA (Europe)
Area: 51,129 sq km (19,741 sq miles)
Population: 3,922,205
Capital city: Sarajevo
Main languages: Bosnian, Serbian, Croatian
Main religions: Muslim, Orthodox, Roman
Catholic
Government: emerging federal democracy
Currency: 1 marka = 100 pfenninga

BOTSWANA (Africa)
Area: 600,372 sq km (231,743 sq miles)
Population: 1,586,119
Capital city: Gaborone
Main languages: Setswana, Kalanga,
English
Main religions: indigenous, Christian
Government: parliamentary republic
Currency: 1 pula = 100 thebe

BRAZIL (South America)
Area: 8,547,400 sq km (3,300,151 sq miles)
Population: 174,468,575
Capital city: Brasilia
Main language: Portuguese
Main religion: Roman Catholic
Government: federal republic
Currency: 1 real = 100 centavos

BRUNEI (Asia)
Area: 5,770 sq km (2,228 sq miles)
Population: 343,653
Capital city: Bandar Seri Begawan
Main languages: Malay, English, Chinese
Main religions: Muslim, Buddhist
Government: constitutional sultanate (a type
of monarchy)
Currency: 1 Bruneian dollar = 100 cents

**Bosnia and
Herzegovina**

Botswana

Brazil

Brunei

Bulgaria

Burkina Faso

Burma (Myanmar)

*CFA = Communaute Financiere Africaine

GAZETTEER OF STATES CONTINUED:

Burundi

Cambodia

Cameroon

Canada

Cape Verde

Central African Republic

Chad

BULGARIA (Europe)
Area: 110,910 sq km (42,822 sq miles)
Population: 7,707,495
Capital city: Sofia
Main language: Bulgarian
Main religions: Bulgarian Orthodox, Muslim
Government: republic
Currency: 1 lev = 100 stotinki

BURKINA FASO (Africa)
Area: 274,200 sq km (105,869 sq miles)
Population: 12,272,289
Capital city: Ouagadougou
Main languages: Moore, Jula, French
Main religions: Muslim, indigenous
Government: republic
Currency: 1 CFA* franc = 100 centimes

BURMA (MYANMAR) (Asia)
Area: 678,500 sq km (261,969 sq miles)
Population: 50,438,300
Capital city: Rangoon
Main language: Burmese
Main religion: Buddhist
Government: military dictatorship
Currency: 1 kyat = 100 pyas

BURUNDI (Africa)
Area: 27,830 sq km (10,745 sq miles)
Population: 6,223,897
Capital city: Bujumbura
Main languages: Kirundi, French, Swahili
Main religions: Christian, indigenous
Government: republic
Currency: 1 Burundi franc = 100 centimes

CAMBODIA (Asia)
Area: 181,040 sq km (69,900 sq miles)
Population: 12,491,501
Capital city: Phnom Penh
Main language: Khmer
Main religion: Buddhist
Government: constitutional monarchy
Currency: 1 new riel = 100 sen

CAMEROON (Africa)
Area: 475,440 sq km (183,567 sq miles)
Population: 15,803,220
Capital city: Yaounde
Main languages: Cameroon Pidgin English, Ewondo, Fula, French, English
Main religions: indigenous, Christian, Muslim
Government: republic
Currency: 1 CFA* franc = 100 centimes

CANADA (North America)
Area: 9,970,610 sq km (3,849,653 sq miles)
Population: 31,592,805
Capital city: Ottawa
Main languages: English, French
Main religions: Roman Catholic, Protestant
Government: federal democracy
Currency: 1 Canadian dollar = 100 cents

CAPE VERDE (Africa)
Area: 4,033 sq km (1,557 sq miles)
Population: 405,163
Capital city: Praia
Main languages: Crioulo*, Portuguese

Main religions: Roman Catholic, Protestant
Government: republic
Currency: 1 Cape Verdean escudo = 100 centavos

CENTRAL AFRICAN REPUBLIC (Africa)
Area: 622,436 sq km (240,322 sq miles)
Population: 3,576,884
Capital city: Bangui
Main languages: Sangho, French
Main religions: indigenous, Christian, Muslim
Government: republic
Currency: 1 CFA* franc = 100 centimes

CHAD (Africa)
Area: 1,284,000 sq km (495,752 sq miles)
Population: 8,707,078
Capital city: Ndjamena
Main languages: Arabic, Sara, French
Main religions: Muslim, Christian, indigenous
Government: republic
Currency: 1 CFA* franc = 100 centimes

CHILE (South America)
Area: 756,626 sq km (292,133 sq miles)
Population: 15,328,467
Capital city: Santiago
Main language: Spanish
Main religions: Roman Catholic, Protestant
Government: republic
Currency: 1 Chilean peso = 100 centavos

CHINA (Asia)
Area: 9,596,960 sq km (3,705,386 sq miles)
Population: 1,273,111,290
Capital city: Beijing
Main languages: Mandarin Chinese, Yue, Wu
Main religions: Taoist, Buddhist
Government: Communist state
Currency: 1 yuan = 10 jiao

COLOMBIA (South America)
Area: 1,138,910 sq km (439,733 sq miles)
Population: 40,349,388
Capital city: Bogota
Main language: Spanish
Main religion: Roman Catholic
Government: republic
Currency: 1 Colombian peso = 100 centavos

COMOROS (Africa)
Area: 1,862 sq km (719 sq miles)
Population: 596,202
Capital city: Moroni
Main languages: Comorian*, French, Arabic
Main religion: Sunni Muslim
Government: republic
Currency: 1 Comoran franc = 100 centimes

CONGO (Africa)
Area: 342,000 sq km (132,046 sq miles)
Population: 2,894,336
Capital city: Brazzaville
Main languages: Munukutuba, Lingala, French
Main religions: Christian, animist
Government: republic
Currency: 1 CFA* franc = 100 centimes

Chile

China

Colombia

Comoros

Congo

Congo (Democratic Republic)

Costa Rica

CFA = Communaute Financiere Africaine; Comorian = a blend of Swahili and Arabic; Crioulo = a blend of Portuguese and West African

Croatia

Cuba

Cyprus

Czech Republic

Denmark

Djibouti

Dominica

CONGO (DEMOCRATIC REPUBLIC) (Africa)
Area: 2,345,410 sq km (905,563 sq miles)
Population: 53,624,718
Capital city: Kinshasa
Main languages: Lingala, Swahili, Kikongo, Tshiluba, French
Main religions: Roman Catholic, Protestant, Kimbanguist, Muslim
Government: transitional
Currency: 1 Congolese franc = 100 centimes

COSTA RICA (North America)
Area: 51,100 sq km (19,730 sq miles)
Population: 3,773,057
Capital city: San Jose
Main language: Spanish
Main religions: Roman Catholic, Evangelical
Government: democratic republic
Currency: 1 Costa Rican colon = 100 centimos

CROATIA (Europe)
Area: 56,538 sq km (21,829 sq miles)
Population: 4,334,142
Capital city: Zagreb
Main language: Croatian
Main religions: Roman Catholic, Orthodox
Government: parliamentary democracy
Currency: 1 kuna = 100 lipas

CUBA (North America)
Area: 110,860 sq km (42,803 sq miles)
Population: 11,184,023
Capital city: Havana
Main language: Spanish
Main religion: Roman Catholic
Government: Communist state
Currency: 1 Cuban peso = 100 centavos

CYPRUS (Europe)
Area: 9,250 sq km (3,571 sq miles)
Population: 762,887
Capital city: Nicosia
Main languages: Greek, Turkish
Main religions: Greek Orthodox, Muslim
Government: republic with a self-proclaimed independent Turkish area
Currency: Greek Cypriot area: 1 Cypriot pound = 100 cents; Turkish Cypriot area: 1 Turkish lira = 100 kurus

CZECH REPUBLIC (Europe)
Area: 78,866 sq km (30,450 sq miles)
Population: 10,264,212
Capital city: Prague
Main language: Czech
Main religion: Roman Catholic
Government: parliamentary democracy
Currency: 1 koruna = 100 haleru

DENMARK (Europe)
Area: 43,094 sq km (16,639 sq miles)
Population: 5,352,815
Capital city: Copenhagen
Main language: Danish
Main religion: Evangelical Lutheran
Government: constitutional monarchy
Currency: 1 Danish krone = 100 oere

DJIBOUTI (Africa)
Area: 23,200 sq km (8,957 sq miles)
Population: 460,700
Capital city: Djibouti
Main languages: Afar, Somali, Arabic, French
Main religion: Muslim
Government: republic
Currency: 1 Djiboutian franc = 100 centimes

DOMINICA (North America)
Area: 751 sq km (290 sq miles)
Population: 70,786
Capital city: Roseau
Main languages: English, French patois
Main religions: Roman Catholic, Protestant
Government: democratic republic
Currency: 1 East Caribbean dollar = 100 cents

DOMINICAN REPUBLIC (North America)
Area: 48,511 sq km (18,731 sq miles)
Population: 8,581,477
Capital city: Santo Domingo
Main language: Spanish
Main religion: Roman Catholic
Government: democratic republic
Currency: 1 Dominican peso = 100 centavos

EAST TIMOR (Asia)
Area: 24,000 sq km (9,266 sq miles)
Population: 737,811
Capital city: Dili
Main languages: Tetun (Tetum), Bahasa Indonesia, Portuguese
Main religions: Roman Catholic, animist
Government: republic
Currency: 1 U.S. dollar = 100 cents

ECUADOR (South America)
Area: 283,560 sq km (109,483 sq miles)
Population: 13,183,978
Capital city: Quito
Main languages: Spanish, Quechua
Main religion: Roman Catholic
Government: republic
Currency: 1 sucre = 100 centavos

EGYPT (Africa)
Area: 1,001,450 sq km (386,660 sq miles)
Population: 69,536,644
Capital city: Cairo
Main language: Arabic
Main religion: Sunni Muslim
Government: republic
Currency: 1 Egyptian pound = 100 piasters

EL SALVADOR (North America)
Area: 21,040 sq km (8,124 sq miles)
Population: 6,237,662
Capital city: San Salvador
Main language: Spanish
Main religion: Roman Catholic
Government: republic
Currency: 1 Salvadoran colon = 100 centavos

EQUATORIAL GUINEA (Africa)
Area: 28,050 sq km (10,830 sq miles)
Population: 486,060
Capital city: Malabo
Main languages: Fang, Bubi, other Bantu

• **Dominican Republic**

East Timor

• **Ecuador**

Egypt

• **El Salvador**

Equatorial Guinea

Eritrea

GAZETTEER OF STATES CONTINUED:

Estonia

Ethiopia

Federated States of Micronesia

Fiji

Finland

France

Gabon

languages, Spanish, French, Pidgin English
Main religion: Christian
Government: republic
Currency: 1 CFA* franc = 100 centimes

ERITREA (Africa)
Area: 117,600 sq km (45,405 sq miles)
Population: 4,298,269
Capital city: Asmara
Main languages: Tigrinya, Afar, Arabic
Main religions: Muslim, Coptic Christian, Roman Catholic, Protestant
Government: transitional
Currency: 1 nafka = 100 cents

ESTONIA (Europe)
Area: 45,226 sq km (17,462 sq miles)
Population: 1,423,316
Capital city: Tallinn
Main languages: Estonian, Russian
Main religions: Evangelical Lutheran, Russian and Estonian Orthodox, other Christian
Government: parliamentary democracy
Currency: 1 Estonian kroon = 100 senti

ETHIOPIA (Africa)
Area: 1,127,127 sq km (435,184 sq miles)
Population: 65,891,874
Capital city: Addis Ababa
Main languages: Amharic, Tigrinya, Arabic
Main religions: Muslim, Ethiopian Orthodox, animist
Government: federal republic
Currency: 1 birr = 100 cents

FEDERATED STATES OF MICRONESIA (Australasia/Oceania)
Area: 702 sq km (271 sq miles)
Population: 134,597
Capital city: Palikir
Main languages: Chuuk, Ponapean, English
Main religions: Roman Catholic, Protestant
Government: democracy
Currency: 1 U.S. dollar = 100 cents

FIJI (Australasia/Oceania)
Area: 18,270 sq km (7,054 sq miles)
Population: 844,330
Capital city: Suva
Main languages: Fijian, Hindustani, English
Main religions: Christian, Hindu
Government: republic
Currency: 1 Fijian dollar = 100 cents

FINLAND (Europe)
Area: 337,030 sq km (130,127 sq miles)
Population: 5,175,783
Capital city: Helsinki
Main language: Finnish
Main religion: Evangelical Lutheran
Government: republic
Currency: 1 euro = 100 cents

FRANCE (Europe)
Area: 547,030 sq km (211,208 sq miles)
Population: 59,551,227
Capital city: Paris
Main language: French

Main religion: Roman Catholic
Government: republic
Currency: 1 euro = 100 cents

GABON (Africa)
Area: 267,670 sq km (103,347 sq miles)
Population: 1,221,175
Capital city: Libreville
Main languages: Fang, Myene, French
Main religions: Christian, animist
Government: republic
Currency: 1 CFA* franc = 100 centimes

GAMBIA, THE (Africa)
Area: 11,300 sq km (4,363 sq miles)
Population: 1,411,205
Capital city: Banjul
Main languages: Mandinka, Fula, Wolof, English
Main religion: Muslim
Government: democratic republic
Currency: 1 dalasi = 100 butut

GEORGIA (Asia)
Area: 69,700 sq km (26,911 sq miles)
Population: 4,989,285
Capital city: Tbilisi
Main languages: Georgian, Russian
Main religions: Georgian Orthodox, Muslim, Russian Orthodox
Government: republic
Currency: 1 lari = 100 tetri

GERMANY (Europe)
Area: 357,021 sq km (137,846 sq miles)
Population: 83,029,536
Capital city: Berlin
Main language: German
Main religions: Protestant, Roman Catholic
Government: federal republic
Currency: 1 euro = 100 cents

GHANA (Africa)
Area: 238,540 sq km (92,100 sq miles)
Population: 19,894,014
Capital city: Accra
Main languages: Twi, Fante, Ga, Hausa, Dagbani, Ewe, Nzemi, English
Main religions: indigenous, Muslim, Christian
Government: democratic republic
Currency: 1 new cedi = 100 pesewas

GREECE (Europe)
Area: 131,940 sq km (50,942 sq miles)
Population: 10,623,835
Capital city: Athens
Main language: Greek
Main religion: Greek Orthodox
Government: parliamentary republic
Currency: 1 euro = 100 cents

GRENADA (North America)
Area: 340 sq km (131 sq miles)
Population: 89,227
Capital city: Saint George's
Main languages: English, French patois
Main religions: Roman Catholic, Protestant
Government: constitutional monarchy
Currency: 1 East Caribbean dollar = 100 cents

Gambia, The

Georgia

Germany

Ghana

Greece

Grenada

Guatemala

*CFA = Communaute Financiere Africaine

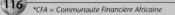

Guinea

Guinea-Bissau

Guyana

• **Haiti**

Honduras

Hungary

Iceland

GUATEMALA (North America)
Area: 108,890 sq km (42,042 sq miles)
Population: 12,974,361
Capital city: Guatemala City
Main languages: Spanish, Amerindian languages including Quiche, Kekchi, Cakchiquel, Mam
Main religions: Roman Catholic, Protestant, indigenous Mayan beliefs
Government: democratic republic
Currency: 1 quetzal = 100 centavos

GUINEA (Africa)
Area: 245,860 sq km (94,927 sq miles)
Population: 7,613,870
Capital city: Conakry
Main languages: Fuuta Jalon, Mallinke, Susu, French
Main religion: Muslim
Government: republic
Currency: 1 Guinean franc = 100 centimes

GUINEA-BISSAU (Africa)
Area: 36,120 sq km (13,946 sq miles)
Population: 1,315,822
Capital city: Bissau
Main languages: Crioulo*, Balante, Pulaar, Mandjak, Mandinka, Portuguese
Main religions: indigenous, Muslim
Government: republic
Currency: 1 CFA* franc = 100 centimes

GUYANA (South America)
Area: 214,970 sq km (83,000 sq miles)
Population: 697,181
Capital city: Georgetown
Main languages: Guyanese Creole, English, Amerindian languages, Caribbean Hindi
Main religions: Christian, Hindu
Government: republic
Currency: 1 Guyanese dollar = 100 cents

HAITI (North America)
Area: 27,750 sq km (10,714 sq miles)
Population: 6,964,549
Capital city: Port-au-Prince
Main languages: Haitian Creole, French
Main religions: Roman Catholic, Protestant, Voodoo
Government: republic
Currency: 1 gourde = 100 centimes

HONDURAS (North America)
Area: 112,090 sq km (43,278 sq miles)
Population: 6,406,052
Capital city: Tegucigalpa
Main language: Spanish
Main religion: Roman Catholic
Government: republic
Currency: 1 lempira = 100 centavos

HUNGARY (Europe)
Area: 93,030 sq km (35,919 sq miles)
Population: 10,106,017
Capital city: Budapest
Main language: Hungarian
Main religions: Roman Catholic, Calvinist
Government: parliamentary democracy
Currency: 1 forint = 100 filler

ICELAND (Europe)
Area: 103,000 sq km (39,768 sq miles)
Population: 277,906
Capital city: Reykjavik
Main language: Icelandic
Main religion: Evangelical Lutheran
Government: republic
Currency: 1 Icelandic krona = 100 aurar

INDIA (Asia)
Area: 3,287,590 sq km (1,269,339 sq miles)
Population: 1,029,991,145
Capital city: New Delhi
Main languages: Hindi, English, Bengali, Urdu, over 1,600 other languages and dialects
Main religions: Hindu, Muslim
Government: federal republic
Currency: 1 Indian rupee = 100 paise

INDONESIA (Asia)
Area: 1,919,440 sq km (741,096 sq miles)
Population: 228,437,870
Capital city: Jakarta
Main languages: Bahasa Indonesia, English, Dutch, Javanese
Main religion: Muslim
Government: republic
Currency: 1 Indonesian rupiah = 100 sen

IRAN (Asia)
Area: 1,648,000 sq km (636,293 sq miles)
Population: 66,128,965
Capital city: Tehran
Main languages: Farsi and other Persian dialects, Azeri
Main religions: Shi'a Muslim, Sunni Muslim
Government: Islamic republic
Currency: 10 Iranian rials = 1 toman

IRAQ (Asia)
Area: 437,072 sq km (168,754 sq miles)
Population: 23,331,985
Capital city: Baghdad
Main languages: Arabic, Kurdish
Main religion: Muslim
Government: developing parliamentary republic
Currency: 1 Iraqi dinar = 1,000 fils

IRELAND (Europe)
Area: 70,280 sq km (27,135 sq miles)
Population: 3,840,838
Capital city: Dublin
Main languages: English, Irish (Gaelic)
Main religion: Roman Catholic
Government: republic
Currency: 1 euro = 100 cents

ISRAEL (Asia)
Area: 20,770 sq km (8,019 sq miles)
Population: 5,938,093
Capital city: Jerusalem
Main languages: Hebrew, Arabic
Main religions: Jewish, Muslim
Government: parliamentary democracy
Currency: 1 Israeli shekel = 100 agorot

ITALY (Europe)
Area: 301,230 sq km (116,305 sq miles)

India

Indonesia

Iran

Iraq

Ireland

Israel

Italy

*CFA = Communaute Financiere Africaine;
Crioulo = a blend of Portuguese and West African

GAZETTEER OF STATES CONTINUED:

Ivory Coast

Population: 57,679,825
Capital city: Rome
Main language: Italian
Main religion: Roman Catholic
Government: republic
Currency: 1 euro = 100 cents

IVORY COAST (Africa)
Area: 322,460 sq km (124,502 sq miles)
Population: 16,393,221
Capital city: Yamoussoukro
Main languages: Baoule, Dioula, French
Main religions: Christian, Muslim, animist
Government: republic
Currency: 1 CFA* = 100 centimes

Jamaica

JAMAICA (North America)
Area: 10,990 sq km (4,243 sq miles)
Population: 2,665,636
Capital city: Kingston
Main languages: Southwestern Caribbean Creole, English
Main religion: Protestant
Government: parliamentary democracy
Currency: 1 Jamaican dollar = 100 cents

JAPAN (Asia)
Area: 377,835 sq km (145,882 sq miles)
Population: 126,771,662
Capital city: Tokyo
Main language: Japanese
Main religions: Shinto, Buddhist
Government: constitutional monarchy
Currency: 1 yen = 100 sen

Japan

JORDAN (Asia)
Area: 92,190 sq km (35,585 sq miles)
Population: 5,153,378
Capital city: Amman
Main languages: Arabic, English
Main religion: Sunni Muslim
Government: constitutional monarchy
Currency: 1 Jordanian dinar = 1,000 fils

Jordan

KAZAKHSTAN (Asia)
Area: 2,717,300 sq km (1,049,150 sq miles)
Population: 16,731,303
Capital city: Astana
Main languages: Kazakh, Russian
Main religions: Muslim, Russian Orthodox
Government: republic
Currency: 1 Kazakhstani tenge = 100 tiyn

Kazakhstan

KENYA (Africa)
Area: 582,650 sq km (224,961 sq miles)
Population: 30,765,916
Capital city: Nairobi
Main languages: Swahili, English, Bantu languages
Main religions: Christian, indigenous
Government: republic
Currency: 1 Kenyan shilling = 100 cents

Kenya

KIRIBATI (Australasia/Oceania)
Area: 717 sq km (277 sq miles)
Population: 94,149
Capital city: Bairiki (on Tarawa island)
Main languages: Gilbertese, English
Main religions: Roman Catholic, Protestant

Kiribati

Government: republic
Currency: 1 Australian dollar = 100 cents

KOSOVO (Europe)
Area: 10,908 sq km (4,212 sq miles)
Population: 2,100,000
Capital city: Pristina
Main languages: Albanian, Serbian, Bosnian
Main religions: Muslim, Serbian Orthodox, Roman Catholic
Government: parliamentary republic
Currency: 1 euro = 100 cents

Kosovo

KUWAIT (Asia)
Area: 17,820 sq km (6,880 sq miles)
Population: 2,041,961
Capital city: Kuwait City
Main languages: Arabic, English
Main religion: Muslim
Government: monarchy
Currency: 1 Kuwaiti dinar = 1,000 fils

Kuwait

KYRGYZSTAN (Asia)
Area: 198,500 sq km (76,641 sq miles)
Population: 4,753,003
Capital city: Bishkek
Main languages: Kyrgyz, Russian
Main religions: Muslim, Russian Orthodox
Government: republic
Currency: 1 Kyrgyzstani som = 100 tyiyn

Kyrgyzstan

LAOS (Asia)
Area: 236,800 sq km (91,428 sq miles)
Population: 5,638,967
Capital city: Vientiane
Main languages: Lao, French, English
Main religions: Buddhist, animist
Government: Communist state
Currency: 1 new kip = 100 at

Laos

LATVIA (Europe)
Area: 64,589 sq km (24,938 sq miles)
Population: 2,385,231
Capital city: Riga
Main languages: Latvian, Russian
Main religions: Lutheran, Roman Catholic, Russian Orthodox
Government: parliamentary democracy
Currency: 1 Latvian lat = 100 santims

Latvia

LEBANON (Asia)
Area: 10,400 sq km (4,015 sq miles)
Population: 3,627,774
Capital city: Beirut
Main languages: Arabic, French, English
Main religions: Muslim, Christian
Government: republic
Currency: 1 Lebanese pound = 100 piasters

Lebanon

LESOTHO (Africa)
Area: 30,350 sq km (11,718 sq miles)
Population: 2,177,062
Capital cities: Maseru, Lobamba
Main languages: Sesotho, English, Zulu, Xhosa
Main religions: Christian, indigenous
Government: constitutional monarchy
Currency: 1 loti = 100 lisente

LIBERIA (Africa)
Area: 111,370 sq km (43,000 sq miles)

Lesotho

*CFA = Communaute Financiere Africaine

Liberia

Population: 3,225,837
Capital city: Monrovia
Main languages: Kpelle, English, Bassa
Main religions: indigenous, Christian, Muslim
Government: republic
Currency: 1 Liberian dollar – 100 cents

LIBYA (Africa)
Area: 1,759,540 sq km (679,358 sq miles)
Population: 5,240,599
Capital city: Tripoli
Main languages: Arabic, Italian, English
Main religion: Sunni Muslim
Government: military rule
Currency: 1 Libyan dinar = 1,000 dirhams

Libya

LIECHTENSTEIN (Europe)
Area: 160 sq km (62 sq miles)
Population: 32,528
Capital city: Vaduz
Main languages: German, Alemannic
Main religion: Roman Catholic
Government: constitutional monarchy
Currency: 1 Swiss franc = 100 centimes

Liechtenstein

LITHUANIA (Europe)
Area: 65,200 sq km (25,174 sq miles)
Population: 3,610,535
Capital city: Vilnius
Main languages: Lithuanian, Polish, Russian
Main religions: Roman Catholic, Lutheran, Russian Orthodox
Government: democracy
Currency: 1 Lithuanian litas = 100 centas

Lithuania

LUXEMBOURG (Europe)
Area: 2,586 sq km (998 sq miles)
Population: 442,972
Capital city: Luxembourg
Main languages: Luxemburgish, German, French
Main religion: Roman Catholic
Government: constitutional monarchy
Currency: 1 euro = 100 cents

Luxembourg

MACEDONIA (Europe)
Area: 25,333 sq km (9,781 sq miles)
Population: 2,046,209
Capital city: Skopje
Main languages: Macedonian, Albanian
Main religions: Macedonian Orthodox, Muslim
Government: emerging democracy
Currency: 1 Macedonian denar = 100 deni

Macedonia

MADAGASCAR (Africa)
Area: 587,040 sq km (226,656 sq miles)
Population: 15,982,563
Capital city: Antananarivo
Main languages: Malagasy, French
Main religions: indigenous beliefs, Christian
Government: republic
Currency: 1 Malagasy franc = 100 centimes

Madagascar

MALAWI (Africa)
Area: 118,480 sq km (45,745 sq miles)
Population: 10,548,250
Capital city: Lilongwe
Main languages: Chichewa, English
Main religions: Protestant, Roman Catholic, Muslim

Government: parliamentary democracy
Currency: 1 Malawian kwacha = 100 tambala

MALAYSIA (Asia)
Area: 329,750 sq km (127,316 sq miles)
Population: 22,229,040
Capital city: Kuala Lumpur
Main languages: Bahasa Melayu, English, Chinese dialects, Tamil
Main religions: Muslim, Buddhist, Daoist
Government: constitutional monarchy
Currency: 1 ringgit = 100 sen

MALDIVES (Asia)
Area: 300 sq km (116 sq miles)
Population: 310,764
Capital city: Male
Main languages: Maldivian, English
Main religion: Sunni Muslim
Government: republic
Currency: 1 rufiyaa = 100 laari

MALI (Africa)
Area: 1,240,000 sq km (478,764 sq miles)
Population: 11,008,518
Capital city: Bamako
Main languages: Bambara, Fulani, Songhai, French
Main religion: Muslim
Government: republic
Currency: 1 CFA* franc = 100 centimes

MALTA (Europe)
Area: 316 sq km (122 sq miles)
Population: 394,583
Capital city: Valletta
Main languages: Maltese, English
Main religion: Roman Catholic
Government: democratic republic
Currency: 1 Maltese lira – 100 cents

MARSHALL ISLANDS
(Australasia/Oceania)
Area: 181 sq km (70 sq miles)
Population: 70,822
Capital city: Majuro
Main languages: Marshallese, English
Main religion: Protestant
Government: republic
Currency: 1 U.S. dollar = 100 cents

MAURITANIA (Africa)
Area: 1,030,700 sq km (397,953 sq miles)
Population: 2,747,312
Capital city: Nouakchott
Main languages: Arabic, Wolof, French
Main religion: Muslim
Government: republic
Currency: 1 ouguiya = 5 khoums

MAURITIUS (Africa)
Area: 1,860 sq km (718 sq miles)
Population: 1,189,825
Capital city: Port Louis
Main languages: Mauritius Creole French, French, Hindi, Bhojpuri, Urdu, Tamil, English
Main religions: Hindu, Christian, English
Government: parliamentary democracy
Currency: 1 Mauritian rupee = 100 cents

Malawi

Malaysia

Maldives

Mali

Malta

Marshall Islands

Mauritania

*CFA = Communaute Financiere Africaine

GAZETTEER OF STATES CONTINUED:

Mauritius

Mexico

Moldova

Monaco

Mongolia

Montenegro

Morocco

MEXICO (North America)
Area: 1,972,550 sq km (761,602 sq miles)
Population: 101,879,171
Capital city: Mexico City
Main languages: Spanish, Mayan, Nahuatl
Main religion: Roman Catholic
Government: federal republic
Currency: 1 New Mexican peso = 100 centavos

MOLDOVA (Europe)
Area: 33,843 sq km (13,067 sq miles)
Population: 4,431,570
Capital city: Chisinau
Main languages: Moldovan, Russian, Gagauz
Main religion: Eastern Orthodox
Government: republic
Currency: 1 Moldovan leu = 100 bani

MONACO (Europe)
Area: 1.95 sq km (0.75 sq miles)
Population: 31,842
Capital city: Monaco
Main languages: French, Monegasque, Italian
Main religion: Roman Catholic
Government: constitutional monarchy
Currency: 1 euro = 100 cents

MONGOLIA (Asia)
Area: 1,565,000 sq km (604,247 sq miles)
Population: 2,654,999
Capital city: Podgorica
Main language: Khalkha Mongol
Main religion: Tibetan Buddist Lamaist
Government: republic
Currency: 1 tugrik = 100 mongos

MONTENEGRO (Europe)
Area: 14,026 sq km (5,019 sq miles)
Population: 678,177
Capital city: Podgorica
Main language: Montenegrin, Serbian, Bosnian, Albanian
Main religion: Orthodox, Muslim
Government: republic
Currency: 1 euro = 100 cents

MOROCCO (Africa)
Area: 446,550 sq km (172,413 sq miles)
Population: 30,645,305
Capital city: Rabat
Main languages: Arabic, Berber, French
Main religion: Muslim
Government: constitutional monarchy
Currency: 1 Moroccan dirham = 100 centimes

MOZAMBIQUE (Africa)
Area: 801,590 sq km (309,494 sq miles)
Population: 19,371,057
Capital city: Maputo
Main languages: Makua, Tsonga, Portuguese
Main religions: indigenous, Christian, Muslim
Government: republic
Currency: 1 metical = 100 centavos

NAMIBIA (Africa)
Area: 825,418 sq km (318,694 sq miles)
Population: 1,797,677
Capital city: Windhoek

Main languages: Afrikaans, German, English
Main religions: Christian, indigenous
Government: republic
Currency: 1 Namibian dollar = 100 cents

NAURU (Australasia/Oceania)
Area: 21 sq km (8 sq miles)
Population: 12,088
Capital: Yaren
Main languages: Nauruan, English
Main religion: Christian
Government: republic
Currency: 1 Australian dollar = 100 cents

NEPAL (Asia)
Area: 147,181 sq km (56,827 sq miles)
Population: 25,284,463
Capital city: Kathmandu
Main languages: Nepali, Maithili
Main religions: Hindu, Buddhist
Government: constitutional monarchy
Currency: 1 Nepalese rupee = 100 paisa

NETHERLANDS (Europe)
Area: 41,532 sq km (16,036 sq miles)
Population: 15,981,472
Capital cities: Amsterdam, The Hague
Main language: Dutch
Main religion: Christian
Government: constitutional monarchy
Currency: 1 euro = 100 cents

NEW ZEALAND (Australasia/Oceania)
Area: 268,680 sq km (103,737 sq miles)
Population: 3,864,129
Capital city: Wellington
Main languages: English, Maori
Main religion: Christian
Government: parliamentary democracy
Currency: 1 New Zealand dollar = 100 cents

NICARAGUA (North America)
Area: 129,494 sq km (49,998 sq miles)
Population: 4,918,393
Capital city: Managua
Main language: Spanish
Main religion: Roman Catholic
Government: republic
Currency: 1 gold cordoba = 100 centavos

NIGER (Africa)
Area: 1,267,000 sq km (489,189 sq miles)
Population: 10,355,156
Capital city: Niamey
Main languages: Hausa, Djerma, French
Main religion: Muslim
Government: republic
Currency: 1 CFA* franc = 100 centimes

NIGERIA (Africa)
Area: 923,768 sq km (356,667 sq miles)
Population: 126,635,626
Capital city: Abuja
Main languages: Hausa, Yoruba, Igbo, English
Main religions: Muslim, Christian, indigenous
Government: republic
Currency: 1 naira = 100 kobo

Mozambique

Namibia

Nauru

Nepal

Netherlands

New Zealand

Nicaragua

*CFA = Communaute Financiere Africaine

Niger

Nigeria

North Korea

Norway

Oman

Pakistan

Palau

NORTH KOREA (Asia)
Area: 120,540 sq km (46,540 sq miles)
Population: 21,968,228
Capital city: Pyongyang
Main language: Korean
Main religions: Buddhist, Confucianist
Government: authoritarian socialist
Currency: 1 North Korean won = 100 chon

NORWAY (Europe)
Area: 324,220 sq km (125,181 sq miles)
Population: 4,503,440
Capital city: Oslo
Main language: Norwegian
Main religion: Evangelical Lutheran
Government: constitutional monarchy
Currency: 1 Norwegian krone = 100 oere

OMAN (Asia)
Area: 212,460 sq km (82,031 sq miles)
Population: 2,622,198
Capital city: Muscat
Main languages: Arabic, English, Baluchi
Main religion: Muslim
Government: monarchy
Currency: 1 Omani rial = 1,000 baiza

PAKISTAN (Asia)
Area: 803,940 sq km (310,401 sq miles)
Population: 144,616,639
Capital city: Islamabad
Main languages: Punjabi, Sindhi, Urdu, English
Main religion: Muslim
Government: federal republic
Currency: 1 Pakistani rupee = 100 paisa

PALAU (Australasia/Oceania)
Area: 459 sq km (177 sq miles)
Population: 19,092
Capital city: Koror
Main languages: Palauan, English
Main religions: Christian, Modekngei
Government: democratic republic
Currency: 1 U.S. dollar = 100 cents

PANAMA (North America)
Area: 78,200 sq km (30,193 sq miles)
Population: 2,845,647
Capital city: Panama City
Main languages: Spanish, English
Main religions: Roman Catholic, Protestant
Government: democracy
Currency: 1 balboa = 100 centesimos

PAPUA NEW GUINEA
(Australasia/Oceania)
Area: 462,840 sq km (178,703 sq miles)
Population: 5,049,055
Capital city: Port Moresby
Main languages: Tok Pisin, Hiri Motu, English
Main religions: Christian, indigenous
Government: parliamentary democracy
Currency: 1 kina = 100 toea

PARAGUAY (South America)
Area: 406,750 sq km (157,046 sq miles)
Population: 5,734,139
Capital city: Asuncion

Main languages: Guarani, Spanish
Main religion: Roman Catholic
Government: republic
Currency: 1 guarani = 100 centimos

PERU (South America)
Area: 1,285,220 sq km (496,223 sq miles)
Population: 27,483,864
Capital city: Lima
Main languages: Spanish, Quechua, Aymara
Main religion: Roman Catholic
Government: republic
Currency: 1 nuevo sol = 100 centimos

PHILIPPINES (Asia)
Area: 300,000 sq km (115,830 sq miles)
Population: 82,841,518
Capital city: Manila
Main languages: Tagalog, English, Ilocano
Main religion: Roman Catholic
Government: republic
Currency: 1 Philippine peso = 100 centavos

POLAND (Europe)
Area: 312,685 sq km (120,727 sq miles)
Population: 38,633,912
Capital city: Warsaw
Main language: Polish
Main religion: Roman Catholic
Government: democratic republic
Currency: 1 zloty = 100 groszy

PORTUGAL (Europe)
Area: 92,391 sq km (35,672 sq miles)
Population: 10,066,253
Capital city: Lisbon
Main language: Portuguese
Main religion: Roman Catholic
Government: democratic republic
Currency: 1 euro = 100 cents

QATAR (Asia)
Area: 11,437 sq km (4,416 sq miles)
Population: 769,152
Capital city: Doha
Main languages: Arabic, English
Main religion: Muslim
Government: monarchy
Currency: 1 Qatari riyal = 100 dirhams

ROMANIA (Europe)
Area: 237,500 sq km (91,699 sq miles)
Population: 22,364,022
Capital city: Bucharest
Main languages: Romanian, Hungarian, German
Main religion: Romanian Orthodox
Government: republic
Currency: 1 leu = 100 bani

RUSSIA (Europe and Asia)
Area: 17,075,200 sq km (6,592,735 sq miles)
Population: 145,470,197
Capital city: Moscow
Main language: Russian
Main religions: Russian Orthodox, Muslim
Government: federal government
Currency: 1 ruble = 100 kopeks

Panama

**Papua
New Guinea**

Paraguay

• Peru

Philippines

Poland

Portugal

GAZETTEER OF STATES CONTINUED:

Qatar

Samoa

RWANDA (Africa)
Area: 26,338 sq km (10,169 sq miles)
Population: 7,312,756
Capital city: Kigali
Main languages: Kinyarwanda, French, English, Swahili
Main religions: Roman Catholic, Protestant, Adventist
Government: transitional
Currency: 1 Rwandan franc = 100 centimes

SAINT KITTS AND NEVIS (North America)
Area: 269 sq km (104 sq miles)
Population: 38,756
Capital city: Basseterre
Main language: English
Main religions: Protestant, Roman Catholic
Government: constitutional monarchy
Currency: 1 East Caribbean dollar = 100 cents

SAINT LUCIA (North America)
Area: 620 sq km (239 sq miles)
Population: 158,178
Capital city: Castries
Main languages: French patois, English
Main religion: Roman Catholic
Government: parliamentary democracy
Currency: 1 East Caribbean dollar = 100 cents

SAINT VINCENT AND THE GRENADINES (North America)
Area: 389 sq km (150 sq miles)
Population: 115,942
Capital city: Kingstown
Main languages: English, French patois
Main religions: Protestant, Roman Catholic
Government: parliamentary democracy
Currency: 1 East Caribbean dollar = 100 cents

SAMOA (Australasia/Oceania)
Area: 2,860 sq km (1,104 sq miles)
Population: 179,058
Capital city: Apia
Main languages: Samoan, English
Main religion: Christian
Government: constitutional monarchy
Currency: 1 tala = 100 sene

SAN MARINO (Europe)
Area: 61 sq km (24 sq miles)
Population: 27,336
Capital city: San Marino
Main language: Italian
Main religion: Roman Catholic
Government: republic
Currency: 1 euro = 100 cents

SÃO TOMÉ AND PRINCIPE (Africa)
Area: 1,001 sq km (386 sq miles)
Population: 165,034
Capital city: Sao Tome
Main languages: Crioulo* dialects, Portuguese
Main religion: Christian
Government: republic
Currency: 1 dobra = 100 centimos

SAUDI ARABIA (Asia)
Area: 2,149,690 sq km (829,995 sq miles)
Population: 22,757,092

Capital city: Riyadh
Main language: Arabic
Main religion: Muslim
Government: monarchy
Currency: 1 Saudi riyal = 100 halalah

SENEGAL (Africa)
Area: 196,190 sq km (75,749 sq miles)
Population: 10,284,929
Capital city: Dakar
Main languages: Wolof, French, Pulaar
Main religion: Muslim
Government: democratic republic
Currency: 1 CFA* franc = 100 centimes

SERBIA (Europe)
Area: 88,361 sq km (34,116 sq miles)
Population: 7,498,0006
Capital city: Belgrade
Main language: Serbian
Main religion: Orthodox, Catholic, Muslim
Government: republic
Currency: 1 Serbian dinar = 100 paras

SEYCHELLES (Africa)
Area: 455 sq km (176 sq miles)
Population: 79,715
Capital city: Victoria
Main language: Seselwa
Main religion: Roman Catholic
Government: republic
Currency: 1 Seychelles rupee = 100 cents

SIERRA LEONE (Africa)
Area: 71,740 sq km (27,699 sq miles)
Population: 5,426,618
Capital city: Freetown
Main languages: Mende, Temne, Krio, English
Main religions: Muslim, indigenous, Christian
Government: republic
Currency: 1 leone = 100 cents

SINGAPORE (Asia)
Area: 648 sq km (250 sq miles)
Population: 4,300,419
Capital city: Singapore
Main languages: Chinese, Malay, English, Tamil
Main religions: Buddhist, Muslim
Government: parliamentary republic
Currency: 1 Singapore dollar = 100 cents

SLOVAKIA (Europe)
Area: 48,845 sq km (18,859 sq miles)
Population: 5,414,937
Capital city: Bratislava
Main languages: Slovak, Hungarian
Main religion: Roman Catholic
Government: parliamentary democracy
Currency: 1 koruna = 100 halierov

SLOVENIA (Europe)
Area: 20,253 sq km (7,820 sq miles)
Population: 1,930,132
Capital city: Ljubljana
Main language: Slovenian
Main religion: Roman Catholic
Government: democratic republic
Currency: 1 tolar = 100 stotins

• San Marino

Sao Tome and Principe

Saudi Arabia

Senegal

Serbia

Seychelles

Romania

Russia

Rwanda

Saint Kitts and Nevis

Saint Lucia

Saint Vincent and the Grenadines

*CFA = Communaute Financiere Africaine; Crioulo = a blend of Portuguese and West African

Sierra Leone

Singapore

Slovakia

• **Slovenia**

Solomon Islands

Somalia

South Africa

SOLOMON ISLANDS (Australasia/ Oceania)
Area: 28,450 sq km (10,985 sq miles)
Population: 480,442
Capital city: Honiara
Main languages: Solomon pidgin, Kwara'ae, To'abaita, English
Main religion: Christian
Government: parliamentary democracy
Currency: 1 Solomon Islands dollar = 100 cents

SOMALIA (Africa)
Area: 637,657 sq km (246,199 sq miles)
Population: 7,488,773
Capital city: Mogadishu
Main languages: Somali, Arabic, Oromo
Main religion: Sunni Muslim
Government: transitional
Currency: 1 Somali shilling – 100 cents

SOUTH AFRICA (Africa)
Area: 1,219,912 sq km (471,008 sq miles)
Population: 43,586,097
Capital cities: Pretoria, Cape Town, Bloemfontein
Main languages: Zulu, Xhosa, Afrikaans, Pedi, English, Tswana, Sotho, Tsonga, Swati, Venda, Ndebele
Main religions: Christian, indigenous
Government: republic
Currency: 1 rand = 100 cents

SOUTH KOREA (Asia)
Area: 98,480 sq km (38,023 sq miles)
Population: 47,904,370
Capital city: Seoul
Main language: Korean
Main religions: Christian, Buddhist
Government: republic
Currency: 1 South Korean won = 100 chun

SPAIN (Europe)
Area: 504,750 sq km (194,884 sq miles)
Population: 40,037,995
Capital city: Madrid
Main languages: Castilian Spanish, Catalan
Main religion: Roman Catholic .
Government: constitutional monarchy
Currency: 1 euro = 100 cents

SRI LANKA (Asia)
Area: 65,610 sq km (25,332 sq miles)
Population: 19,408,635
Capital cities: Colombo, Sri Jayewardenepura Kotte
Main languages: Sinhala, Tamil, English
Main religions: Buddhist, Hindu
Government: republic
Currency: 1 Sri Lankan rupee = 100 cents

SUDAN (Africa)
Area: 2,505,810 sq km (967,493 sq miles)
Population: 36,080,373
Capital city: Khartoum
Main languages: Arabic, English
Main religions: Sunni Muslim, indigenous
Government: Islamic republic
Currency: 1 Sudanese dinar = 100 piastres

SURINAM (South America)
Area: 163,270 sq km (63,039 sq miles)
Population: 433,998
Capital city: Paramaribo
Main languages: Sranang Tongo, Dutch, English
Main religions: Christian, Hindu, Muslim
Government: republic
Currency: 1 Surinamese guilder, gulden or florin = 100 cents

SWAZILAND (Africa)
Area: 17,363 sq km (6,704 sq miles)
Population: 1,104,343
Capital cities: Mbabane, Lobamba
Main languages: Swati, English
Main religions: Protestant, indigenous, Muslim
Government: monarchy
Currency: 1 lilangeni = 100 cents

SWEDEN (Europe)
Area: 449,964 sq km (173,731 sq miles)
Population: 8,875,053
Capital city: Stockholm
Main language: Swedish
Main religion: Lutheran
Government: constitutional monarchy
Currency: 1 Swedish krona = 100 oere

SWITZERLAND (Europe)
Area: 41,290 sq km (15,942 sq miles)
Population: 7,283,274
Capital city: Bern
Main languages: German, French, Italian
Main religions: Roman Catholic, Protestant
Government: federal republic
Currency: 1 Swiss franc, franken or frano = 100 centimes, rappen or centesimi

SYRIA (Asia)
Area: 185,180 sq km (71,498 sq miles)
Population: 16,728,808
Capital city: Damascus
Main languages: Arabic, Kurdish
Main religions: Muslim, Christian
Government: republic under military regime
Currency: 1 Syrian pound = 100 piastres

TAJIKISTAN (Asia)
Area: 143,100 sq km (55,251 sq miles)
Population: 6,578,681
Capital city: Dushanbe
Main languages: Tajik, Russian
Main religion: Sunni Muslim
Government: republic
Currency: 1 somoni = 100 dirams

TANZANIA (Africa)
Area: 945,087 sq km (364,898 sq miles)
Population: 36,232,074
Capital cities: Dar es Salaam, Dodoma
Main languages: Swahili, English, Sukuma
Main religions: Christian, Muslim, indigenous
Government: republic
Currency: 1 Tanzanian shilling = 100 cents

THAILAND (Asia)
Area: 514,000 sq km (198,455 sq miles)
Population: 61,797,751

South Korea

• **Spain**

Sri Lanka

Sudan

Surinam

Swaziland

Sweden

*CFA = Communaute Financiere Africaine

GAZETTEER OF STATES CONTINUED:

Switzerland

Syria

Tajikistan

Tanzania

Thailand

Togo

Tonga

Capital city: Bangkok
Main languages: Thai, English, Chaochow
Main religion: Buddhist
Government: constitutional monarchy
Currency: 1 baht = 100 satang

TOGO (Africa)
Area: 56,785 sq km (21,925 sq miles)
Population: 5,153,088
Capital city: Lome
Main languages: Mina, Ewe, Kabye, French
Main religions: indigenous, Christian, Muslim
Government: republic
Currency: 1 CFA* franc = 100 centimes

TONGA (Australasia/Oceania)
Area: 748 sq km (289 sq miles)
Population: 104,227
Capital city: Nukualofa
Main languages: Tongan, English
Main religion: Christian
Government: constitutional monarchy
Currency: 1 pa'anga = 100 seniti

TRINIDAD AND TOBAGO (North America)
Area: 5,128 sq km (1,980 sq miles)
Population: 1,169,682
Capital city: Port-of-Spain
Main languages: English, French, Spanish, Hindi
Main religions: Christian, Hindu
Government: republic
Currency: 1 Trinidad and Tobago dollar = 100 cents

TUNISIA (Africa)
Area: 163,610 sq km (63,170 sq miles)
Population: 9,705,102
Capital city: Tunis
Main languages: Arabic, French
Main religion: Muslim
Government: republic
Currency: 1 Tunisian dinar = 1,000 millimes

TURKEY (Europe and Asia)
Area: 780,580 sq km (301,382 sq miles)
Population: 66,493,970
Capital city: Ankara
Main language: Turkish
Main religion: Muslim
Government: democratic republic
Currency: 1 Turkish lira = 100 kurus

TURKMENISTAN (Asia)
Area: 488,100 sq km (188,455 sq miles)
Population: 4,603,244
Capital city: Ashgabat (Ashkhabad)
Main languages: Turkmen, Russian
Main religion: Muslim
Government: republic
Currency: 1 Turkmen manat = 100 tenesi

TUVALU (Australasia/Oceania)
Area: 26 sq km (10 sq miles)
Population: 10,991
Capital city: Funafuti
Main languages: Tuvaluan, English
Main religion: Congregationalist

Government: constitutional monarchy
Currency: 1 Tuvaluan dollar or 1 Australian dollar = 100 cents

UGANDA (Africa)
Area: 236,040 sq km (91,135 sq miles)
Population: 23,985,712
Capital city: Kampala
Main languages: Luganda, English, Swahili
Main religions: Christian, Muslim, indigenous
Government: republic
Currency: 1 Ugandan shilling = 100 cents

UKRAINE (Europe)
Area: 603,700 sq km (233,089 sq miles)
Population: 49,153,027
Capital city: Kiev
Main languages: Ukrainian, Russian
Main religion: Ukrainain Orthodox
Government: republic
Currency: 1 hryvnia = 100 kopiykas

UNITED ARAB EMIRATES (Asia)
Area: 82,880 sq km (32,000 sq miles)
Population: 2,407,460
Capital city: Abu Dhabi
Main languages: Arabic, English
Main religion: Muslim
Government: federation
Currency: 1 Emirati dirham = 100 fils

UNITED KINGDOM (Europe)
Area: 244,820 sq km (94,525 sq miles)
Population: 59,647,790
Capital city: London
Main language: English
Main religions: Anglican, Roman Catholic
Government: constitutional monarchy
Currency: 1 British pound = 100 pence

UNITED STATES OF AMERICA (North America)
Area: 9,629,091 sq km (3,717,792 sq miles)
Population: 278,058,881
Capital city: Washington D.C.
Main language: English
Main religions: Protestant, Roman Catholic
Government: federal republic
Currency: 1 U.S. dollar = 100 cents

URUGUAY (South America)
Area: 176,220 sq km (68,039 sq miles)
Population: 3,360,105
Capital city: Montevideo
Main language: Spanish
Main religion: Roman Catholic
Government: republic
Currency: 1 Uruguayan peso = 100 centesimos

UZBEKISTAN (Asia)
Area: 447,400 sq km (172,741 sq miles)
Population: 25,155,064
Capital city: Tashkent
Main languages: Uzbek, Russian
Main religions: Muslim, Eastern Orthodox
Government: republic
Currency: 1 Uzbekistani sum = 100 tyyn

Trinidad and Tobago

Tunisia

Turkey

Turkmenistan

Tuvalu

Uganda

Ukraine

United Arab Emirates

United Kingdom

United States of America

Uruguay

Uzbekistan

Vanuatu

VANUATU (Australasia/Oceania)
Area: 12,189 sq km (4,706 sq miles)
Population: 192,910
Capital city: Port-Vila
Main languages: Bislama, French, English
Main religion: Christian
Government: republic
Currency: 1 vatu = 100 centimes

VATICAN CITY (Europe)
Area: 0.44 sq km (0.17 sq miles)
Population: 880
Capital city: Vatican City
Main languages: Italian, Latin
Main religion: Roman Catholic
Government: led by the Pope
Currency: 1 euro = 100 cents

VENEZUELA (South America)
Area: 912,050 sq km (352,143 sq miles)
Population: 23,916,810
Capital city: Caracas
Main language: Spanish
Main religion: Roman Catholic
Government: federal republic
Currency: 1 bolivar = 100 centimos

VIETNAM (Asia)
Area: 329,560 sq km (127,243 sq miles)
Population: 79,939,014
Capital city: Hanoi
Main languages: Vietnamese, French, English, Khmer, Chinese
Main religion: Buddhist
Government: Communist state
Currency: 1 new dong = 100 xu

YEMEN (Asia)
Area: 527,970 sq km (203,849 sq miles)
Population: 18,078,035
Capital city: Sana
Main language: Arabic
Main religion: Muslim
Government: republic
Currency: 1 Yemeni rial = 100 fils

YUGOSLAVIA (Europe)
Area: 102,350 sq km (39,517 sq miles)
Population: 10,677,290
Capital city: Belgrade
Main language: Serbian
Main religions: Orthodox, Muslim
Government: republic
Currency: 1 Yugoslavian new dinar = 100 paras

ZAMBIA (Africa)
Area: 752,614 sq km (290,584 sq miles)
Population: 9,770,199
Capital city: Lusaka
Main languages: Bemba, Tonga, Nyanja, English
Main religions: Christian, Muslim, Hindu
Government: republic
Currency: 1 Zambian kwacha = 100 ngwee

ZIMBABWE (Africa)
Area: 390,580 sq km (150,803 sq miles)
Population: 11,365,366
Capital city: Harare
Main languages: Shona, Ndebele, English
Main religions: Christian, indigenous
Government: republic
Currency: 1 Zimbabwean dollar = 100 cents

Vatican City

Venezuela

Vietnam

Yemen

Zambia

Zimbabwe

The United Nations

The United Nations (U.N.) is an organization which aims to bring countries together to work for peace and development. Of the world's 194 states, 192 belong to the U.N. Those that don't belong are Kosovo and the Vatican City.

Internet links

For a link to a website where you can test your flag knowledge by playing a game where you have to match countries and their flags, go to **www.usborne-quicklinks.com**

Kofi Annan, the former Secretary-General of the U.N., with U.N. ambassador Pele

TIME ZONES

When it's midday in Rio de Janeiro, it's midnight in Tokyo. This is because the Earth is divided into different time zones. Within each zone, people usually set their clocks to the same time. If you fly between two zones, you change your watch to the time in the new zone.

Dividing up time

There are 25 main time zones. They are separated by one-hour intervals and there is a new time zone every 15 degrees of longitude. There are 12 one-hour zones both ahead of and behind Greenwich Mean Time, or GMT, which is the time at the Prime Meridian Line.

Governments can change their countries' time zones. So, for convenience, whole countries usually keep the same local time instead of sticking to the zones exactly. For example, China could be divided into several time zones, but instead the whole country keeps the same time. A few areas, such as India, use non-standard half hour deviations.

Summer time

Some countries adjust their clocks in summer. For example, in the U.K. all clocks go forward one hour. This is known as Daylight Saving Time or Summer Time. It is a way of getting more out of the days by having an extra hour of daylight in the evening. It reduces energy use as people don't use as much electricity for lights.

Changing dates

On the opposite side of the world from the Prime Meridian Line is the International Date Line, which runs mostly through the Pacific Ocean and bends to avoid the land. Places to the west of it are 24 hours ahead of places to the east. This means that if you travel east across it you lose a day and if you travel west across it you gain a day.

This map shows the time zones. The times at the top of the map tell you the time in the different zones when it is noon at the Prime Meridian Line. There are two midnight zones, one for each day on either side of the International Date Line. The numbers in circles tell you how many hours ahead of or behind Greenwich Mean Time an area is.

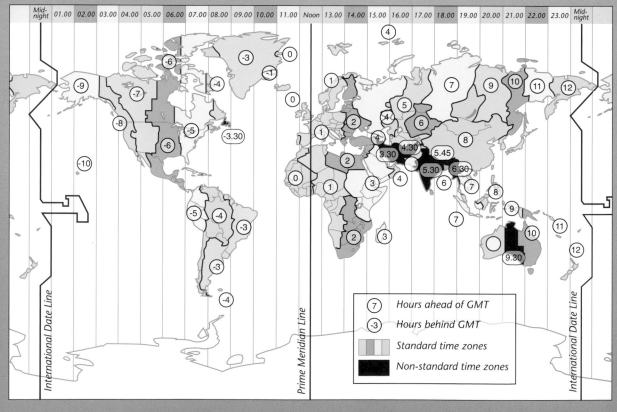

126

GENERAL INDEX

Answers to geography quiz (pages 110–111)

Mystery places

Top left: La Sagrada Familia church in Barcelona, Spain
Top right: The Taj Mahal near Agra, India
Middle left: The Golden Gate Bridge in San Francisco, U.S.A.
Middle right: The Acropolis in Athens, Greece
Bottom: The CN Tower in Toronto, Canada

Quick quiz

1. Japan
2. 6 a.m.
3. Australia
4. North America
5. Czech Republic
6. Lake Baikal, Russia
7. Vatican City
8. Costa Rica
9. Nigeria
10. Ankara

Survival challenge

1. b. An umbrella would not be useful as it doesn't rain in Antarctica. It's also the world's windiest continent, so an umbrella wouldn't last long! You would need sunglasses and sunscreen, however, as the reflection of the sun off snow is dazzling and can cause sunburn.

2. b. Extra clothes would help to conserve your sweat, which cools down your skin, and resting in the shade (if there is any) would help your body stay as cool as possible. Being active, talking or singing would cause your body to lose moisture and your mouth to dry out – which would make you even thirstier.

3. All of them. Six-eyed crab spiders are one of the most venomous types of spiders in the world. Their bites are so severe that they can cause death. Button spiders have a bite which is very painful, though not lethal, while a bite from a violin spider causes painful swelling.

4. c. A bear will only attack if it thinks you are a threat to it. If you moved away slowly, not making any sudden movements, it would probably leave you alone. You should only lie down (preferably curled into a ball) and play dead if the bear actually takes a swipe at you.

MAP INDEX

This is an index of the places and features named on the maps. Each entry consists of the following parts: the name (given in bold type), the country or region within which it is located (given in italics), the page on which the name can be found (given in bold type), and the grid reference (also given in bold type). For some names, there is also a description explaining what kind of place it is – for example a country, internal administrative area (state or province), national capital or internal capital. To find a place on a map, first find the map indicated by the page reference. Then use the grid reference to find the square containing the name or town symbol. See page 11 for help with using the grid.

a

Abaco, *The Bahamas,* **33 L5**
Abadan, *Iran,* **73 E5**
Abakan, *Russia,* **74 E3**
Abaya, Lake, *Ethiopia,* **103 G2**
Abeche, *Chad,* **98 F6**
Abeokuta, *Nigeria,* **101 F7**
Aberdeen, *United Kingdom,* **88 D2**
Aberystwyth, *United Kingdom,* **88 C3**
Abha, *Saudi Arabia,* **73 D8**
Abidjan, *Ivory Coast,* **101 E7**
Abilene, *U.S.A.,* **32 G4**
Abomey, *Benin,* **101 F7**
Abu Dhabi, *United Arab Emirates, national capital,* **73 F7**
Abuja, *Nigeria, national capital,* **101 G7**
Abu Kamal, *Syria,* **72 D5**
Abu Simbel, *Egypt,* **99 H4**
Acapulco, *Mexico,* **34 E4**
Accra, *Ghana, national capital,* **101 E7**
Acklins Island, *The Bahamas,* **33 L6**
Aconcagua, *Argentina,* **44 E6**
Adana, *Turkey,* **72 C4**
Adapazari, *Turkey,* **91 J3**
Ad Dakhla, *Western Sahara,* **100 B4**
Ad Dammam, *Saudi Arabia,* **73 F6**
Addis Ababa, *Ethiopia, national capital,* **103 G2**
Adelaide, *Australia, internal capital,* **54 G6**
Aden, *Yemen,* **73 E9**
Aden, Gulf of, *Africa/Asia,* **73 E9**
Admiralty Islands, *Papua New Guinea,* **65 L4**
Adrar, *Algeria,* **100 E3**
Adriatic Sea, *Europe,* **90 E3**
Adzope, *Ivory Coast,* **101 E7**
Aegean Sea, *Europe,* **91 H4**
Afghanistan, *Asia, country,* **70 A4**
Africa, **20–21**
Agadez, *Niger,* **98 C5**
Agadir, *Morocco,* **100 D2**
Agra, *India,* **70 D5**
Agrigento, *Italy,* **90 E4**
Agua Prieta, *Mexico,* **34 C1**
Aguascalientes, *Mexico,* **34 D3**
Agulhas, Cape, *South Africa,* **104 C6**
Agulhas Negras, Mount, *Brazil,* **44 K4**
Ahaggar Mountains, *Algeria,* **100 G4**
Ahmadabad, *India,* **71 C6**
Ahvaz, *Iran,* **73 E5**
Aix-en-Provence, *France,* **89 F6**
Aizawl, *India,* **71 G6**
Ajaccio, *France,* **89 G6**
Ajdabiya, *Libya,* **98 F2**
Ajmer, *India,* **70 C5**
Akhisar, *Turkey,* **91 H4**
Akita, *Japan,* **69 P3**
Akjoujt, *Mauritania,* **100 C5**
Akola, *India,* **71 D6**
Aksaray, *Turkey,* **91 K4**
Aksu, *China,* **70 E2**
Alabama, *U.S.A., internal admin. area,* **33 J4**
Al Amarah, *Iraq,* **73 E5**
Aland Islands, *Finland,* **86 F3**
Alanya, *Turkey,* **91 J4**
Al Aqabah, *Jordan,* **73 C6**
Alaska, *U.S.A., internal admin. area,* **30 D2**

Alaska, Gulf of, *North America,* **30 E3**
Alaska Peninsula, *U.S.A.,* **30 D3**
Alaska Range, *U.S.A.,* **30 D2**
Alavus, *Finland,* **86 G3**
Al Ayn, *United Arab Emirates,* **73 G7**
Albacete, *Spain,* **89 D7**
Albania, *Europe, country,* **91 F3**
Albany, *Australia,* **54 C7**
Albany, *Georgia, U.S.A.,* **33 K4**
Albany, *New York, U.S.A., internal capital,* **33 M2**
Al Bayda, *Libya,* **98 F2**
Alberta, *Canada, internal admin. area,* **30 H3**
Albert, Lake, *Africa,* **103 F3**
Albino Point, *Angola,* **104 B3**
Alboran Island, *Spain,* **89 D7**
Alborg, *Denmark,* **87 D4**
Albuquerque, *U.S.A.,* **32 E3**
Aldabra Group, *Seychelles,* **105 J1**
Aleppo, *Syria,* **72 C4**
Alesund, *Norway,* **86 C3**
Aleutian Islands, *U.S.A.,* **31 A3**
Alexander Archipelago, *Canada,* **30 F3**
Alexander Bay, *South Africa,* **104 C5**
Alexandria, *Egypt,* **99 G2**
Algeciras, *Spain,* **89 C7**
Algeria, *Africa, country,* **100 F3**
Algiers, *Algeria, national capital,* **100 F1**
Al Hillah, *Iraq,* **72 D5**
Al Hoceima, *Morocco,* **100 E1**
Al Hudaydah, *Yemen,* **73 D9**
Ali Bayramli, *Azerbaijan,* **72 E4**
Alicante, *Spain,* **89 D7**
Alice Springs, *Australia,* **54 F4**
Aligarh, *India,* **70 D5**
Al Jawf, *Libya,* **98 F4**
Al Khums, *Libya,* **98 D2**
Al Kut, *Iraq,* **73 E5**
Allahabad, *India,* **70 E5**
Almaty, *Kazakhstan,* **70 D2**
Almeria, *Spain,* **89 D7**
Almetyevsk, *Russia,* **85 G3**
Almirante, *Panama,* **35 H6**
Al Mubarrez, *Saudi Arabia,* **73 E6**
Al Mukalla, *Yemen,* **73 E9**
Alor Setar, *Malaysia,* **64 B2**
Alps, *Europe,* **90 D2**
Al Qamishli, *Syria,* **72 D4**
Alta, *Norway,* **86 G1**
Altai Mountains, *Asia,* **68 D1**
Altamira, *Brazil,* **43 H4**
Altay, *China,* **70 F1**
Altay, *Mongolia,* **68 E1**
Altun Mountains, *China,* **70 G3**
Aluksne, *Latvia,* **87 H4**
Alytus, *Lithuania,* **87 H5**
Amadjuak Lake, *Canada,* **31 M2**
Amami, *Japan,* **69 L5**
Amarillo, *U.S.A.,* **32 F3**
Amazon, *South America,* **43 H4**
Amazon Delta, *Brazil,* **43 J3**
Ambanja, *Madagascar,* **105 J2**
Ambato, *Ecuador,* **42 C4**
Amber, Cape, *Madagascar,* **105 J2**
Ambilobe, *Madagascar,* **105 J2**
Ambon, *Indonesia,* **65 G4**
Ambositra, *Madagascar,* **105 J4**

American Samoa, *Oceania, dependency,* **52 F6**
America, United States of, *North America, country,* **32 F3**
Amiens, *France,* **88 E4**
Amman, *Jordan, national capital,* **73 C5**
Amravati, *India,* **71 D6**
Amritsar, *India,* **70 C4**
Amsterdam, *Netherlands, national capital,* **88 F3**
Am Timan, *Chad,* **98 F6**
Amu Darya, *Asia,* **72 H4**
Amundsen Gulf, *Canada,* **30 G1**
Amundsen Sea, *Antarctica,* **109 Q3**
Amur, *Asia,* **75 G3**
Anadyr, *Russia,* **75 J2**
Anadyr, Gulf of, *Asia,* **75 K2**
Analalava, *Madagascar,* **105 J2**
Anambas Islands, *Indonesia,* **64 C3**
Anchorage, *U.S.A.,* **30 E2**
Ancona, *Italy,* **90 E3**
Andaman Islands, *India,* **71 G8**
Andaman Sea, *Asia,* **66 C5**
Andara, *Namibia,* **104 D3**
Andes, *South America,* **44 E5**
Andorra, *Europe, country,* **89 E6**
Andorra la Vella, *Andorra, national capital,* **89 E6**
Andreanof Islands, *U.S.A.,* **31 B3**
Androka, *Madagascar,* **105 H5**
Andros, *The Bahamas,* **33 L6**
Aneto, Pico de, *Spain,* **89 E6**
Angel Falls, *Venezuela,* **42 F2**
Angers, *France,* **88 D5**
Angkor, *Cambodia,* **66 D5**
Angoche, *Mozambique,* **105 G3**
Angola, *Africa, country,* **104 C2**
Angra do Heroismo, *Azores,* **100 K10**
Angren, *Uzbekistan,* **70 C2**
Anguilla, *North America,* **34 M4**
Anjouan Island, *Comoros,* **105 H2**
Ankara, *Turkey, national capital,* **91 K3**
Annaba, *Algeria,* **100 G1**
An Najaf, *Iraq,* **73 D5**
Annapolis, *U.S.A., internal capital,* **33 L3**
An Nasiriyah, *Iraq,* **73 E5**
Anqing, *China,* **69 J4**
Anshan, *China,* **69 J4**
Antalaha, *Madagascar,* **105 K2**
Antalya, *Turkey,* **91 J4**
Antalya, Gulf of, *Turkey,* **91 J4**
Antananarivo, *Madagascar, national capital,* **105 J3**
Antarctica, **109 B4**
Antarctic Peninsula, *Antarctica,* **109 T2**
Anticosti Island, *Canada,* **31 N4**
Antigua and Barbuda, *North America, country,* **34 M4**
Antofagasta, *Chile,* **44 D4**
Antsalova, *Madagascar,* **105 H3**
Antsirabe, *Madagascar,* **105 J3**
Antsiranana, *Madagascar,* **105 J2**
Antwerp, *Belgium,* **88 F4**
Aomori, *Japan,* **69 P2**
Aoraki, *New Zealand,* **55 P8**
Apalachee Bay, *U.S.A.,* **33 K5**
Aparri, *Philippines,* **67 H4**
Apatity, *Russia,* **86 K2**

Apennines, *Italy,* **90 E3**
Apia, *Samoa, national capital,* **52 F6**
Appalachian Mountains, *U.S.A.,* **33 K3**
Aqsay, *Kazakhstan,* **85 G3**
Aqtau, *Kazakhstan,* **72 F3**
Aqtobe, *Kazakhstan,* **85 H3**
Arabian Desert, *Africa,* **99 H3**
Arabian Peninsula, *Asia,* **73 E7**
Arabian Sea, *Asia,* **73 G8**
Aracaju, *Brazil,* **43 L6**
Arad, *Romania,* **91 G2**
Araguaia, *Brazil,* **43 H6**
Araguaina, *Brazil,* **43 J5**
Arak, *Iran,* **72 E5**
Aral, *Kazakhstan,* **72 H2**
Aral Sea, *Asia,* **72 G2**
Arapiraca, *Brazil,* **43 L5**
Araraquara, *Brazil,* **44 J4**
Araure, *Venezuela,* **42 E2**
Arbil, *Iraq,* **72 D4**
Arctic Ocean, **108 A4**
Ardabil, *Iran,* **72 E4**
Arendal, *Norway,* **86 D4**
Arequipa, *Peru,* **42 D7**
Argentina, *South America, country,* **45 E7**
Argentino, Lake, *Argentina,* **45 D10**
Arhus, *Denmark,* **87 D4**
Arica, *Chile,* **44 D3**
Arica, Gulf of, *South America,* **42 D7**
Arizona, *U.S.A., internal admin. area,* **32 D4**
Arkansas, *U.S.A.,* **33 G3**
Arkansas, *U.S.A., internal admin. area,* **33 H4**
Arkhangelsk, *Russia,* **74 C2**
Armenia, *Asia, country,* **72 D3**
Armidale, *Australia,* **55 K6**
Arnhem, *Netherlands,* **88 F4**
Arnhem Land, *Australia,* **54 F2**
Arqalyq, *Kazakhstan,* **72 J1**
Ar Ramadi, *Iraq,* **72 D5**
Ar Raqqah, *Syria,* **72 C4**
Aruba, *North America,* **35 K5**
Aru Islands, *Indonesia,* **65 J5**
Arusha, *Tanzania,* **103 G4**
Arzamas, *Russia,* **84 E2**
Asahikawa, *Japan,* **69 P2**
Asansol, *India,* **71 F6**
Ashgabat (Ashkhabad), *Turkmenistan, national capital,* **72 G4**
Asia, **21**
Asir, *Saudi Arabia,* **73 D7**
Asmara, *Eritrea, national capital,* **99 J5**
Assab, *Eritrea,* **99 K6**
Assumption, *Seychelles,* **105 J1**
Astana, *Kazakhstan, national capital,* **74 D3**
Astove, *Seychelles,* **105 J2**
Astrakhan, *Russia,* **85 F4**
Asuncion, *Paraguay, national capital,* **44 G5**
Aswan, *Egypt,* **99 H4**
Aswan High Dam, *Egypt,* **99 H4**
Asyut, *Egypt,* **99 H3**
Atacama Desert, *Chile,* **44 E3**
Atalaia do Norte, *Brazil,* **42 D4**

Livorno, *Italy,* 90 D3
Liwale, *Tanzania,* 103 G5
Ljubljana, *Slovenia, national capital,*
90 E2
Llanos, *South America,* 42 D2
Lloydminster, *Canada,* 30 J3
Lobamba, *Lesotho, national capital,*
104 F5
Lodz, *Poland,* 87 F6
Lofoten, *Norway,* 86 E1
Logan, Mount, *Canada,* 30 F2
Logrono, *Spain,* 89 D6
Loire, *France,* 88 E5
Loja, *Ecuador,* 42 C4
Lokan Reservoir, *Finland,* 86 H2
Lolland, *Denmark,* 87 D5
Lombok, *Indonesia,* 64 E5
Lome, *Togo, national capital,* 101 F7
London, *Canada,* 31 L4
London, *United Kingdom, national capital,*
88 D4
Londonderry, *United Kingdom,* 88 C3
Londrina, *Brazil,* 44 H4
Long Island, *The Bahamas,* 33 L6
Long Xuyen, *Vietnam,* 66 E5
Lopez, Cape, *Gabon,* 102 A4
Lop Lake, *China,* 70 G2
Lord Howe Island, *Australia,* 55 L6
Los Angeles, *Chile,* 45 D7
Los Angeles, *U.S.A.,* 32 C4
Los Mochis, *Mexico,* 34 C2
Louangphrabang, *Laos,* 66 D4
Loubomo, *Congo,* 102 B4
Louga, *Senegal,* 101 B5
Louisiana, *U.S.A., internal admin. area,*
33 H4
Lower California, *Mexico,* 34 B2
Loyalty Islands, *New Caledonia,* 55 N4
Luacano, *Angola,* 104 D2
Luanda, *Angola, national capital,* 104 B1
Luangwa, *Africa,* 104 F2
Luanshya, *Zambia,* 104 E2
Lubango, *Angola,* 104 B2
Lubbock, *U.S.A.,* 32 F4
Lublin, *Poland,* 87 G6
Lubny, *Ukraine,* 84 C3
Lubumbashi, *Democratic Republic of
Congo,* 102 E6
Lucena, *Philippines,* 67 H5
Lucerne, *Switzerland,* 90 D2
Lucira, *Angola,* 104 B2
Lucknow, *India,* 70 E5
Luderitz, *Namibia,* 104 C5
Ludhiana, *India,* 70 D4
Ludza, *Latvia,* 87 H4
Luena, *Angola,* 104 C2
Luganville, *Vanuatu,* 55 N3
Lugo, *Spain,* 89 C6
Luhansk, *Ukraine,* 84 D4
Luiana, *Angola,* 104 D3
Lukulu, *Zambia,* 104 D2
Lumbala Kaquengue, *Angola,* 104 D2
Lumbala Nguimbo, *Angola,* 104 D2
Lundazi, *Zambia,* 105 F2
Lupilichi, *Mozambique,* 105 G2
Lusaka, *Zambia, national capital,* 104 E3
Lutsk, *Ukraine,* 87 H6
Luxembourg, *Europe, country,* 88 F4
Luxembourg, *Luxembourg, national
capital,* 88 F4
Luxor, *Egypt,* 99 H3
Luzhou, *China,* 68 G5
Luzon, *Philippines,* 67 H4
Luzon Strait, *Philippines,* 67 H4
Lviv, *Ukraine,* 87 H6
Lyon, *France,* 89 F5
Lysychansk, *Ukraine,* 84 D4

m

Maan, *Jordan,* 73 C5
Maastricht, *Netherlands,* 88 F4
Macae, *Brazil,* 44 K4
Macapa, *Brazil,* 43 H3
Macau, *China,* 69 H6
Macedonia, *Europe, country,* 91 G3
Maceio, *Brazil,* 43 L5

Machakos, *Kenya,* 103 G4
Machala, *Ecuador,* 42 C4
Machu Picchu, *Peru,* 42 D6
Mackay, *Australia,* 55 J4
Mackenzie, *Canada,* 30 G2
Mackenzie Bay, *Canada,* 30 F2
Mackenzie Mountains, *Canada,* 30 F2
Macon, *U.S.A.,* 33 K4
Madagascar, *Africa, country,* 105 J4
Madang, *Papua New Guinea,* 65 L5
Madeira, *Atlantic Ocean,* 100 B2
Madeira, *Brazil,* 42 F5
Madingou, *Congo,* 102 B4
Madison, *U.S.A., internal capital,* 33 J2
Madras, *India,* 71 E8
Madrid, *Spain, national capital,* 89 D6
Madurai, *India,* 71 D9
Maevatanana, *Madagascar,* 105 J3
Mafeteng, *Lesotho,* 104 E5
Mafia Island, *Tanzania,* 103 H5
Magadan, *Russia,* 75 H3
Magangue, *Colombia,* 42 D2
Magdalena, *Bolivia,* 44 F2
Magdeburg, *Germany,* 88 G3
Magellan, Strait of, *South America,* 45 E10
Magnitogorsk, *Russia,* 85 H3
Mahajanga, *Madagascar,* 105 J3
Mahalapye, *Botswana,* 104 E4
Mahilyow, *Belarus,* 87 J5
Mai-Ndombe, Lake, *Democratic Republic
of Congo,* 102 C4
Maine, *U.S.A., internal admin. area,*
33 N1
Maine, Gulf of, *U.S.A.,* 33 N2
Maio, *Cape Verde,* 101 M11
Majorca, *Spain,* 89 E7
Majuro, *Marshall Islands, national capital,*
52 E4
Makarikari, *Botswana,* 104 D4
Makassar Strait, *Indonesia,* 65 E4
Makeni, *Sierra Leone,* 101 C7
Makgadikgadi Pans, *Botswana,* 104 D4
Makhachkala, *Russia,* 72 E3
Makkovik, *Canada,* 31 P3
Makokou, *Gabon,* 102 B3
Makumbako, *Tanzania,* 103 F5
Makurdi, *Nigeria,* 102 A2
Mala, *Peru,* 42 C6
Malabo, *Equatorial Guinea,
national capital,* 102 A3
Maladzyechna, *Belarus,* 87 H5
Malaga, *Spain,* 89 C7
Malaimbandy, *Madagascar,* 105 J4
Malakal, *Sudan,* 103 F2
Malakula, *Vanuatu,* 55 N3
Malang, *Indonesia,* 64 D5
Malanje, *Angola,* 104 C1
Malar, Lake, *Sweden,* 86 F4
Malatya, *Turkey,* 72 C4
Malawi, *Africa, country,* 105 F2
Malawi, Lake, *Africa,* 103 F6
Malaysia, *Asia, country,* 64 B2
Maldives, *Asia, country,* 71 C9
Male, *Maldives, national capital,* 71 C10
Malegaon, *India,* 71 C6
Mali, *Africa, country,* 100 E5
Malindi, *Kenya,* 103 H4
Malmo, *Sweden,* 87 E5
Malpelo Island, *Colombia,* 42 B3
Malta, *Europe, country,* 90 E4
Mamoudzou, *Mayotte,* 105 J2
Mamuno, *Botswana,* 104 D4
Man, *Ivory Coast,* 101 D7
Manado, *Indonesia,* 65 F3
Managua, *Nicaragua, national capital,*
35 G5
Manakara, *Madagascar,* 105 J4
Manama, *Bahrain, national capital,* 73 F6
Manaus, *Brazil,* 43 G4
Manchester, *United Kingdom,* 88 D3
Manchuria, *China,* 69 K2
Mandalay, *Burma,* 66 C3
Mandera, *Kenya,* 103 H3
Mandritsara, *Madagascar,* 105 J3

Mandurah, *Australia,* 54 C6
Mangalore, *India,* 71 C8
Mania, *Madagascar,* 105 J3
Manicouagan Reservoir, *Canada,* 31 N3
Manila, *Philippines, national capital,*
67 H5
Manisa, *Turkey,* 91 H4
Man, Isle of, *Europe,* 88 C3
Manitoba, *Canada, internal admin. area,*
31 K3
Manitoba, Lake, *Canada,* 31 K3
Manizales, *Colombia,* 42 C2
Manja, *Madagascar,* 105 H4
Mannar, *Sri Lanka,* 71 E9
Mannar, Gulf of, *Asia,* 71 D9
Mannheim, *Germany,* 88 G4
Mansa, *Zambia,* 104 E2
Manta, *Ecuador,* 42 B4
Manzhouli, *China,* 75 F3
Mao, *Chad,* 98 E6
Maoke Range, *Indonesia,* 65 J4
Maputo, *Mozambique, national capital,*
105 F5
Maraba, *Brazil,* 43 J5
Maracaibo, *Venezuela,* 42 D1
Maracaibo, Lake, *Venezuela,* 42 D2
Maracay, *Venezuela,* 42 E1
Maradi, *Niger,* 98 C6
Maranon, *Peru,* 42 C4
Marathon, *Canada,* 31 L4
Mar del Plata, *Argentina,* 45 G7
Margarita Island, *Venezuela,* 42 F1
Margherita Peak, *Africa,* 102 E3
Marib, *Yemen,* 73 E8
Maribor, *Slovenia,* 90 E2
Marie Byrd Land, *Antarctica,* 109 Q3
Mariental, *Namibia,* 104 C4
Marijampole, *Lithuania,* 87 G5
Marilia, *Brazil,* 44 J4
Marimba, *Angola,* 104 C1
Mariupol, *Ukraine,* 84 D4
Marka, *Somalia,* 103 H3
Marmara, Sea of, *Turkey,* 91 J3
Maroantsetra, *Madagascar,* 105 J3
Maroua, *Cameroon,* 102 B1
Marquesas Islands, *French Polynesia,*
53 K5
Marrakech, *Morocco,* 100 D2
Marra, Mount, *Sudan,* 98 F6
Marsa Matruh, *Egypt,* 99 G2
Marseille, *France,* 89 F6
Marshall Islands, *Oceania, country,* 52 D3
Martapura, *Indonesia,* 64 D4
Martinique, *North America,* 34 M5
Mary, *Turkmenistan,* 72 H4
Maryland, *U.S.A., internal admin. area,*
33 L3
Masaka, *Uganda,* 103 F4
Masasi, *Tanzania,* 103 G6
Masbate, *Philippines,* 67 H5
Maseru, *Lesotho, national capital,* 104 E5
Mashhad, *Iran,* 72 G4
Masirah Island, *Oman,* 73 G7
Massachusetts, *U.S.A.,
internal admin. area,* 33 M2
Massangena, *Mozambique,* 105 F4
Massawa, *Eritrea,* 99 J5
Massif Central, *France,* 89 E5
Massinga, *Mozambique,* 105 G4
Masvingo, *Zimbabwe,* 104 F4
Matagalpa, *Nicaragua,* 35 G5
Matala, *Angola,* 104 B2
Matamoros, *Mexico,* 34 E2
Matanzas, *Cuba,* 35 H4
Mataram, *Indonesia,* 64 E5
Mataro, *Spain,* 89 E6
Matehuala, *Mexico,* 34 D3
Mato Grosso, Plateau of, *Brazil,* 43 G6
Matsuyama, *Japan,* 69 M4
Maturin, *Venezuela,* 42 F2
Maui, *U.S.A.,* 33 P7
Maun, *Botswana,* 104 D3
Mauritania, *Africa, country,* 100 C5
Mauritius, *Indian Ocean, country,* 105 L3
Mavinga, *Angola,* 104 D3
Mayotte, *Africa,* 105 J2

Mazar-e Sharif, *Afghanistan,* 70 B3
Mazatlan, *Mexico,* 34 C3
Mazyr, *Belarus,* 87 J5
Mbabane, *Swaziland, national capital,*
104 F5
Mbala, *Zambia,* 104 F1
Mbale, *Uganda,* 103 F3
Mbandaka, *Democratic Republic of Congo,*
102 C3
Mbarara, *Uganda,* 103 F4
Mbeya, *Tanzania,* 103 F5
Mbuji-Mayi, *Democratic Republic of
Congo,* 102 D5
McClintock Channel, *Canada,* 30 J1
McClure Strait, *Canada,* 30 G1
McKinley, Mount, *U.S.A.,* 30 D2
Mead, Lake, *U.S.A.,* 32 D3
Mecca, *Saudi Arabia,* 73 C7
Mecula, *Mozambique,* 105 G2
Medan, *Indonesia,* 64 A3
Medellin, *Colombia,* 42 C2
Medford, *U.S.A.,* 32 B2
Medina, *Saudi Arabia,* 73 C7
Mediterranean Sea, *Africa/Europe,* 21
Medvezhyegorsk, *Russia,* 86 K3
Meerut, *India,* 70 D5
Meiktila, *Burma,* 66 C3
Meizhou, *China,* 69 J6
Mekele, *Ethiopia,* 103 G1
Meknes, *Morocco,* 100 D2
Mekong, *Asia,* 66 E5
Melaka, *Malaysia,* 64 B3
Melamo, Cape, *Mozambique,* 105 H2
Melanesia, *Oceania,* 52 D5
Melbourne, *Australia, internal capital,*
54 H7
Melilla, *Africa,* 89 D7
Melitopol, *Ukraine,* 84 D4
Melo, *Uruguay,* 44 H6
Melville Island, *Australia,* 54 F2
Melville Island, *Canada,* 30 H1
Melville Peninsula, *Canada,* 31 L2
Memphis, *U.S.A.,* 33 J3
Mendoza, *Argentina,* 44 E6
Menongue, *Angola,* 104 C2
Mentawai Islands, *Indonesia,* 64 A4
Menzel Bourguiba, *Tunisia,* 98 C1
Mergui, *Burma,* 66 C5
Mergui Archipelago, *Burma,* 66 C5
Merida, *Mexico,* 34 G3
Meridian, *U.S.A.,* 33 J4
Merlo, *Argentina,* 44 E6
Mersin, *Turkey,* 72 B4
Meru, *Kenya,* 103 G3
Messina, *Italy,* 90 E4
Messina, *South Africa,* 104 E4
Metz, *France,* 88 F4
Mexicali, *Mexico,* 34 A1
Mexico, *North America, country,* 34 D3
Mexico City, *Mexico, national capital,*
34 E4
Mexico, Gulf of, *North America,* 34 F3
Mexico, Plateau of, *Mexico,* 34 D2
Miami, *U.S.A.,* 33 K5
Michigan, *U.S.A., internal admin. area,*
33 J2
Michigan, Lake, *U.S.A.,* 33 J2
Michurinsk, *Russia,* 84 E3
Micronesia, *Oceania,* 52 C4
Micronesia, Federated States of, *Oceania,*
country, 52 C4
Middlesbrough, *United Kingdom,* 88 D3
Midway Islands, *Pacific Ocean,* 52 F2
Mikkeli, *Finland,* 86 H3
Milan, *Italy,* 90 D2
Milange, *Mozambique,* 105 G3
Mildura, *Australia,* 54 H6
Milwaukee, *U.S.A.,* 33 J2
Minas, *Uruguay,* 44 G6
Mindanao, *Philippines,* 67 H6
Mindelo, *Cape Verde,* 101 M11
Mindoro, *Philippines,* 67 H5
Mingacevir, *Azerbaijan,* 72 E3
Minna, *Nigeria,* 101 G7
Minneapolis, *U.S.A.,* 33 H2
Minnesota, *U.S.A., internal admin. area,*

33 G1
Minorca, *Spain*, 89 E6
Minot, *U.S.A.*, 32 F1
Minsk, *Belarus, national capital*, 87 H5
Miri, *Malaysia*, 64 D3
Mirim Lake, *Brazil*, 44 H6
Miskolc, *Hungary*, 87 G6
Misool, *Indonesia*, 65 H4
Misratah, *Libya*, 98 E2
Mississippi, *U.S.A.*, 33 H4
Mississippi, *U.S.A., internal admin. area*, 33 H4
Mississippi Delta, *U.S.A.*, 33 J5
Missoula, *U.S.A.*, 32 D1
Missouri, *U.S.A.*, 32 G2
Missouri, *U.S.A., internal admin. area*, 33 H3
Mistassini, Lake, *Canada*, 31 M3
Mitwaba, *Democratic Republic of Congo*, 102 E5
Mkushi, *Zambia*, 104 E2
Mmabatho, *South Africa*, 104 E5
Moanda, *Gabon*, 102 B4
Mobile, *U.S.A.*, 33 J4
Mochudi, *Botswana*, 104 E4
Mocuba, *Mozambique*, 105 G3
Modena, *Italy*, 90 D2
Mogadishu, *Somalia, national capital*, 103 J3
Mogao Caves, *China*, 68 E2
Mohilla Island, *Comoros*, 105 H2
Mo i Rana, *Norway*, 86 E2
Mojave Desert, *U.S.A.*, 32 C4
Moldova, *Europe, country*, 91 J2
Moldoveanu, Mount, *Romania*, 84 C4
Molepolole, *Botswana*, 104 E4
Mollendo, *Peru*, 42 D7
Molokai, *U.S.A.*, 35 P7
Molopo, *Africa*, 104 D5
Molucca Sea, *Indonesia*, 65 F4
Mombasa, *Kenya*, 103 G4
Monaco, *Europe, country*, 89 F6
Monastir, *Tunisia*, 98 D1
Monchegorsk, *Russia*, 86 K2
Monclova, *Mexico*, 34 D2
Moncton, *Canada*, 31 N4
Mongo, *Chad*, 98 E6
Mongolia, *Asia, country*, 68 F1
Mongu, *Zambia*, 104 D3
Monrovia, *Liberia, national capital*, 101 C7
Montalvo, *Ecuador*, 42 C4
Montana, *U.S.A., internal admin. area*, 32 E1
Montauban, *France*, 89 E5
Montego Bay, *Jamaica*, 35 J4
Montenegro, *Europe, country*, 91 F3
Monterrey, *Mexico*, 34 D2
Montes Claros, *Brazil*, 44 K3
Montevideo, *Uruguay, national capital*, 44 G6
Montgomery, *U.S.A., internal capital*, 33 J4
Montpelier, *U.S.A., internal capital*, 33 M2
Montpellier, *France*, 89 E6
Montreal, *Canada*, 31 M4
Montserrat, *North America*, 34 M4
Monywa, *Burma*, 66 C3
Moose Jaw, *Canada*, 30 J3
Mopti, *Mali*, 101 E6
Moree, *Australia*, 55 J5
Morelia, *Mexico*, 34 D4
Morocco, *Africa, country*, 100 D2
Morogoro, *Tanzania*, 103 G5
Morombe, *Madagascar*, 105 H4
Moroni, *Comoros, national capital*, 105 H2
Morotai, *Indonesia*, 65 G3
Morpara, *Brazil*, 44 K2
Moscow, *Russia, national capital*, 84 D2
Moshi, *Tanzania*, 103 G4
Mosquitos, Gulf of, *North America*, 35 H5
Mossendjo, *Congo*, 102 B4
Mossoro, *Brazil*, 43 L5
Most, *Czech Republic*, 90 E1
Mostaganem, *Algeria*, 100 F1

Mostar, *Bosnia and Herzegovina*, 90 F3
Mosul, *Iraq*, 72 D4
Moulmein, *Burma*, 66 C4
Moundou, *Chad*, 102 C2
Mount Gambier, *Australia*, 54 H7
Mount Hagen, *Papua New Guinea*, 65 K5
Mount Isa, *Australia*, 54 G4
Mount Li, *China*, 68 G4
Moyale, *Ethiopia*, 103 G3
Moyobamba, *Peru*, 42 C5
Mozambique, *Africa, country*, 105 F3
Mozambique, *Mozambique*, 105 H3
Mozambique Channel, *Africa*, 105 G4
Mpika, *Zambia*, 104 F2
Mtwara, *Tanzania*, 103 H6
Mudanjiang, *China*, 69 L2
Mueda, *Mozambique*, 105 G2
Mufulira, *Zambia*, 104 E2
Multan, *Pakistan*, 70 C4
Mumbai, *India*, 71 C7
Mumbue, *Angola*, 104 C2
Munhango, *Angola*, 104 C2
Munich, *Germany*, 88 G4
Munster, *Germany*, 88 F4
Murcia, *Spain*, 89 D7
Murmansk, *Russia*, 86 K1
Murom, *Russia*, 84 E2
Murray, *Australia*, 54 G6
Murzuq, *Libya*, 98 D3
Muscat, *Oman, national capital*, 73 G7
Mutare, *Zimbabwe*, 105 F3
Mutoko, *Zimbabwe*, 104 F3
Mutsamudu, *Comoros*, 105 H2
Mutshatsha, *Democratic Republic of Congo*, 102 D6
Mwali, *Comoros*, 105 H2
Mwanza, *Tanzania*, 103 F4
Mwene-Ditu, *Democratic Republic of Congo*, 102 D5
Mweru, Lake, *Africa*, 104 E1
Mwinilunga, *Zambia*, 104 D2
Myanmar, *Asia, country*, 66 C3
Myitkyina, *Burma*, 66 C2
Mykolayiv, *Ukraine*, 84 C4
Mysore, *India*, 71 D8
Mzuzu, *Malawi*, 105 F2

n

Naberezhnyye Chelny, *Russia*, 85 G2
Nabeul, *Tunisia*, 90 D4
Nacala, *Mozambique*, 105 H2
Nador, *Morocco*, 89 D8
Naga, *Philippines*, 67 H5
Nagasaki, *Japan*, 69 L4
Nagoya, *Japan*, 69 N3
Nagpur, *India*, 71 D6
Nain, *Canada*, 31 N3
Nairobi, *Kenya, national capital*, 103 G4
Najran, *Saudi Arabia*, 73 D8
Nakhodka, *Russia*, 69 M2
Nakhon Ratchasima, *Thailand*, 66 D5
Nakhon Sawan, *Thailand*, 66 D4
Nakhon Si Thammarat, *Thailand*, 66 D6
Nakuru, *Kenya*, 103 G4
Nalchik, *Russia*, 72 D3
Namangan, *Uzbekistan*, 70 C2
Namib Desert, *Africa*, 104 B3
Namibe, *Angola*, 104 B3
Namibia, *Africa, country*, 104 C4
Nam Lake, *China*, 70 G4
Nampo, *North Korea*, 69 L3
Nampula, *Mozambique*, 105 G3
Namsos, *Norway*, 86 D2
Namur, *Belgium*, 88 F4
Nanaimo, *Canada*, 30 G4
Nanchang, *China*, 69 J5
Nancy, *France*, 88 F4
Nanded, *India*, 71 D7
Nanjing, *China*, 69 J4
Nanning, *China*, 68 G6
Nanping, *China*, 69 J5
Nantes, *France*, 89 D5
Napier, *New Zealand*, 55 Q7
Naples, *Italy*, 90 E3
Narmada, *India*, 71 C6

Narva, *Estonia*, 86 J4
Narvik, *Norway*, 86 F1
Nashik, *India*, 71 C6
Nashville, *U.S.A., internal capital*, 33 J3
Nasi Lake, *Finland*, 86 G3
Nassau, *The Bahamas, national capital*, 33 L5
Nasser, Lake, *Egypt*, 99 H4
Natal, *Brazil*, 43 L5
Natitingou, *Benin*, 101 F6
Natuna Islands, *Indonesia*, 64 C3
Nauru, *Oceania, country*, 52 D5
Navapolatsk, *Belarus*, 87 J5
Navoiy, *Uzbekistan*, 70 B2
Nawabshah, *Pakistan*, 70 B5
Naxcivan, *Azerbaijan*, 72 E4
Nazca, *Peru*, 42 D6
Nazret, *Ethiopia*, 103 G2
Ndalatando, *Angola*, 104 B1
Ndele, *Central African Republic*, 102 D2
Ndjamena, *Chad, national capital*, 98 E6
Ndola, *Zambia*, 104 E2
Near Islands, *U.S.A.*, 31 A3
Nebraska, *U.S.A., internal admin. area*, 32 F2
Necochea, *Argentina*, 45 G7
Negombo, *Sri Lanka*, 71 D9
Negro, *Brazil*, 42 F4
Negro, Cape, *Peru*, 42 B5
Negros, *Philippines*, 67 H6
Neiva, *Colombia*, 42 C3
Nekemte, *Ethiopia*, 103 G2
Nellore, *India*, 71 E8
Nelson, *New Zealand*, 55 P8
Nelspruit, *South Africa*, 104 F5
Nema, *Mauritania*, 101 D5
Neman, *Europe*, 87 G5
Nepal, *Asia, country*, 70 E5
Netherlands, *Europe, country*, 88 F3
Netherlands Antilles, *North America, dependency*, 35 L5
Nettilling Lake, *Canada*, 31 M2
Neuquen, *Argentina*, 45 E7
Nevada, *U.S.A., internal admin. area*, 32 C3
Nevers, *France*, 89 E5
New Amsterdam, *Guyana*, 43 G2
Newark, *U.S.A.*, 33 M2
New Britain, *Papua New Guinea*, 65 M5
New Brunswick, *Canada, internal admin. area*, 31 N4
New Caledonia, *Oceania*, 55 M4
Newcastle, *Australia*, 55 K6
Newcastle upon Tyne, *United Kingdom*, 88 D3
New Delhi, *India, national capital*, 70 D5
Newfoundland, *Canada*, 31 P4
Newfoundland, *Canada, internal admin. area*, 31 N3
New Guinea, *Asia/Oceania*, 65 J4
New Hampshire, *U.S.A., internal admin. area*, 33 M2
New Ireland, *Papua New Guinea*, 65 M4
New Jersey, *U.S.A., internal admin. area*, 33 M3
New Mexico, *U.S.A., internal admin. area*, 32 E4
New Orleans, *U.S.A.*, 33 J5
New Plymouth, *New Zealand*, 55 P7
Newport, *United Kingdom*, 88 D4
New Siberia Islands, *Russia*, 75 H2
New South Wales, *Australia, internal admin. area*, 54 H6
New York, *U.S.A.*, 33 M2
New York, *U.S.A., internal admin. area*, 33 M2
New Zealand, *Australasia, country*, 55 Q8
Ngami, Lake, *Botswana*, 104 D4
Ngaoundere, *Cameroon*, 102 B2
Ngoma, *Zambia*, 104 E3
Nha Trang, *Vietnam*, 66 E5
Niagara Falls, *North America*, 31 M4
Niamey, *Niger, national capital*, 101 F6
Nias, *Indonesia*, 64 A3
Nicaragua, *North America, country*, 35 G5
Nicaragua, Lake, *Nicaragua*, 35 H5

Nice, *France*, 89 F6
Nicobar Islands, *India*, 71 G9
Nicosia, *Cyprus, national capital*, 91 K5
Nieuw Nickerie, *Surinam*, 43 G2
Niger, *Africa*, 101 G7
Niger, *Africa, country*, 98 D5
Niger Delta, *Nigeria*, 101 G8
Nigeria, *Africa, country*, 101 F7
Niigata, *Japan*, 69 N3
Nikopol, *Ukraine*, 84 C4
Niksic, *Yugoslavia*, 91 F3
Nile, *Africa*, 99 H3
Nile Delta, *Egypt*, 99 H2
Nimes, *France*, 89 F6
Ningbo, *China*, 69 K5
Niono, *Mali*, 101 D6
Nioro du Sahel, *Mali*, 101 D5
Nipigon, Lake, *Canada*, 31 L4
Nis, *Yugoslavia*, 91 G3
Nitra, *Slovakia*, 87 F6
Niue, *Oceania*, 52 G6
Nizhniy Novgorod, *Russia*, 84 E2
Nizhniy Tagil, *Russia*, 85 H2
Njazidja, *Comoros*, 105 H2
Njinjo, *Tanzania*, 103 G5
Nkongsamba, *Cameroon*, 102 A3
Nogales, *Mexico*, 34 B1
Nokaneng, *Botswana*, 104 D3
Norfolk Island, *Australia*, 55 N5
Norilsk, *Russia*, 74 F2
Norrkoping, *Sweden*, 86 F4
North America, 20
North Bay, *Canada*, 31 M4
North Cape, *New Zealand*, 55 P6
North Cape, *Norway*, 86 J1
North Carolina, *U.S.A., internal admin. area*, 33 K3
North Dakota, *U.S.A., internal admin. area*, 32 F1
Northern Ireland, *United Kingdom, internal admin. area*, 88 C3
Northern Mariana Islands, *Oceania*, 52 B3
Northern Territory, *Australia, internal admin. area*, 54 F3
North European Plain, *Russia*, 84 D3
North Frisian Islands, *Europe*, 88 F3
North Island, *New Zealand*, 55 Q7
North Korea, *Asia, country*, 69 L2
North Sea, *Europe*, 88 E2
North West Cape, *Australia*, 54 B4
Northwest Territories, *Canada, internal admin. area*, 30 G2
Norway, *Europe, country*, 86 D3
Norwegian Sea, *Europe*, 86 C2
Norwich, *United Kingdom*, 88 E3
Nosy Be, *Madagascar*, 105 J2
Nosy Boraha, *Madagascar*, 105 J3
Nottingham, *United Kingdom*, 88 D3
Nouadhibou, *Mauritania*, 100 B4
Nouakchott, *Mauritania, national capital*, 100 B5
Noumea, *New Caledonia*, 55 N4
Nova Iguacu, *Brazil*, 44 K4
Nova Mambone, *Mozambique*, 105 G4
Novara, *Italy*, 90 D2
Nova Scotia, *Canada, internal admin. area*, 31 N4
Novaya Zemlya, *Russia*, 74 C2
Novgorod, *Russia*, 86 J4
Novi Sad, *Yugoslavia*, 91 F2
Novocherkassk, *Russia*, 84 E4
Novo Mesto, *Slovenia*, 90 E2
Novorossiysk, *Russia*, 72 C3
Novosibirsk, *Russia*, 74 E3
Novyy Urengoy, *Russia*, 74 D2
Nubian Desert, *Africa*, 99 H4
Nueva Loja, *Ecuador*, 42 C3
Nukualofa, *Tonga, national capital*, 52 F7
Nukus, *Uzbekistan*, 72 G3
Nullarbor Plain, *Australia*, 54 E6
Nunavut, *Canada, internal admin. area*, 31 K2
Nungo, *Mozambique*, 105 G2
Nunivak Island, *U.S.A.*, 30 C3
Nuqui, *Colombia*, 42 C2
Nuremberg, *Germany*, 88 G4

San Sebastian, *Spain*, 89 D6
Santa Clara, *Cuba*, 35 H3
Santa Cruz, *Bolivia*, 44 F3
Santa Cruz, *Ecuador*, 42 N10
Santa Cruz Islands, *Solomon Islands*,
   55 N2
Santa Elena, *Venezuela*, 42 F3
Santa Fe, *Argentina*, 44 F6
Santa Fe, *U.S.A., internal capital*, 32 E3
Santa Maria, *Brazil*, 44 H5
Santa Marta, *Colombia*, 42 D1
Santander, *Spain*, 89 D6
Santarem, *Brazil*, 43 H4
Santa Rosa, *Argentina*. 45 F7
Santiago, *Chile, national capital*, 44 D6
Santiago, *Dominican Republic*, 35 K4
Santiago, *Panama*, 35 H6
Santiago de Compostela, *Spain*, 89 B6
Santiago de Cuba, *Cuba*, 35 J3
Santiago del Estero, *Argentina*, 44 F5
Santo Antao, *Cape Verde*, 101 L11
Santo Domingo, *Dominican Republic,
   national capital*, 35 L4
Santo Domingo de los Colorados, *Ecuador*,
   42 C4
San Valentin, Mount, *Chile*, 45 D9
Sanya, *China*, 68 G7
Sao Francisco, *Brazil*, 43 L5
Sao Jose do Rio Preto, *Brazil*, 44 J4
Sao Luis, *Brazil*, 43 K4
Sao Miguel, *Azores*, 100 K10
Sao Nicolau, *Cape Verde*, 101 M11
Sao Paulo, *Brazil*, 44 J4
Sao Roque, Cape, *Brazil*, 43 L4
Sao Tiago, *Cape Verde*, 101 M11
Sao Tome, *Sao Tome and Principe,
   national capital*, 101 G8
Sao Tome and Principe, *Africa, country*,
   101 G8
Sapporo, *Japan*, 69 P2
Saqqara, *Egypt*, 99 H3
Sarajevo, *Bosnia and Herzegovina,
   national capital*, 91 F3
Saransk, *Russia*, 84 F3
Sarapul, *Russia*, 85 G2
Saratov, *Russia*, 85 F3
Saratov Reservoir, *Russia*, 85 F3
Sardinia, *Italy*, 90 D3
Sargodha, *Pakistan*, 70 C4
Sarh, *Chad*, 102 C2
Sarremaa, *Estonia*, 86 G4
Saskatchewan, *Canada,
   internal admin. area*, 30 J3
Saskatoon, *Canada*, 30 J3
Sassari, *Italy*, 90 D3
Satu Mare, *Romania*, 91 G2
Saudi Arabia, *Asia, country*, 73 E7
Sault Ste. Marie, *Canada*, 31 L4
Saurimo, *Angola*, 104 D1
Savannah, *U.S.A.*, 33 K4
Savannakhet, *Laos*, 66 D4
Sawu, *Indonesia*, 65 F6
Sawu Sea, *Indonesia*, 65 F5
Schwerin, *Germany*, 88 G3
Scotland, *United Kingdom,
   internal admin. area*, 88 C2
Seattle, *U.S.A.*, 32 B1
Seeheim, *Namibia*, 104 C5
Sefadu, *Sierra Leone*, 101 C7
Seg, Lake, *Russia*, 86 K3
Segou, *Mali*, 101 D6
Seine, *France*, 88 E4
Sekondi-Takoradi, *Ghana*, 101 E8
Selebi-Phikwe, *Botswana*, 104 E4
Selibabi, *Mauritania*, 101 C5
Selvas, *Brazil*, 42 E5
Semarang, *Indonesia*, 64 D5
Semenov, *Russia*, 84 E2
Semiozernoe, *Kazakhstan*, 85 J3
Sendai, *Japan*, 69 P3
Senegal, *Africa*, 101 C5
Senegal, *Africa, country*, 101 B6
Seoul, *South Korea, national capital*,
   69 L3
Serang, *Indonesia*, 64 C5
Seremban, *Malaysia*, 64 B3

Sergiyev Posad, *Russia*, 84 D2
Serov, *Russia*, 85 J2
Serowe, *Botswana*, 104 E4
Serpukhov, *Russia*, 84 D3
Serres, *Greece*, 91 G3
Sesheke, *Zambia*, 104 D3
Setif, *Algeria*, 100 G1
Setubal, *Portugal*, 89 B7
Sevastopol, *Ukraine*, 91 K2
Severn, *United Kingdom*, 88 D3
Severnaya Zemlya, *Russia*, 75 F2
Severomorsk, *Russia*, 86 K1
Sevettijarvi, *Finland*, 86 J1
Seville, *Spain*, 89 C7
Seward, *U.S.A.*, 30 E2
Seward Peninsula, *U.S.A.*, 30 C2
Seychelles, *Indian Ocean, country*, 105 J1
Seydhisfjordhur, *Iceland*, 86 Q2
Sfax, *Tunisia*, 98 D2
Shalqar, *Kazakhstan*, 72 G2
Shanghai, *China*, 69 K4
Shannon, *Ireland*, 88 C3
Shantou, *China*, 69 J6
Shaoguan, *China*, 69 H6
Sharjah, *United Arab Emirates*, 73 G6
Sharm el Sheikh, *Egypt*, 99 H3
Shasta, Mount, *U.S.A.*, 32 B2
Sheffield, *United Kingdom*, 88 D3
Shenyang, *China*, 69 K2
Shepetivka, *Ukraine*, 87 H6
Shetland Islands, *United Kingdom*,
   88 D1
Shieli, *Kazakhstan*, 72 J3
Shihezi, *China*, 70 F2
Shijiazhuang, *China*, 69 H3
Shikoku, *Japan*, 69 M4
Shillong, *India*, 70 G5
Shiraz, *Iran*, 73 F6
Shishaldin Volcano, *U.S.A.*, 31 C3
Shiyan, *China*, 68 H4
Shizuoka, *Japan*, 69 N3
Shkoder, *Albania*, 91 F3
Shreveport, *U.S.A.*, 33 H4
Shumen, *Bulgaria*, 91 H3
Shymkent, *Kazakhstan*, 70 B2
Sialkot, *Pakistan*, 70 C4
Siauliai, *Lithuania*, 87 G5
Sibiti, *Congo*, 102 B4
Sibiu, *Romania*, 91 H2
Sibolga, *Indonesia*, 64 A3
Sibu, *Malaysia*, 64 D3
Sicily, *Italy*, 90 E4
Sicuani, *Peru*, 42 D6
Sidi-Bel-Abbes, *Algeria*, 100 E1
Sidon, *Lebanon*, 72 C5
Sidra, Gulf of, *Africa*, 98 E2
Sierra Leone, *Africa, country*, 101 C7
Sierra Morena, *Spain*, 89 C7
Sierra Nevada, *Spain*, 89 D7
Sierra Nevada, *U.S.A.*, 32 B3
Siglufjordhur, *Iceland*, 86 P2
Siguiri, *Guinea*, 101 D6
Sikasso, *Mali*, 101 D6
Sikhote Alin Range, *Russia*, 69 N1
Siling Lake, *China*, 70 F4
Simao, *China*, 68 F6
Simeulue, *Indonesia*, 64 A3
Simferopol, *Ukraine*, 91 K2
Simpson Desert, *Australia*, 54 G4
Sinai, *Egypt*, 99 H3
Sinai, Mount, *Egypt*, 99 H3
Sincelejo, *Colombia*, 42 C2
Sines, *Portugal*, 89 B7
Singapore, *Asia, country*, 64 B3
Singapore, *Singapore, national capital*,
   64 B3
Sinnamary, *French Guiana*, 43 H2
Sinuiju, *North Korea*, 69 K2
Sioux City, *U.S.A.*, 33 G2
Sioux Falls, *U.S.A.*, 33 G2
Sirjan, *Iran*, 73 G6
Sittwe, *Burma*, 66 B3
Sivas, *Turkey*, 72 C4
Skagen, *Denmark*, 87 D4
Skagerrak, *Europe*, 87 C4
Skelleftea, *Sweden*, 86 G2

Skikda, *Algeria*, 100 G1
Skopje, *Macedonia, national capital*,
   91 G3
Skyros, *Greece*, 91 H4
Slavonski Brod, *Croatia*, 90 F2
Sligo, *Ireland*, 88 B3
Sliven, *Bulgaria*, 91 H3
Slovakia, *Europe, country*, 87 F6
Slovenia, *Europe, country*, 90 E2
Slovyansk, *Ukraine*, 84 D4
Slupsk, *Poland*, 87 F5
Slutsk, *Belarus*, 87 H5
Smallwood Reservoir, *Canada*, 31 N3
Smola, *Norway*, 86 C3
Smolensk, *Russia*, 87 J5
Sobradinho Reservoir, *Brazil*, 43 K6
Sobral, *Brazil*, 43 K4
Sochi, *Russia*, 72 C3
Society Islands, *French Polynesia*, 53 J5
Socotra, *Yemen*, 73 F9
Sodankyla, *Finland*, 86 H2
Sodertalje, *Sweden*, 86 F4
Sofia, *Bulgaria, national capital*, 91 G3
Sohag, *Egypt*, 99 H3
Sokhumi, *Georgia*, 72 D3
Sokode, *Togo*, 101 F7
Sokoto, *Nigeria*, 101 G6
Solapur, *India*, 71 D7
Solikamsk, *Russia*, 85 H2
Solomon Islands, *Oceania, country*,
   52 D5
Solomon Sea, *Papua New Guinea*,
   65 M5
Solwezi, *Zambia*, 104 E2
Somalia, *Africa, country*, 103 J2
Somerset Island, *Canada*, 31 K1
Songea, *Tanzania*, 103 G6
Songo, *Mozambique*, 105 F3
Son La, *Vietnam*, 66 D3
Sorong, *Indonesia*, 65 H4
Soroti, *Uganda*, 103 F3
Soroya, *Norway*, 86 G1
Sotra, *Norway*, 86 C3
Souk Ahras, *Algeria*, 90 C4
Sousse, *Tunisia*, 98 D1
South Africa, *Africa, country*, 104 D6
South America, 20
Southampton, *United Kingdom*, 88 D4
Southampton Island, *Canada*, 31 L2
South Australia, *Australia,
   internal admin. area*, 54 F5
South Bend, *U.S.A.*, 33 J2
South Carolina, *U.S.A.,
   internal admin. area*, 33 K4
South China Sea, *Asia*, 67 F5
South Dakota, *U.S.A., internal admin. area*,
   32 F2
South East Cape, *Australia*, 54 J8
Southend-on-Sea, *United Kingdom*, 88 E4
Southern Ocean, 20–21
Southern Sierra Madre, *Mexico*, 34 D4
South Georgia, *Atlantic Ocean*, 45 L10
South Island, *New Zealand*, 55 N8
South Korea, *Asia, country*, 69 L3
South Orkney Islands, *Atlantic Ocean*,
   45 J12
South Sandwich Islands, *Atlantic Ocean*,
   45 N10
South Shetland Islands, *Atlantic Ocean*,
   45 G12
South West Cape, *New Zealand*, 55 N9
Spain, *Europe, country*, 89 D7
Split, *Croatia*, 90 F3
Spokane, *U.S.A.*, 32 C1
Spratly Islands, *Asia*, 67 F5
Springfield, *Illinois, U.S.A., internal
   capital*, 33 J3
Springfield, *Massachusetts, U.S.A.*,
   33 M2
Springfield, *Missouri, U.S.A.*, 33 H3
Springs, *South Africa*, 104 E5
Sri Jayewardenepura Kotte, *Sri Lanka,
   national capital*, 71 E9
Sri Lanka, *Asia, country*, 71 E9
Srinagar, *India*, 70 C4
Standerton, *South Africa*, 104 E5

Stanley, *Falkland Islands*, 45 G10
Stara Zagora, *Bulgaria*, 91 H3
Staryy Oskol, *Russia*, 84 D3
Stavanger, *Norway*, 86 C4
Stavropol, *Russia*, 72 D2
Steinkjer, *Norway*, 86 D2
Stellenbosch, *South Africa*, 104 C6
Sterlitamak, *Russia*, 85 H3
Stewart Island, *New Zealand*, 55 N9
Stockholm, *Sweden, national capital*,
   86 F4
Stoeng Treng, *Cambodia*, 66 E5
Stoke-on-Trent, *United Kingdom*, 88 D3
Stora Lule Lake, *Sweden*, 86 F2
Storavan Lake, *Sweden*, 86 F2
Stor Lake, *Sweden*, 86 E3
Stornoway, *United Kingdom*, 88 C2
Stranraer, *United Kingdom*, 88 C3
Strasbourg, *France*, 88 F4
Sturt Stony Desert, *Australia*, 54 G5
Stuttgart, *Germany*, 88 G4
Subotica, *Yugoslavia*, 91 F2
Suceava, *Romania*, 91 H2
Sucre, *Bolivia, national capital*, 44 E3
Sudan, *Africa, country*, 99 G5
Sudbury, *Canada*, 31 L4
Suez, *Egypt*, 99 H3
Suez Canal, *Egypt*, 99 H2
Suhar, *Oman*, 73 G7
Sukkur, *Pakistan*, 70 B5
Sukses, *Namibia*, 104 C4
Sula, *Norway*, 86 C3
Sula Islands, *Indonesia*, 65 G4
Sullana, *Peru*, 42 B4
Sulu Archipelago, *Philippines*, 67 H6
Sulu Sea, *Asia*, 67 G6
Sumatra, *Indonesia*, 64 B3
Sumba, *Indonesia*, 65 E5
Sumbawa, *Indonesia*, 64 E5
Sumqayit, *Azerbaijan*, 72 E3
Sumy, *Ukraine*, 84 C3
Sunderland, *United Kingdom*, 88 D3
Sundsvall, *Sweden*, 86 F3
Superior, Lake, *U.S.A.*, 33 J1
Sur, *Oman*, 73 G7
Surabaya, *Indonesia*, 64 D5
Surakarta, *Indonesia*, 64 D5
Surat, *India*, 71 C6
Surgut, *Russia*, 74 D2
Surigao, *Philippines*, 67 J6
Surinam, *South America, country*, 43 G3
Surt, *Libya*, 98 E2
Sutherland Falls, *New Zealand*, 55 N8
Suva, *Fiji, national capital*, 55 Q3
Suwalki, *Poland*, 87 G5
Suwon, *South Korea*, 69 L3
Svalbard, *Norway*, 74 A2
Svolvaer, *Norway*, 86 E1
Svyetlahorsk, *Belarus*, 87 J5
Swakopmund, *Namibia*, 104 B4
Swan Islands, *Honduras*, 35 H4
Swansea, *United Kingdom*, 88 D4
Swaziland, *Africa, country*, 104 F5
Sweden, *Europe, country*, 86 E3
Swift Current, *Canada*, 30 J3
Swindon, *United Kingdom*, 88 D4
Switzerland, *Europe, country*, 90 C2
Sydney, *Australia, internal capital*,
   55 K6
Sydney, *Canada*, 31 N4
Syktyvkar, *Russia*, 85 G1
Sylhet, *Bangladesh*, 71 G6
Syracuse, *Italy*, 90 E4
Syracuse, *U.S.A.*, 33 L2
Syr Darya, *Asia*, 72 H2
Syria, *Asia, country*, 72 C4
Syrian Desert, *Asia*, 73 C5
Syzran, *Russia*, 85 F3
Szczecin, *Poland*, 87 E5
Szeged, *Hungary*, 87 G7
Szekesfehervar, *Hungary*, 87 F7
Szombathely, *Hungary*, 87 F7

t

Tabora, *Tanzania*, 103 F5
Tabriz, *Iran*, 72 E4

Tabuk, *Saudi Arabia,* 73 C6
Tacloban, *Philippines,* 67 J5
Tacna, *Peru,* 42 D7
Tacoma, *U.S.A.,* 32 B1
Tacuarembo, *Uruguay,* 44 G6
Tademait Plateau, *Algeria,* 100 F3
Tadmur, *Syria,* 72 C5
Taegu, *South Korea,* 69 L3
Taejon, *South Korea,* 69 L3
Tagus, *Europe,* 89 B7
Tahat, Mount, *Algeria,* 100 G4
Tahiti, *French Polynesia,* 53 J6
Tahoua, *Niger,* 98 C6
Taian, *China,* 69 J3
Tai Lake, *China,* 69 J4
Taimyr Peninsula, *Russia,* 75 F2
Taiping, *Malaysia,* 64 B3
Taiwan Strait, *Asia,* 69 J6
Taiyuan, *China,* 68 H3
Taizz, *Yemen,* 73 D9
Tajikistan, *Asia, country,* 70 B3
Taj Mahal, *India,* 70 D5
Tajumulco, *Guatemala,* 34 F4
Taklimakan Desert, *China,* 70 E3
Talara, *Peru,* 42 B4
Talaud Islands, *Indonesia,* 65 G3
Talca, *Chile,* 45 D7
Taldyqorghan, *Kazakhstan,* 70 D1
Tallahassee, *U.S.A., internal capital,* 33 K4
Tallinn, *Estonia, national capital,* 86 H4
Taltal, *Chile,* 44 D5
Tamale, *Ghana,* 101 E7
Tamanrasset, *Algeria,* 100 G4
Tambacounda, *Senegal,* 101 C6
Tambov, *Russia,* 84 E3
Tampa, *U.S.A.,* 33 K5
Tampere, *Finland,* 86 G3
Tampico, *Mexico,* 34 E3
Tana, Lake, *Ethiopia,* 103 G1
Tandil, *Argentina,* 45 G7
Tanga, *Tanzania,* 103 G5
Tanganyika, Lake, *Africa,* 102 E5
Tangier, *Morocco,* 100 D1
Tangshan, *China,* 69 J3
Tanimbar Islands, *Indonesia,* 65 H5
Tanjungkarang-Telukbetung, *Indonesia,* 64 C5
Tanjungredeb, *Indonesia,* 64 E3
Tanta, *Egypt,* 99 H2
Tan-Tan, *Morocco,* 100 C3
Tanzania, *Africa, country,* 103 F5
Tapachula, *Mexico,* 34 F5
Tapajos, *Brazil,* 43 G4
Tarakan, *Indonesia,* 64 E3
Taranto, *Italy,* 90 F3
Taraz, *Kazakhstan,* 70 C2
Targu Mures, *Romania,* 91 H2
Tarija, *Bolivia,* 44 F4
Tarim Basin, *China,* 70 E3
Tarkwa, *Ghana,* 101 E7
Tarnow, *Poland,* 87 G6
Tarragona, *Spain,* 89 E6
Tartagal, *Argentina,* 44 F4
Tartu, *Estonia,* 86 H4
Tartus, *Syria,* 72 C5
Tashkent, *Uzbekistan, national capital,* 70 B2
Tasmania, *Australia, internal admin. area,* 55 J8
Tasman Sea, *Australasia,* 55 L7
Tataouine, *Tunisia,* 98 D2
Taunggyi, *Burma,* 66 C3
Taupo, Lake, *New Zealand,* 55 Q7
Taurus Mountains, *Turkey,* 91 J4
Tavoy, *Burma,* 66 C5
Tawau, *Malaysia,* 65 E3
Taytay, *Philippines,* 67 G5
Taza, *Morocco,* 100 E2
Tbilisi, *Georgia, national capital,* 72 D3
Tchibanga, *Gabon,* 102 B4
Tebessa, *Algeria,* 100 G1
Tegal, *Indonesia,* 64 C5
Tegucigalpa, *Honduras, national capital,* 35 G5
Tehran, *Iran, national capital,* 72 F4
Tehuacan, *Mexico,* 34 E4

Tehuantepec, Gulf of, *Mexico,* 34 E4
Tehuantepec, Isthmus of, *Mexico,* 34 E4
Tekirdag, *Turkey,* 91 H3
Tel Aviv-Yafo, *Israel,* 73 B5
Teller, *U.S.A.,* 30 C2
Temuco, *Chile,* 45 D7
Ten Degree Channel, *India,* 71 G9
Tenerife, *Canary Islands,* 100 B3
Tenkodogo, *Burkina Faso,* 101 E6
Tennessee, *U.S.A.,* 33 J3
Tennessee, *U.S.A., internal admin. area,* 33 J3
Teofilo Otoni, *Brazil,* 44 K3
Teotihuacan, *Mexico,* 34 E4
Terceira, *Azores,* 100 K10
Teresina, *Brazil,* 43 K4
Ternate, *Indonesia,* 65 G3
Terni, *Italy,* 90 D3
Ternopil, *Ukraine,* 87 H6
Terra Firma, *South Africa,* 104 D5
Terracotta Army, *China,* 68 G4
Teseney, *Eritrea,* 99 J5
Tete, *Mozambique,* 105 F3
Tetouan, *Morocco,* 100 D1
Tetovo, *Macedonia,* 91 G3
Texarkana, *U.S.A.,* 33 H4
Texas, *U.S.A., internal admin. area,* 32 G4
Thailand, *Asia, country,* 66 D4
Thailand, Gulf of, *Asia,* 66 D6
Thai Nguyen, *Vietnam,* 66 E3
Thames, *United Kingdom,* 88 D4
Thanh Hoa, *Vietnam,* 66 E4
Thar Desert, *Asia,* 70 B5
Thasos, *Greece,* 91 H3
Thaton, *Burma,* 66 C4
Thessaloniki, *Greece,* 91 G3
Thies, *Senegal,* 101 B6
Thika, *Kenya,* 103 G4
Thimphu, *Bhutan, national capital,* 70 F5
Thompson, *Canada,* 31 K3
Three Points, Cape, *Africa,* 101 E8
Thunder Bay, *Canada,* 31 L4
Tianjin, *China,* 69 J3
Tibesti Mountains, *Africa,* 98 E4
Tibet, *China,* 70 F4
Tibet, Plateau of, *China,* 70 F4
Tidjikja, *Mauritania,* 100 C5
Tien Shan, *Asia,* 70 D2
Tierra del Fuego, *South America,* 45 E10
Tighina, *Moldova,* 91 J2
Tigris, *Asia,* 73 E5
Tijuana, *Mexico,* 34 A1
Tikal, *Guatemala,* 34 G4
Tikhvin, *Russia,* 86 K4
Tillaberi, *Niger,* 101 F6
Timbuktu, *Mali,* 101 E5
Timisoara, *Romania,* 91 G2
Timor, *Asia,* 65 G6
Timor Sea, *Asia/Australasia,* 65 G6
Tindouf, *Algeria,* 100 D3
Tirana, *Albania, national capital,* 91 F3
Tiraspol, *Moldova,* 91 J2
Tiruchchirappalli, *India,* 71 D8
Titicaca, Lake, *South America,* 42 E7
Tlemcen, *Algeria,* 100 E2
Toamasina, *Madagascar,* 105 J3
Tobago, *Trinidad and Tobago,* 34 M5
Toba, Lake, *Indonesia,* 64 A3
Tobol, *Asia,* 85 K2
Tobolsk, *Russia,* 85 K2
Tobyl, *Kazakhstan,* 85 J3
Tocantins, *Brazil,* 43 J4
Togo, *Africa, country,* 101 F7
Tokelau, *Oceania,* 52 F5
Tokyo, *Japan, national capital,* 69 N3
Tolanaro, *Madagascar,* 105 J5
Toledo, *Spain,* 89 D7
Toledo, *U.S.A.,* 33 K2
Toledo Bend Reservoir, *U.S.A.,* 33 H4
Toliara, *Madagascar,* 105 H4
Tolyatti, *Russia,* 85 F3
Tolybay, *Kazakhstan,* 85 J3
Tomakomai, *Japan,* 69 P2
Tombouctou, *Mali,* 101 E5

Tomsk, *Russia,* 74 E3
Tonga, *Oceania, country,* 52 F6
Tongliao, *China,* 69 K2
Tonkin, Gulf of, *Asia,* 66 E4
Tonle Sap, *Cambodia,* 66 D5
Toowoomba, *Australia,* 55 K5
Topeka, *U.S.A., internal capital,* 33 G3
Top, Lake, *Russia,* 86 K2
Topoli, *Kazakhstan,* 85 G4
Torghay, *Kazakhstan,* 85 J4
Tornio, *Finland,* 86 H2
Toronto, *Canada, internal capital,* 31 M4
Torrens, Lake, *Australia,* 54 G6
Torreon, *Mexico,* 34 D2
Torres Strait, *Australasia,* 54 H2
Tortuga Island, *Venezuela,* 42 E1
Toubkal, *Morocco,* 100 D2
Tougan, *Burkina Faso,* 101 E6
Touggourt, *Algeria,* 100 G2
Toulon, *France,* 89 F6
Toulouse, *France,* 89 E6
Tours, *France,* 88 E5
Townsville, *Australia,* 54 J3
Toyama, *Japan,* 69 N3
Tozeur, *Tunisia,* 98 C2
Trabzon, *Turkey,* 72 C3
Tralee, *Ireland,* 88 B3
Transantarctic Mountains, *Antarctica,* 109 S4
Transylvanian Alps, *Romania,* 91 G2
Trapani, *Italy,* 90 E4
Trento, *Italy,* 90 D2
Trenton, *U.S.A., internal capital,* 33 M2
Tres Arroyos, *Argentina,* 45 F7
Tres Marias Reservoir, *Brazil,* 44 J3
Tres Puntas, Cape, *Argentina,* 45 E9
Trieste, *Italy,* 90 E2
Trincomalee, *Sri Lanka,* 71 E9
Trinidad, *Bolivia,* 44 F2
Trinidad, *Trinidad and Tobago,* 34 M5
Trinidad and Tobago, *North America, country,* 34 M5
Tripoli, *Lebanon,* 72 C5
Tripoli, *Libya, national capital,* 98 D2
Trivandrum, *India,* 71 D9
Trnava, *Slovakia,* 87 F6
Trois-Rivieres, *Canada,* 31 M4
Tromso, *Norway,* 86 F1
Trondheim, *Norway,* 86 D3
Troyes, *France,* 88 F4
Trujillo, *Peru,* 42 C5
Tsau, *Botswana,* 104 D4
Tses, *Namibia,* 104 C5
Tshabong, *Botswana,* 104 D5
Tshane, *Botswana,* 104 D4
Tshikapa, *Democratic Republic of Congo,* 102 D5
Tshwane, *Botswana,* 104 D4
Tsimlyansk Reservoir, *Russia,* 84 E4
Tsiroanomandidy, *Madagascar,* 105 J3
Tsumeb, *Namibia,* 104 C3
Tuamotu Archipelago, *French Polynesia,* 53 K6
Tubmanburg, *Liberia,* 101 C7
Tubruq, *Libya,* 98 F2
Tubuai Islands, *French Polynesia,* 53 J7
Tucson, *U.S.A.,* 32 D4
Tucupita, *Venezuela,* 42 F2
Tucurui Reservoir, *Brazil,* 43 J4
Tugela Falls, *South Africa,* 104 E5
Tuguegarao, *Philippines,* 67 H4
Tula, *Russia,* 84 D3
Tulcea, *Romania,* 91 J2
Tulsa, *U.S.A.,* 33 G3
Tumaco, *Colombia,* 42 C3
Tumbes, *Peru,* 42 B4
Tunduma, *Tanzania,* 103 F5
Tunduru, *Tanzania,* 103 G6
Tunis, *Tunisia, national capital,* 98 D1
Tunisia, *Africa, country,* 98 C2
Tunja, *Colombia,* 42 D2
Tupelo, *U.S.A.,* 33 J4
Tupiza, *Bolivia,* 44 E4
Turbat, *Pakistan,* 73 H6
Turbo, *Colombia,* 42 C2
Turin, *Italy,* 90 C2

Turkana, Lake, *Africa,* 103 G3
Turkey, *Asia, country,* 72 C4
Turkistan, *Kazakhstan,* 70 B2
Turkmenabat, *Turkmenistan,* 72 H4
Turkmenbasy, *Turkmenistan,* 72 F3
Turkmenistan, *Asia, country,* 72 G4
Turks and Caicos Islands, *North America,* 35 K3
Turku, *Finland,* 86 G3
Turpan, *China,* 70 F2
Turpan Depression, *China,* 70 G2
Tuscaloosa, *U.S.A.,* 33 J4
Tuvalu, *Oceania, country,* 52 E5
Tuxtla Gutierrez, *Mexico,* 34 F4
Tuzla, *Bosnia and Herzegovina,* 91 F2
Tuz, Lake, *Turkey,* 91 K4
Tver, *Russia,* 84 D2
Twin Falls, *U.S.A.,* 32 D2
Tynda, *Russia,* 75 G3
Tyrrhenian Sea, *Europe,* 90 D3
Tyumen, *Russia,* 85 K2

U

Ubangi, *Africa,* 102 C3
Uberaba, *Brazil,* 44 J3
Uberlandia, *Brazil,* 44 J3
Ubon Ratchathani, *Thailand,* 66 D4
Ucayali, *Peru,* 42 D5
Udaipur, *India,* 71 C6
Uddevalla, *Sweden,* 86 D4
Udon Thani, *Thailand,* 66 D4
Uele, *Democratic Republic of Congo,* 102 D3
Ufa, *Russia,* 85 H3
Uganda, *Africa, country,* 103 F3
Uitenhage, *South Africa,* 104 E6
Ujung Pandang, *Indonesia,* 65 E5
Ukhta, *Russia,* 74 C2
Ukraine, *Europe, country,* 84 C4
Ulan Bator, *Mongolia, national capital,* 68 G1
Ulanhot, *China,* 69 K1
Ulan Ude, *Russia,* 75 F3
Ulm, *Germany,* 88 G4
Uluru, *Australia,* 54 F5
Ulyanovsk, *Russia,* 85 F3
Uman, *Ukraine,* 87 J6
Ume, *Sweden,* 86 F2
Umea, *Sweden,* 86 G3
Umnak Island, *U.S.A.,* 31 C3
Umtata, *South Africa,* 104 E6
Unalaska Island, *U.S.A.,* 31 C3
Ungava Bay, *Canada,* 31 N3
Ungava Peninsula, *Canada,* 31 M2
Unimak Island, *U.S.A.,* 31 C3
United Arab Emirates, *Asia, country,* 73 F7
United Kingdom, *Europe, country,* 88 D3
United States of America, *North America, country,* 32 F3
Upington, *South Africa,* 104 D5
Uppsala, *Sweden,* 86 F4
Ural, *Asia,* 85 G4
Ural Mountains, *Russia,* 85 H2
Uray, *Russia,* 85 J1
Urganch, *Uzbekistan,* 70 A2
Urmia, *Iran,* 72 E4
Uruapan, *Mexico,* 34 D4
Urucui, *Brazil,* 43 K5
Uruguaiana, *Brazil,* 44 G5
Uruguay, *South America, country,* 44 G6
Urumqi, *China,* 70 F2
Usak, *Turkey,* 91 J4
Ushuaia, *Argentina,* 45 E10
Uskemen, *Kazakhstan,* 74 E3
Utah, *U.S.A., internal admin. area,* 32 D3
Utsjoki, *Finland,* 86 H1
Utsunomiya, *Japan,* 69 N3
Uy, *Asia,* 85 J3
Uyuni, *Bolivia,* 44 E4
Uzbekistan, *Asia, country,* 74 D3
Uzhhorod, *Ukraine,* 87 G6

V

Vaasa, *Finland,* 86 G3
Vadodara, *India,* 71 C6

ACKNOWLEDGEMENTS

Every effort has been made to trace the copyright holders of the material in this book. If any rights have been omitted, the publishers offer to rectify this in any subsequent edition, following notification. The publishers are grateful to the following organizations and individuals for their contributions and permission to reproduce material (t=top, m=middle, b=bottom, l=left, r=right):

Cover © Jacques Descloitres, MODIS Land Science Team; (globe) © Digital Vision; **Endpapers** © Ric Ergenbright/CORBIS; **p1** © Jim Zuckerman/CORBIS; **p2–3** © Art Wolfe/Science Photo Library; **p4–5** Stephen Moncrieff, Digital Vision; **p4** (tr) © Geospace/Science Photo Library; **p6** (bl) © CNES, 1988 Distribution SPOT Image/Science Photo Library; (mr) Stephen Moncrieff; **p7** (tm & tr) European Map Graphics Ltd; (b) © Paul A. Souders/CORBIS; **p8–9** (background) © Digital Vision; **p8** (mr) PHOTO ESA; **p9** (tl) © NERC Satellite Station, University of Dundee www.sat.dundee.ac.html; (br) Science Photo Library/European Space Agency; **p10** (b) Stephen Moncrieff; (tr) © Dan Guravich/CORBIS; **p11** (bl) European Map Graphics Ltd; (tr) © W. Perry Conway/CORBIS; **p12** (b) © Christopher Cormack/CORBIS; **p13** Stephen Moncrieff, Craig Asquith; **p14** (tr) © Bill Ross/CORBIS; (b) Craig Asquith; **p15** Craig Asquith; **p16–17** European Map Graphics Ltd; **p22–23** © Richard Cummins/CORBIS; **p23** (br) © W. Perry Conway/CORBIS; **p24** (tr) © Worldsat International/Science Photo Library; (m) © NASA/JSC; (b) © Raymond Gehman/CORBIS; **p25** © NASA/CORBIS; **p26–27** (b) © Richard Cummins/CORBIS; **p26** (t) © Dave G. Houser/CORBIS; **p27** (tr) © Joe McDonald/CORBIS; **p28** (l) © Angelo Hornak/CORBIS; (tr) © Carl & Ann Purcell/CORBIS; **p29** (tl) © Schafer & Hill/GettyImages; (br) © Michael & Patricia Fogden/CORBIS; **p36–37** © Galen Rowell/CORBIS; **p37** (tr) © Eye Ubiquitous/CORBIS; **p38** (m) © Julian Baum & David Angus/Science Photo Library; (bl) © Yann Arthus-Bertrand/CORBIS; (mr) © NASA/JSC; **p39** (r) © CNES, 1986 Distribution SPOT Image/Science Photo Library; (bl) © CNES, Distribution SPOT Image/Science Photo Library; **p40–41** (b) © Robert Frerck/GettyImages; **p40** (tr) Claus Meyer/GettyImages; **p41** (tl) Walter Bibikow/GettyImages; (tr) Peter Oxford/BBC Wild; **p46–47** © Still Pictures/Pascal Kobeh; **p47** (br) © Bates Littlehales/CORBIS; **p48–49** (b) © Amos Nachoum/CORBIS; **p48** (ml) © 1995, Worldsat International and J. Knighton/Science Photo Library; (tr) © NASA/JSC; **p49** (tr) © CNES, Distribution SPOT Image/Science Photo Library; (ml) © CORBIS; **p50** © Yoshio Tomii/Bruce Coleman; **p51** (tr) © Klein/Hubert/Still Pictures; (bl) © Zefa visual media; **p56–57** © Michael S. Yamashita/CORBIS; **p57** (br) © Keren Su/CORBIS; **p58** (tr) © Worldsat International/Science Photo Library; (m) © CNES, 1986 Distribution SPOT Image/Science Photo Library; (b) © Liu Liqun/CORBIS; **p59** (t) © NASA JPL; (br) © CNES, 1987 Distribution SPOT Image/Science Photo Library; **p60** (l) © Keren Su/CORBIS; (tr) © Keren Su/China Span/Alamy; **p61** (tl) © www.pictor.com; (b) © Papilio/CORBIS; **p62** (tr) © Richard T. Nowitz/CORBIS; (b) © Archivo Iconografico, S.A./CORBIS; **p63** (ml) © www.pictor.com; (tr) © Wolfgang Kaehler/CORBIS; (b) © Brian & Cherry Alexander Photography; **p76–77** © Digital Vision; **p77** (br) Agripicture/© Peter Dean; **p78–79** © Peter Adams/GettyImages; **p78** (tr) NASA/GSFC/MITI/ERSDAC/JAROS, & U.S./Japan ASTER Science Team; (ml) © NASA GSFC Scientific Visualization Studio; **p79** (tr) © CNES, 1994 Distribution SPOT Image/Science Photo Library; (m) © German Remote Sensing Data Center; **p80** (tr) © The Art Archive/Historiska Muséet Stockholm/Dagli Orti; (bl) © Enzo & Paolo Ragazzini/CORBIS; **p81** (t) © Zefa visual media; (br) © Frans Lanting/Minden Pictures; **p82** © Paul Hardy/corbisstockmarket.com; **p83** (t) © Bob Krist/CORBIS; (b) © Araldo de Luca/CORBIS; **p92–93** © Tom Brakefield/CORBIS; **p93** (br) © Gallo Images/CORBIS; **p94** (tr) © Worldsat International/Science Photo Library; (bl) © Yann Arthus-Bertrand/CORBIS; (br) © NASA JPL; **p95** (r) © Jacques Descloitres, MODIS Land Science Team; (bl) © NASA/JSC; **p96** © Roger Wood/CORBIS; **p97** (ml) © Charles O'Rear/CORBIS; (tr) © Wolfgang Kaehler/CORBIS; (b) © Karl Ammann/CORBIS; **p106** (tr) © Worldsat International/Science Photo Library; (m) © Jan Jordan; **p107** (t) © NRSC Ltd/Science Photo Library; (b) © Digital Vision; **p110–111** (b) © Paul A. Souders/CORBIS; **p110** (tl) © Peter M. Wilson/CORBIS; (tm) © Joe McDonald/CORBIS; (ml) © Charles O'Rear/CORBIS; (mr) © Vanni Archive/CORBIS; **p111** (br) Galen Rowell/CORBIS; **p112–125** (background) © Digital Vision; (Afghanistan, Bahrain, Comoros, Rwanda, Turkmenistan and East Timor flags) © Shipmate Flags, Vlaardingen, The Netherlands; (all other flags) © Flag Enterprises Ltd; **p125** (b) AFP Photos/Henry Ray Abrams; **p126** (b) Craig Asquith.

Managing editor: Gillian Doherty
Managing designer: Mary Cartwright
Cover design by Zöe Wray
With thanks to Ruth King